THE FIFTH VICTIM

FBI TASK FORCE S.W.O.R.D.
BOOK 1

D.D. BLACK

DARKNESS AND LIGHT PUBLISHING

A Note on Setting and Characters

While many locations in this book are true to life, some details of the settings have been changed.

Any resemblances between characters in this book and actual people are purely coincidental, including the dog, Ranger, a character I wish were real but is entirely a creation of my imagination.

Thanks for reading,

D.D. Black

The price of anything is the amount of life you exchange for it.
- Henry David Thoreau

We are all in the gutter, but some of us are looking at the stars.
- Oscar Wilde

I think that one of these days... you're going to have to find out where you want to go. And then you've got to start going there. But immediately. You can't afford to lose a minute.
- JD Salinger

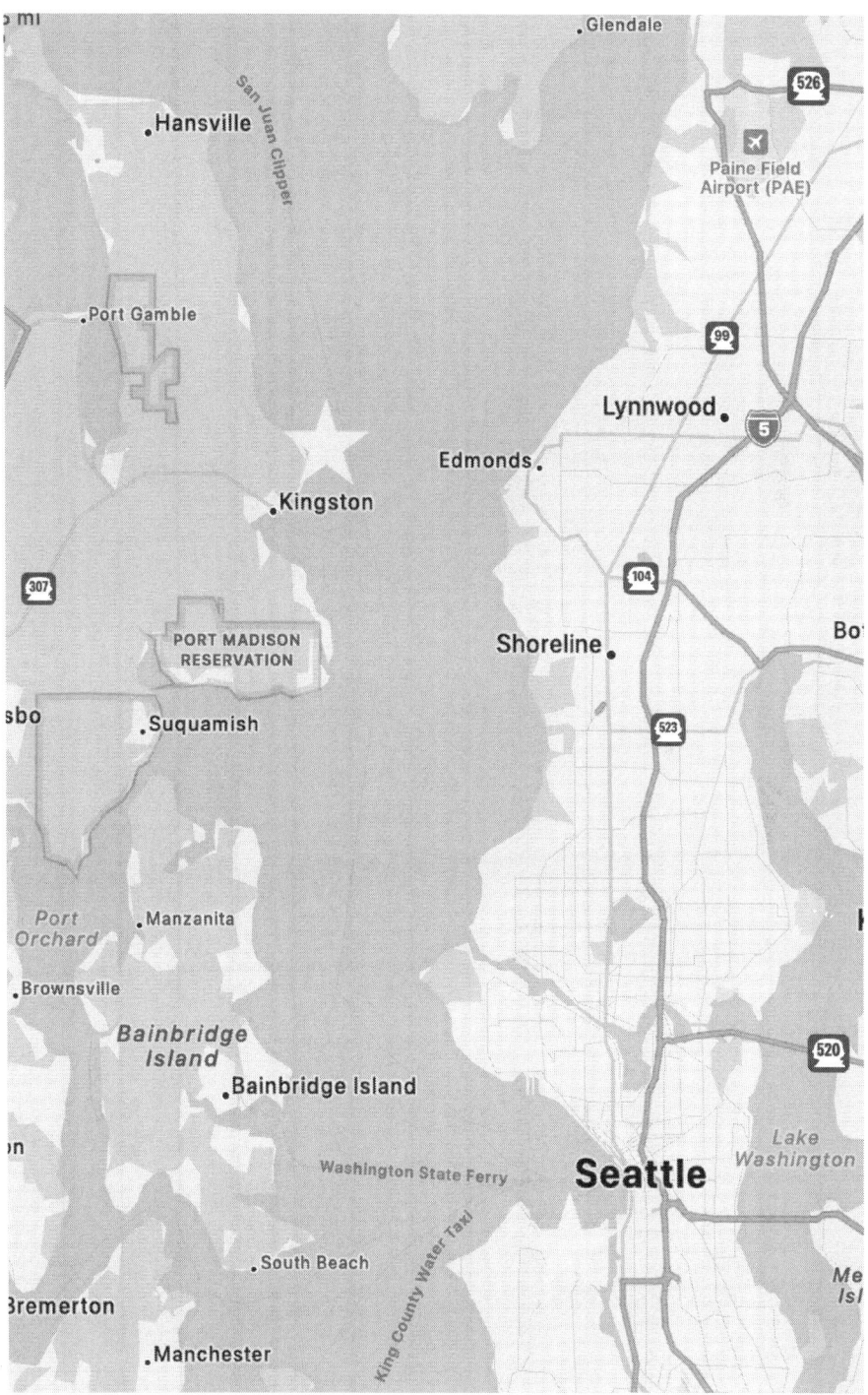

PART 1

A MOTLEY CREW

CHAPTER ONE

University District

Seattle, Washington

"WHY ARE YOU DOING THIS?"

With quick, precise movements, she moved across the room and sat on a chair next to the bed, then stared into the professor's pale green eyes. "I am the gatherer of light."

The man bound to the bed was brilliant. In fact, Professor Isaac Orion was a genius, a man for whom *not knowing* was the worst kind of suffering. Now his face contorted, the fear that had haunted his eyes converging with a look of overwhelming confusion.

She wondered whether his bafflement alone might kill him.

"Wha... wha... what?" he stammered. "What is a gatherer of light?"

"Silence, please." She had no intention of explaining something he didn't need to understand.

She covered his mouth with a thick swath of blue duct tape. He would never speak through this body again.

Blue silk covered the windows. Blue candles burned on the bedside table next to a stack of the professor's books. Carrying in a blue rug would have been impractical, but she'd brought a bag of dried blue flowers—hydrangeas, cornflowers, and delphiniums—and sprinkled them with love all across the floor. Even the incense, which she'd ordered special for the occasion, gave off a bluish smoke.

She stood and moved quickly but silently to her small black duffel bag, which sat by the door of Orion's bedroom. The second syringe was ready and she removed it carefully from its box. Again she crossed the room and sat next to the professor, the embodiment of the Blue on earth.

Twisting his head as far as it would go, Orion caught a glimpse of the syringe as she set it on the bedside table. He kicked and thrashed, but it was no use. She'd studied knots like she'd studied most everything.

"Don't worry," she said. "That's for later."

Returning to the bag, she retrieved a vial of blue-tinted oil. Leaning over the bound professor, she used the dropper to place a few beads on his forehead and a couple on each cheek. With her gloved hand, she rubbed them in.

"Just relax," she said quietly. "It won't harm you. Let it seep into you, meld with your brilliance, your consciousness, with all you've ever thought and known and that which does the thinking, does the knowing."

Orion breathed heavily through his nose.

She returned to the bag and got out a glass jar of blue ink. On the wall opposite Orion's bed, she began to paint a series of symbols with a thin calligraphy brush. She'd practiced this moment for years, mastering the gentle strokes over thousands of repetitions.

She could hear Orion trying to cry out, but the tape didn't loosen and his screams remained muffled.

When she'd finished writing, she stepped back to admire her work.

She turned back to Orion. "It says, *Amro bodhiananda nia g'uo agando.*" She knew he wouldn't understand its meaning. Only a few dozen people on earth did.

Dr. Isaac Orion spoke three languages, but this wasn't one of them. A forty-two year old quantum physicist, he was the most famous professor at the University of Washington. Originally from Chicago, he'd excelled at math and science from a young age, earning his PhD in physics from MIT when he was only twenty-four. Now he managed a small lab focusing on experiments with quantum entanglement and teleportation.

With everything ready, she sat next to him and reached for the syringe.

His brow contorted. Sweat dripped down his cheeks.

He tried to kick, tried to shout, tried to free himself. But it was no use.

With her free hand, she touched his forehead. "Professor, I see that you are struggling to understand. Don't. There is nothing for you to fear, there is nothing more you need to know, or learn, or do. I am the gatherer of light. I must claim blue. And *you* are blue."

Time slowed. She moved her hand deliberately, its weight heavy in the air, a gentle grip on the syringe.

The injection went as planned. Right into the fleshy part of Orion's thigh. Five hundred milligrams was enough to put down an 800-pound horse. Professor Isaac Orion would be dead in thirty seconds.

He wouldn't suffer. He would not feel a thing.

She set the syringe back in the box and closed her eyes.

She inhaled deeply, drawing in the professor's history, his brilliance—both the natural intelligence he'd been born with and that which he'd acquired through decades of study. She claimed every moment of his life, absorbed all that he was, imbibed his very soul.

As he died she sat in silence, visualizing every facet of the blue light filling her, becoming her.

Royal blue, pastel blue, rich navy blue, eggshell blue.

As his light was extinguished, hers burned brighter.

"Amro bodhiananda nia g'uo agando."

Her hands and feet tingled. Her chest filled with a kind of pride it had never known, the pride of wisdom hard earned.

She was becoming.

"Amro bodhiananda."

She stood and covered his body with a large swatch of royal blue silk, then gathered her belongings.

Her mind blazed with a transcendent intelligence as old as time, older even than that.

It was working.

CHAPTER TWO

Kingston, Washington

Two Weeks Later

CLAIRE ANDERSON SHIFTED in the chair, a smile spreading across her face. "It's *all* final, Susan. Soon, anyway. The ink should be dry on the divorce late next week, and my last day of work is the end of the month."

Susan, her therapist, beamed at her, dropping her usual look of neutrality in favor of a rare, genuine smile. "I'm happy for you, Claire. You've been through *a lot* to get to this place."

Claire folded her hands in her lap. "Still can't believe it. Ten days of work to go. The divorce, well, that's been over a year coming. Nothing left there. But I thought I'd retire from the FBI when I was old and gray. Well, gray-*er*." She brushed back her hair, which was sandy blonde with just a hint of gray. "Leaving behind the job that's *making* it gray, well, that oughta help."

At forty-six years old, she was retiring from the FBI. With

her twins in college and her twelve-year-old son Benny settling into his new school for children with special needs, she was about to experience a kind of freedom she'd been craving for years, but had never thought truly possible.

Time for her garden. Time for her book club. Time to see if she had what it took to write her *own* books. Maybe even time to join a wine club.

"We're almost at the end of our session," Susan said, crossing her left leg over her right. "Is there anything else you'd like to discuss today?"

"I don't think so," Claire said. Even after a year of therapy, she still didn't feel entirely comfortable leading the conversation. She usually left the prodding to Susan.

And Susan was usually ready. "How about Brian? The divorce is almost final, but how is co-parenting going?"

Claire ran a finger over a tiny wrinkle in her cream-colored slacks, as though she could iron out the imperfection. Five minutes left in her session and the last thing she wanted to discuss was her soon-to-be ex-husband. "Brian? Co-parenting. Everything is fine. Really. It's fine."

"Claire, c'mon. I know you're professionally trained to read witnesses when they're lying to you, but I've done a little training myself." Susan nodded up at the row of framed diplomas on her wall. "When I mentioned Brian, you grimaced as though you'd just tasted something foul."

Claire let out a long breath. Not a sigh, not quite anyway. She'd stopped sighing about Brian months ago. She was just… tired. Tired of talking about him. Tired of dealing with his lawyers. Tired of holding everything together. "He's making a little bit more of an effort," she said. "Roughly every other weekend—not *every*—like we'd agreed. A Seahawks game, a video game expo over in Seattle. He still cancels on Benny half the time, though." She felt the heat rising in her chest. "Selfish ba—" She stopped herself.

Susan handed her a box of tissues.

"I've told you before," Claire continued, "Brian's a decent guy—wasn't abusive, didn't drink or smoke or have affairs. I just... don't know if I can ever get over my resentment about how he feels about Benny, despite his recent efforts."

"I understand. It would be a lot for anyone to move past."

When Claire was five months pregnant, they'd found out Benny would be born with Down syndrome. To her, it had been like hearing he'd have brown hair instead of the blonde hair shared by their twin girls, who were seven at the time. Or that he'd be into art and music rather than history and politics. Sure, she knew he'd come with unique circumstances, but so did *every* child.

But to Brian, Benny had been "a problem." Another burden, another issue, another *thing to deal with*. Brian had raised his concerns right there in the doctor's office, and he'd never treated Benny the way he'd treated the twins. Brian's reaction formed a tiny fissure in their marriage. Twelve years of little earthquakes separated them further, and Claire was no longer willing to jump the chasm.

Susan looked down at her watch. "I'm sorry to say, that's our time for today. But I'll see you in two weeks."

Claire stood, adjusting her suit blazer, which matched her cream colored pants.

"And remember," Susan continued, "if you hear that perfectionist voice trying to run things, you know—*I have to do this right, failure is not an option, I am the only one holding everything together*—try to replace it with a more positive one."

"I will," Claire said, but she was already wandering toward the door, eyes scanning the messages that had come in on the work phone she kept silenced during the fifty-minute session.

She had two missed calls and a text that read *Call Me*, all from her direct supervisor, Gerald Hightower, Assistant Special Agent in Charge of the FBI Field Office in Seattle. Her ASAC knew she was off limits between 8 and 8:50 AM every other Monday, so the messages put her on high alert.

"Claire?" Susan's voice cut through her thoughts, which were racing through a dozen possibilities about what new crisis could have caused Hightower to call twice and text.

She looked up briefly. "Sorry, yes, and thank you."

"Claire. Your other phone."

Claire turned and accepted her personal cell phone from Susan's outstretched hand. She'd left it on the side table next to the box of tissues. "Thanks."

The screen was bright with a new text message: *Blimey! They've taken me back in the fold.*

The message was from a number that wasn't in her contacts, an area code she didn't recognize. Probably a mistaken text. A wrong number.

Holding her personal phone on top of her work phone, she tapped out a quick reply: *Number not in contacts. Who is this?*

Out in the hallway of the little office complex, she tucked her personal phone away in her purse and called Hightower back on her work phone. The phone rang as she walked past an insurance agency and an architectural firm, making her way out into the gray drizzle of a cold February day.

"Agent Anderson," Hightower said when he answered. "Sorry, I realized you were engaged, but this one, well…"

Claire stopped halfway across the parking lot, letting the drizzle hit her. *Damn.* She knew that tone. Knew that turn of phrase. She could almost see Hightower. He'd be standing in his office, closing his eyes briefly as though the weight of the world rested on his shoulders.

This one, well… meant that a fresh new horror had crossed his desk. She'd heard the phrase a couple times a year for the last decade, and each time it meant that whatever nightmare he'd just learned of was about to become hers as well.

Except that this time she had an out. Heading toward her

car, she pressed her phone to her ear. "Ten days, Hightower. Don't stick me with something new with ten days to go. And please, call me Claire. Consider it a going away present."

"We've got a situation here," he said. "It's bad, Claire."

As she got into the car and turned it on, the phone automatically connected to the sound system. She pulled out toward the Kingston-Edmonds ferry, which was only a few blocks from her therapist's office. "I'm sure you do. But... ten days."

"I know it's easy to say, 'Not my problem,' but—"

"That's not fair. You know I've always taken on everything that crossed my desk, but I can hear it in your voice, this is something bad."

"You're the woman for this one. Really." Hightower was trying to sound upbeat, even optimistic, like a used car salesman trying to get rid of the worst lemon on the lot. "The latest victim is on your side of the water. Port Angeles. And—"

Claire turned down the gentle hill toward the ferry dock. "The *latest* victim?"

"Hit my desk early this morning. We believe the woman in Port Angeles is the third victim of a serial killer the Oregon office is calling 'The Color Killer.'"

"Hold on," Claire said, hitting the mute button on her dash.

She rolled down her window and waved her ferry pass at the woman in the booth, then drove right onto the bottom deck of the boat that would take her to Edmonds, just north of Seattle. The ferries had been running behind lately, but this morning luck was on her side. She'd set up her sessions with Susan to end at the perfect time to catch the 9:15, which could get her to the office by a little after 10.

"Okay, I'm back," she said as she turned off the car. "*The Color Killer*, you said? Is this a racial thing?"

"Not at all. That at least would be something we've seen before. Something we could understand and profile. This one, well..."

Damn. There it was again. The phrase she dreaded. "What?" Claire demanded.

"This case is much stranger. Connects to the case in Seattle from last week. The professor. Orion. The blue crime scene."

Claire knew that a professor had been murdered in the University District, but it hadn't crossed her desk because the Seattle PD was handling it. "You promised I'd have a say over what I took on during my last six weeks. And you know I'm still wrapping up paperwork from the thing in Port Townsend. Hell, I feel like I'm still wrapping up paperwork from last century."

Hightower said nothing.

"Not to mention the fact that I was *shot* a couple months ago."

Still he said nothing.

He had her trapped. She owed Hightower a lot, and he knew as well as anyone that her curiosity always got the better of her. She sighed. "I'll be in soon. And I'll hear you out."

"Thank you, Claire. That's all I can ask. You know I wouldn't have called if it wasn't important. Plus, your old friend is gonna be on it."

He was trying to make his voice sound light again, but she wasn't buying it. In twenty years in the FBI, she'd made a few friends, sure, but there was something in the way he said it that made her skeptical. "Who?"

"Oh, you'll see."

Then it clicked. As she ended the call, his face flashed through her mind. It was fleshy, red-cheeked, and wore a smile that said, *I know the world's secrets, but will only share them on two conditions: First, that I've downed two pints of lager, and second, that you've acknowledged my genius.*

It was the face of criminal psychologist Fitz Pembroke, III. It had been years since she'd seen him. But she should have known it was Fitz. *Blimey!* Who else would have texted that?

She got out of her car and headed up the stairs to the ferry café for a cappuccino.

She texted him back: *That you, Fitz?*

It was much too early for a glass of wine, but if she'd be speaking with Fitz, she'd need another caffeinated beverage.

And maybe a doughnut.

CHAPTER THREE

AS SHE PULLED into the parking garage of the FBI Headquarters in downtown Seattle, Claire tapped the command button on her console. "Text Sofia."

The bright and cheery AI phone helper replied, "Okay. What would you like to say to Sofia?"

Sofia was a neighboring college student still living with her parents. She'd been helping out since she was fifteen, was always reliable, and welcomed a call at any hour. Most importantly, Benny loved her. And since Brian moved out, Claire had been relying on Sofia more than ever.

"Hey there, Sof. Benny's bus drops him early today. Noon because it's a half day for some random reason. Anyway, I'd hoped to get home to surprise him but, well, something came up at work. There are hot dogs in the fridge, and I cut up a pineapple. His favorite. Thanks."

She waited as the friendly voice repeated her message. "Send it?" it asked sweetly.

"Yes."

"Done," the car responded with synthetic enthusiasm.

"Um, thanks," she said, awkwardly.

Claire loved finding new efficiencies—new ways to save a minute here or five minutes there—and speech-to-text was her latest favorite. It felt wrong to not thank the helpful voice assistant inside her phone. But it felt *equally* wrong to thank it.

Her message received a thumbs up emoji and Claire responded with a row of heart emojis after she'd parked. From the parking garage she took the elevator up to street level, planning to grab another cappuccino in the lobby before her trip up to the fourth floor to see Hightower.

But she didn't even make it to the back of the line. There at the window, staring into the lobby from the sidewalk and grinning like the arrogant bastard that he was, was Fitzgerald Pembroke, III.

His face was just as fleshy and red as usual, but most of it was now covered by a medium length, salt-and-pepper beard. He wore the same brown sports-coat he'd been wearing the last time they'd worked together, and it didn't look like he'd washed or ironed it since.

He waved eagerly, gesturing for her to join him outside. Against her better judgment, she did, taking the revolving door out onto the sidewalk.

"Well, Claire Anderson," he said, "as I live and wheeze."

"Fitz. The man who put the 'broke' in Pembroke." She leaned in and gave his large frame a half-hearted hug. He smelled of stale lager covered up with an overwhelming cologne. Wood and leather. Probably *Aramis,* she thought, a popular cologne in the seventies and eighties that now signaled pretentiousness from yards away. "What are you doing here? The state finally revoke your psychiatrist's license?"

Despite her playful dislike for him, she had a fondness for English accents. Fitz's was a mix of the Queen's English he was surrounded by as a boy and a more working-class Cockney accent he'd picked up during countless hours at the pubs. Plus, he'd lived in Washington for ten years, so he'd taken on a few pronunciations specific to the Pacific Northwest, too.

So even though his accent never came across as stuffy or uptight, his words achieved that nicely. "Very funny, Claire-bear. I've come once again to rescue your lackluster federal investigators with my brilliance. Sounds like they've got a real psycho on their hands, so they called in the best."

Claire smirked and looked past Fitz, scanning the street in an exaggerated manner. "The best? So they're bringing in Becky Reynolds from Quantico?"

"Once again, very funny." He plucked a dark bronze coin from his pocket and initiated a coin walk. Precise maneuvering sent the coin in a fluid dance over his knuckles, jumping from finger to finger.

A skill he must have honed through hours and hours of sedentary practice, Claire thought.

Claire grew serious. "Hightower didn't say much about the case. Did he tell you anything?"

"Very little, actually. So far, just getting my bearings on the agents he wants on this thing. There's a new guy. Out of Idaho, apparently. What you Americans might call a *cowboy*. Real Gary Cooper, John Wayne type. Plus there's a girl from Portland. Orchid or Sunflower or something."

"Girl?"

"Twenty-something. I didn't mean 'girl' with any disrespect. Hightower says she's brilliant, but, at my age, anyone under thirty is a *girl*."

He and Claire were about the same age, but Fitz *did* look older by about a decade. His cheeks were saggy, his eyes puffy, and he'd gained a bit of weight since she'd last seen him, and not just from the beard. "Fitz, never call any woman over the age of twelve a *girl*, got it? Especially one employed by the FBI. Now, tell me what you know about her."

"Apparently she got kicked out of CIRG."

Claire frowned. "For what?" CIRG, the Cyber Initiative and Resource Group, was one of the fastest-growing areas of the FBI, and Claire couldn't help but wonder what one had to do to get kicked out of it, especially if she was as brilliant as Hightower had told Fitz she was.

Fitz chuckled, then put on his high-British accent, trying to sound stuffy and formal. "*Apparently they had concerns about her level of engagement and commitment to the unit's mission.* Despite being one of the most brilliant technical minds of her generation, her *lack of consistent effort was viewed as incompatible with the high-stakes, high-performance expectations of the CIRG.*"

"Where are you getting that from?" Claire asked. "And what does it mean?"

"Hightower read me a bit of her file," Fitz said. "And it means she's a slacker."

They took the revolving door into the lobby and Claire stopped next to a large potted tree. The line for coffee was too long, so she'd have to make do with whatever Hightower had in his office.

She frowned at Fitz. "So Hightower wants to stick me with an arrogant British profiler with a drinking problem and too much cologne, a millennial John Wayne who just arrived in town, and a Gen Z'er who couldn't keep a gig with the unit that takes anyone who can code?"

Fitz looped his arm through hers like they were about to go on a pleasant stroll around Green Lake on a Sunday afternoon. "Crikey, Claire, your job description reads like that of a babysitter."

She wished she was back at home, tending to her garden and waiting for Benny to get home from school. "Be straight with me, Fitz. I've got less than two weeks left and the last thing I can deal with is… well, you know. One of those cases that…" She trailed off, unwilling to complete the thought.

But, as usual, Fitz read right through her and wasn't shy

about speaking it. "One of those cases that gets under your skin? That finds that place deep inside you, the place that shudders at the thought of chaos, of disorder. A case that makes you look at your color-coded files and your pens all facing the same way, your perfect little roses and tidy rows of your garden, your neatly-pressed cream-color suits and your controlled little life and says, 'Yooo-hoooo, Claire-bear, the world is chaotic and dangerous and disordered and deeply imperfect.'"

He paused, a smirk playing on his lips as the coin continued its roll over his knuckles.

"Yeah," he continued, "two-to-one odds says it is *exactly* that kind of case. But here's the rub, Claire. The real world isn't a neatly arranged puzzle where every piece fits. It's a jigsaw puzzle dumped out on the table, edges frayed, pieces missing, pieces from different puzzles added." He grinned. "And the box lid with the picture on it? The dog shredded that years ago. The real world is messy, unpredictable, and sometimes it's downright ugly." He flicked the edge of her blazer. "Suits get wrinkled, Claire. And that terrifies you, doesn't it? Because the minute you let the chaos in, you risk letting that fortress you've built come crumbling down."

She wanted to tell him to go to hell, but she didn't. Truth was, Fitz was right, at least partially. She'd always wished the world was a little better than it was, a little neater than it was. That the puzzle pieces would fit together a little better than they ever actually did.

But what Fitz didn't know was that she'd battled through that for decades, that she hadn't let it keep her from doing her job.

They stopped at the elevator and Fitz stepped back, holding up the coin. He shot her a challenging look, his words sharp but his eyes soft, almost compassionate. "See this coin?"

Claire cocked her head. "Sure."

"It's a Roman *Aureus* from the first century AD, the reign of Julius Caesar."

"How much did that set your *father* back?" She said it with a bit of a sneer. Even though Fitz joked about being the only broke person from a very wealthy British family, she knew it still ate at him.

Fitz smirked. "It set him back plenty, I'm sure. My point is, Caesar thought he could control everything, be dictator in perpetuity, and we all know what happened to him. Stabbed fifty-seven times. You go about controlling every piece of your life and your life will rise up against you. Don't you realize that it's the chaos, the uncertainty, the disarray that keeps things interesting? Babysit me and the youngsters. At the very least, as your dime-store therapist might say, it'll be *an opportunity for growth*."

"I'm almost surprised you flunked out of Oxford and Cambridge."

"Hey, that's not fair." He stepped back, taking mock offense. "I didn't flunk out of anywhere. I was one of the top students at both of those fine British institutions of higher learning."

She raised an eyebrow.

"I did not 'flunk out,'" Fitz insisted. "I was *expelled*. There's an important difference."

The elevator dinged its arrival and she met Fitz's eyes, which were bright blue and, even though she never would have admitted it, sparkled with an intelligence she respected.

"We've gotta get to the meeting with Hightower. For once, just give it to me straight, Fitz. What am I walking into?"

He stepped aside to allow her to lead the way into the elevator. "An ambush, my dear. An ambush."

CHAPTER FOUR

FITZ WAS RIGHT.

The meeting wasn't in Hightower's office, which Claire had always found imposing enough on its own. Instead, it was in Conference Room B, which meant that this case already involved more higher-ups than she was comfortable with.

She wouldn't miss the old, outdated FBI building when she retired, but she *would* miss Conference Room B. One of the only rooms to get a complete renovation in the last decade, it was dominated by a large, polished mahogany table surrounded by high-backed leather chairs. The walls were a stark, clinical white offset by multiple large screens whose glossy black surfaces reflected the harsh, sterile glare of recessed lighting. Everything felt sterile, neat, symmetrical, and orderly.

She loved it.

The meeting hadn't started, but, as she walked in, Claire felt they'd been waiting for her to arrive.

Hightower nodded from the head of the table, his onyx black head gleaming like a polished 8-ball under the lights.

Next to him sat EJ Ley, Special Agent in Charge of the Seattle Field Office, one of the top ten positions in the national

FBI hierarchy and Hightower's direct supervisor. She wore her usual black on black on black, which matched her straight black hair and contrasted with her pale skin. There were rumors that for half of her career she'd spent nights at the office, and Claire doubted she'd seen the sun for most of it. But her presence at the meeting was a surprise.

Next to Ley sat a man in his thirties whose entire face looked like it had been carved from tanned marble. He had the jawline of a Disney prince and the scowl of a Disney villain. She guessed that this was the agent from Idaho Fitz had called a "John Wayne type."

On the wall to her right was the massive disembodied face of Nancy McNamara, Special Agent in Charge of Oregon, displayed on a flatscreen. Her presence meant that the case had already gone interstate.

Fitz pulled out a chair, offering it to Claire with a dramatic flourish, like an overly-formal waiter at a French restaurant neither of them could afford.

Hightower didn't waste any time getting to the point. "We have three victims. Linked, as of this morning, to an interstate serial killer designated UnSub 19. The second murder occurred in Coos Bay, Oregon..." he nodded up toward the screen... "hence SAC McNamara's presence."

Hightower jabbed a thumb at the younger man. "Jack Russo, Field Agent from Idaho, spent the last two years out of the Salt Lake City office. This is his first day. Welcome, Agent Russo."

Jack nodded, but his facial expression didn't change. Claire wasn't sure if he was bored or serious. Either way, it appeared as though his disposition had been carved out of the same stone as his jawline.

"SAC Ley is here to observe, stay abreast of the situation," Hightower concluded.

"I won't be intruding," Ley said, her words fast and clipped. "As you know, after the recent terrorist attack at Lumen Field, many of our best agents were re-assigned to CTD. Counterterrorism is again a major priority. This little squad is all we've got to bring down UnSub 19. I'm in town this week and I'll be in touch with Hightower at least twice daily." She stood and let her eyes land on each member of the team. "If it leaks, or details are shared with the public poorly, this is the kind of case the media can feed on for weeks. Do *not* let this one get out of hand. We don't want our office looking like a clown show." With that, she patted Hightower on the back and walked out.

"Finally, everyone," Hightower continued as she closed the door behind her. "This is Claire Anderson, Supervisory Special Agent, and Fitz Pembroke, formerly of the Behavioral Analysis Unit, now an independent criminal psychologist, profiler, and all-around genius, both self-proclaimed and third-party verified."

Fitz offered a Queen-of-England wave.

Claire gave a curt nod. "Tell us about the case, sir."

Hightower stood and tapped the button on a remote control. The second screen lit up, displaying what initially looked like a peaceful spa in a nice hotel whose decorator was obsessed with the color blue—blue curtains, blue bedspread, blue flower petals strewn on the floor.

"Victim one. Isaac Orion. UW Professor. Aged 42. Murdered in his University District neighborhood home fourteen days ago. February 6th. Found by police the following day when he didn't show up for a big presentation. Was sedated with etomidate, then killed by a massive overdose of opioids. No pain. No torture."

He clicked the button and the picture on the screen changed to a photo of a series of symbols painted on the wall in blue.

"This was on the wall opposite the victim's bed," Hightower continued. "So far it's indecipherable, and it may be gibberish."

Claire could sense Fitz was about to interrupt. He had difficulty containing himself, especially when he had a chance to show off some special knowledge that everyone else in the room lacked.

Hightower held up his index finger in Fitz's general direction. "You'll get your shot. Lemme finish."

He clicked the remote again and the photo changed to a scene similar to the first image except that this room was all black, the victim's face that of an older man, maybe late seventies. He had a few strands of thin black hair and Claire thought she might recognize him.

"Sal Cardinelli," Hightower said. "Sub-boss of the Chicago mob in the eighties. Pushed out by a new wave of younger crooks in ninety-five and relocated to the Pacific Northwest, where he was a small-time player in sports gambling and prostitution. Been living a quiet life in Coos Bay, Oregon since 2005. Murdered five days after Professor Orion. Same drugs in his system. Same everything except for the black and the markings on the wall you see here." He clicked and the image changed to a series of symbols that looked similar to the last, but painted in black.

Hightower clicked again, this time revealing an all-white room and the body of an older woman on a small bed.

"Third victim: Sister Marybeth Peters, killed February 16th, four days ago. Our Lady of the Olympic Abbey, a rural Trappistine monastery and working dairy farm in Port Angeles, Washington."

"What's Trappistine mean?" The question was from Jack, the younger man with the stone jawline.

"A Roman Catholic contemplative religious order," Fitz said before anyone else could reply. "It's a strict order of nuns and monks. Poverty, silence, manual labor." He chuckled. "I'll give it a pass, thanks."

Hightower looked annoyed by their back-and-forth. "Sister Peters was killed in the same way. Subdued with etomidate, then suffered an opioid-induced cardiac arrest."

He clicked one final time, revealing another series of symbols, this time written in white on a wall of simple gray stone.

Hightower walked back to his chair and sat heavily, shaking his head in disgust. It was the physical expression of his phrase, *This one, well...*

"Three murders, ten days apart. Seattle, then Coos Bay, Oregon, then back to Washington State. Zero connections between the victims so far. Zero obvious patterns in the movement of the killer." He let his eyes fall on Claire. "I'd like you to take on the role of Supervisory Special Agent and oversee the crew." He nodded at Fitz, then at Jack. "You'll have a technical analyst, too. Violet Wei."

That reminded Claire. From what Fitz had said, she'd thought this highly-touted tech guru would be at the meeting. "Where is she?" Claire asked.

Hightower looked a bit embarrassed. "She's not much of a meeting-person."

Claire didn't understand what that meant, but at the moment it was the least of her concerns. In past cases, Hightower would have summarized what leads and evidence they had, what work local officers had done before the FBI swooped in and grabbed the case. But he hadn't said anything, which meant he didn't *have* anything.

"Witnesses?" Claire asked. "Evidence? Video surveillance? Motive? Anything on the meaning of the colors?"

Hightower looked up. "We had a newer profiler take a stab when you were on your way in." He clicked again and the screen displayed a brief report.

Claire read the report along with everyone else in the room, interrupted several times by Fitz's mocking laughter.

Preliminary Subject Profile - Case 1023-B

The perpetrator, henceforth designated as UnSub 19 (Unknown Subject 19), displays a preference for theatrics, as evidenced by the distinct color schemes (blue, black, and white) at each crime scene. UnSub 19 appears to be meticulous, perhaps even obsessive, given the careful execution of the murders and the elaborate staging. The method of killing, via painless injection, suggests a level of empathy towards the victims or perhaps a tendency to shy away from overt violence. There exists a possibility that the color-coded rooms may represent some form of coded message or symbolism. It may be hypothesized that UnSub 19 has a background in arts or design, and possibly in the medical field or with access to medical equipment. Further investigation is necessary for more conclusive profiling.

Others were still reading when Fitz could no longer contain himself. "That reads like a toddler wrote it. And the insight... I mean, 'There exists a possibility that the color-coded rooms may represent some form of coded message or symbolism.' Ya think!?"

Hightower shot a piercing look at Fitz. "You are here to move us forward, not give an opinion on past efforts. Got it?"

He must really need the paycheck, Claire thought when Fitz didn't open his mouth to respond.

She stood up and looked from the new guy, Jack, to Fitz, then let her eyes land on Hightower. "So lemme get this straight: We've got three intricately-staged murders ten days apart, you have no leads, and you want me to bring this home before I retire?"

Hightower frowned. "Please sit down. You said you'd hear me out."

Claire sat and folded her arms.

Fitz had said she was walking into an ambush and, as usual, he'd been right.

CHAPTER FIVE

"FIRST IMPRESSIONS. Just a sentence or two from each of you." Hightower pointed at the screen, where Nancy McNamara had been watching silently. "You first."

"I went to the Coos Bay scene myself," McNamara began. "Sal Cardinelli being murdered was enough to get me out of bed. We spent three days looking into his death as a possible mob hit." She shook her head. "That was before we learned about Isaac Orion being killed in Seattle and the obvious similarities. Cardinelli lived in a little beach house. He had one of those video doorbell alarm systems, but it had been disabled. Neighbors saw nothing. Folks who knew him said he had no enemies in the area. Friendliest guy you'd ever meet. Has a bodyguard, but he was at the gym at the time of the killing. We believe the killer studied their routines as the bodyguard was with Cardinelli all but maybe six hours per week."

"I'll add," Hightower said, "that the monastery does not have surveillance and that the alarm system at Orion's house had also been disabled. Other evidence points to the fact that the killer studied their schedules and routines at length to avoid confrontation." After a pause, he turned to Jack. "Agent Russo, first thoughts?"

Jack Russo ran a hand over his bald head and spoke slowly, in a deep voice that sounded a little older than his age, which Claire put at around thirty. "First impressions? I'd want to double check surveillance. There must be something from a neighbor's house, a gas station, a traffic cam. Something. And witnesses. I'd want a dozen agents knocking on doors and asking questions. Someone saw something. Then I'd look at the murder weapon. The opioids and the etomidate, the latter of which is hard to come by. Surveil all three crime scenes in case the killer returns. Tap the phones at the monastery."

Hightower considered this. "Violet Wei is already working on the surveillance aspect and trying to track any large sales of etomidate. The opioids, well, sadly they will be tougher to track, common as they are."

He pointed at Fitz, whose face had the look of an eager schoolboy who knew the right answer and was waiting impatiently for his turn. "I know you've been holding your tongue. Now's your time."

Fitz pushed his chair back.

"Stay seated," Hightower barked.

Fitz cleared his throat. "We start with the symbols on the wall. The killer is telling us something, but what? It's—"

"It's the scrawlings of a deranged killer," Jack interjected. "Probably made it up between alien abductions."

Fitz frowned and shook his head. "Only thing worse than a gobshite is an American gobshite." He leaned forward, looking at Jack with disdain, almost pity. "They teach you that in special ops? You learn that on one of your black-bag jobs?" Despite Hightower's admonition, Fitz stood. "As someone who speaks five languages, Jackie-boy—and, oh yeah, I looked you up—you should be able to recognize gibberish from real communication when it's painted on a wall in front of you. Those glyphs were consistent and detailed enough to know they're a language, even if *we* can't read it yet." Fitz turned his gaze to Hightower, tugging at his salt-and-pepper beard thoughtfully. "I don't know those symbols, but they are somewhat similar to Sanskrit characters and, in my opinion, one-hundred percent real. And meaningful. *Not* the random scrawlings of a deranged killer. And like I was saying before I was so rudely interrupted, the killer is giving himself away. If he doesn't want to be caught, he at least wants to be understood. We'll bring in linguists from the University of Washington, possibly religious scholars. I know some from my time at Oxford and Cambridge."

"I forget," Jack said, his voice full of derision. "Was it pills or cheating on exams?"

Everyone turned to stare at him.

"Why you were kicked out of Cambridge and Oxford," Jack continued. "Which was it? Pills or cheating?" He stood and leveled his gaze on Fitz. "Yeah, I looked you up, too, old man."

Fitz sat back down. "It was pills," he said, not a hint of shame in his voice. "I didn't need to cheat on exams."

Claire already knew Fitz had past issues with pills. She knew he still enjoyed lager a little too much, but assumed Hightower had confirmed that his last drug rehab had stuck, otherwise he wouldn't be here.

A thick silence hung in the air, and finally Hightower raised his eyes to Claire.

She placed her hands on the table in front of her, interlacing her fingers. "As much fun as it is to listen to ego-maniacal men argue back and forth, I'm going to pass." Hightower tried to interrupt, but she held up an open palm like a stop sign. "Let me finish. I said I'd hear you out, and I did. You know I don't like loose ends, messes. I've got nine and a half days left. Even if we get lucky and solve this thing, it'll be months of paperwork." She stood. "These two are more than capable. Let one of them take the lead on this. I hear Violet Wei is great, too."

Claire walked out of the room, feeling proud of herself for not taking the case, but ashamed for lying. What she hadn't said was that the real reason she didn't want the case was that it gave her *that feeling*.

The feeling she'd had when she was seventeen and knew deep down that her boyfriend was cheating on her weeks before she'd found any proof. The feeling she had walking alone in a dark parking garage at night, or the feeling she had when her phone rang at 2 AM.

It was a dark, dreadful feeling that made her want to seek out something comforting, something joyful, like curling up in bed to watch Netflix, or hanging out in Benny's room so she could absorb some of his infectious joy while he recorded one of his YouTube videos.

It was a feeling that told her to back away from the situation as fast as possible.

In the past, she hadn't always listened.

This time she would.

CHAPTER SIX

Kingston, Washington

THAT EVENING, Benny was halfway through recording a YouTube video when Claire stopped outside his bedroom door to listen. "Bro," he was saying, "here's the thing about pay-to-win games, here's how they get you." He spoke loudly and with a notable lisp—his "s" sounding more like "th"—and his voice carried a joy that could lighten her spirit, no matter what kind of horrific set of crimes she'd worked on that day. "It's a little thing called the dopamine response system. You get halfway through a game, riding little pings of joy. Then, suddenly, you're stuck and you keep losing. For only ninety-nine cents you can continue and get to the next stage, but guess what happens then? Yup, you get stuck again. Drop another ninety-nine cents in the slot and... *ping*! You guessed it. Problem is, turns out ninety-nine cents is pretty close to a dollar and if you go for that ping a few hundred times, suddenly you've spent all your lunch money. Okay, that's it for today, thanks for watching my vid. This is Benny saying keep chill, keep gaming, and, above all else, have an amazing time."

His channel was called *Down with Gaming* and, though it had initially been aimed at gamers living with Down syndrome, his infectious humor and encyclopedic knowledge of video games had made it a hit with a much wider audience.

Claire had been hesitant at first when he'd asked to start a channel. She knew about online bullying and had concerns about privacy. But eventually she'd relented. And she hadn't regretted it. She made sure Benny spent plenty of time off the computer as well, and his success with the channel had made him more happy than she'd ever seen him.

She knocked on the door. "Benny, I'm home."

Half a second later the door swung open. "Hi, mom."

"Whoa, did you grow at school today? What the heck are they feeding you?" Benny was twelve and seemed to be getting taller by the day.

He smiled. "Just regular food."

"So, spinach and liverwurst?"

"Gross. Do you wanna see my latest video? It's not edited yet but…"

"I think I just heard a lot of it through the door, Bean-Bean, how about dinner?"

"Sof gave me three hot dogs when I got home." He paused, considering. "But I'll have three more." He laughed at his own comedic timing, then bounded down the stairs.

He really did look bigger than he had that morning. She liked to think all her children had gotten some of her and their father's best qualities. Benny certainly had a lot of his father in him. He had Brian's sense of humor and lightheartedness, plus his wavy brown hair and ability to eat any amount of food without gaining weight.

She hoped he hadn't inherited Brian's self-centeredness. She got enough of that at work from men like Fitz. Benny did love to hear himself talk, but his talk was playful, funny, and giving to others.

"Mooooom!" It was Benny's voice, calling from the kitchen. "I can't find the juice!"

He'd definitely gotten Brian's impatience, but that didn't bother her much.

∼

A couple hours later, Benny was in his room editing his video and Claire sat in her little office next to the kitchen. Originally it had been a large closet, but now it held a small desk and a laptop. On the wall to her left was a framed map of Washington State, on which a single red star marked the town of Moses Lake, where she'd been born and where her parents had died, along with thirty-five other members of their religious group, in a mass suicide. She'd been one year old and was the only survivor.

For the last half hour her eyes had been wandering back and forth between the blank word document on her screen and a framed t-shirt on the wall above her desk.

It was a warm-up shirt from her time on the UW basketball team. Being five-foot-nine and quite skilled, she'd been good enough to get a scholarship, though she'd lacked the sheer athleticism to become a star. Under the UW logo was coach Shirley Condon's mantra for the team: *Commitment yields excellence, but only love yields transcendent performance.*

The saying stuck with her because, athletically, she had never been the most gifted. But her dogged persistence and her unwillingness to quit had turned her into an excellent shooter. In high school she led the state of Washington in three-point shooting percentage. Commitment had never been a problem for her. It was the second part she struggled with, and she'd had the t-shirt framed a few years after graduating as a reminder that commitment, no matter how total, may not be enough.

Coach Condon stressed that showing up on time, working

hard, was the minimum. She wanted her players to love the game so much that they could transcend those who were merely putting in the work.

Grabbing her iPad and wine glass, she headed out the French doors off the kitchen and sat in the gazebo in her little garden. The night was cool, but she needed the fresh air, and at least it wasn't raining.

Scrolling through her iPad, she opened her email and saw a message from Hightower. The subject read: *Just in Case,* and the email contained only a single attachment.

Damn. It was part of the case file. Specifically, the part with the bios of the victims. Hightower knew Claire well enough to know that she wouldn't be able to resist.

Scrolling through the file, she learned that the first victim, Isaac Orion, was not just the most famous professor at UW, he was a rockstar author and public speaker as well as a consultant for NASA. Although she didn't understand anything about his research—which focused on quantum entanglement and the possibility of an atom existing in two places at once—she could tell he was a big deal.

There were probably a lot of people who wanted the second victim dead. Sal Cardinelli had been a ruthless criminal, suspected in a half dozen murders, but never convicted. What she didn't understand was what possible motivation UnSub 19 could have to make those two men his victims. They seemed from two different worlds.

And the third murder was even stranger. Sister Marybeth Peters lived in a remote monastery, never bothering a soul. Not only that, whereas Orion lived alone and Cardinelli lived in a remote location, Peters lived in confined quarters with dozens of other people. Claire wanted to see photos, videos of the monastery to try to piece together how a killer could have gained access undetected, how he could have set up the room all in white and done her act of evil without anyone noticing.

But no, she was declining the case.

She sipped her wine and scrolled down further in the bio of Marybeth Peters. Then she saw someone she recognized. A much younger version of the victim, it was a picture labeled "Marybeth O'Malley." She knew that face, and that name. At UW over two decades ago, to fulfill her one remaining humanities credit, Claire had taken a class on world religion from a young teacher by that name. O'Malley had been a fairly well known author and speaker on the spiritual aspects and ancient traditions of her religion. According to the file, O'Malley had been divorced in 2001, changed her name back to Marybeth Peters, and had been living in the monastery ever since.

Claire had only had twenty-six 50-minute classes with O'Malley, but they'd been life altering. Claire had always known that she was adopted, but during her freshman year of college she'd learned how her parents had died. Finding out had launched her into a strange relationship with religions. A relationship Marybeth O'Malley had helped heal with her kind, inclusive, and sweeping view of world religions.

Claire set the iPad on the bench and stood, walking through the garden, the damp ground squishing under her feet.

She sipped her wine and paced.

For the better part of the last year she'd imagined herself on the verge of retirement taking nice, relaxed strolls through her summer garden.

Now it was forty degrees out, no blooms were in sight, and she was anything but relaxed.

A feeling of dread had embedded itself in her belly, one she knew from experience there was only one way to dislodge.

CHAPTER SEVEN

Seattle, Washington

The next morning

FITZ AND JACK were halfway through a pissing contest in Hightower's office when Claire walked in, coffee in hand.

"I've got twenty years experience on this kid, boss," Fitz was saying, his voice sounding like he'd just been tossed out of a pub after six pints of lager.

Jack folded his arms. "You're a psych consultant. When was the last time a shrink led a case? It's never happened." He turned to face Fitz. "Not to mention, are you drunk right now?"

Hightower raised an eyebrow at Fitz.

"Absolutely not. I've got some problems, and I'll be the first to admit it. But I do not come in drunk. I cut myself off at midnight. This is just how I sound in the morning."

"It's true," Claire offered. "A case we worked a couple years back, it took me a week to believe he wasn't starting the workday drunk."

Fitz scowled at Jack. "See! I may live life as a scruffy bungler, but I never drink and profile. And thank you, Claire." He turned to Hightower. "Now, how about it, Gerry? I've already gotten through the beginnings of a profile on this sicko and I promise this one is gonna be solved with this—" Fitz tapped his temple with his index finger—"not with *that*." He reached out to squeeze Jack's bicep muscle, which was visible through his thin, crisp white button-up.

Jack glared at him. "Yeah, I have muscles. Wouldn't hurt you to go to the gym every decade or two." He faced Hightower. "I was also valedictorian of my high school, did covert ops all over the world for military intelligence, asset recruitment, and I understand electronic surveillance, wiretaps. And, as you know, I speak five languages and this may well have an international component."

"Well I speak one language," Fitz said, "but if you want I can look up four other ways to tell you to go fu—"

"Boys!" Claire interjected. "The argument's moot."

"Why?" Hightower asked.

Apparently none of them had bothered to wonder why she'd interrupted the meeting. "*I'm* leading the team."

Fitz looked as though his eyes might pop out of his head.

Jack's face showed a flash of surprise, then frustration, but, to Claire's surprise, he pivoted quickly. "Better you than him." He jabbed a thumb toward Fitz.

Though Jack and Fitz were both standing, Hightower sat behind his desk. "Missed us too much?" he asked. He didn't wait for a reply. "You'll be working out of the Boiler Room. Anything you need. Anything." He smiled. "And I'm glad you showed up when you did. I was about to let these two arm wrestle for the gig."

"Arm wrestling," Fitz said, "is as much about sheer girth as it is about muscle." He sized up Jack. "I would have liked my chances."

Jack scoffed.

Hightower stood and folded his arms. "There's a famous old text, Plato's *Republic*. It's about politics and philosophy and the best way to run a city, a state, a country. Now, I got a C+ in philosophy, but I do recall one takeaway. The best person to be in charge is the one who wants it least."

Jack's face showed no expression. Fitz held up a finger as though he might launch a philosophical counter argument, but Hightower silenced him with a glare, then nodded toward Claire. "Bring this thing in, Agent Anderson. It'll be a good going away present for us."

She wasn't sure she wanted to give the FBI a going away present, but she was sure she wanted to solve the case. "I have two conditions," she said. "Vivian Greene. *Kiko*. I want her added to the squad. Need another field agent to balance out these two." She indicated Fitz and Jack.

Hightower frowned. "She's young."

"I know her. She can handle it. She's been through hell and back in this life already."

Claire first met Vivian Kikua "Kiko" Greene when she was invited back to the University of Washington as an FBI alum to give a guest lecture in a criminology class. The bright young student immediately stood out to Claire with her insightful questions.

Then, a few months later, Claire saw Kiko shine in a different light on the UW theater stage. Inhabiting the rambunctious role of the Fool in a Shakespeare production, Kiko revealed impressive acting talent. Claire returned to watch Kiko capture diverse personas perfectly in other productions. Soon she made it a personal goal to mentor Kiko and recruit her unique skills into the FBI, where her chameleon-like abilities would be invaluable. In fact, Kiko had played a key role in solving a recent drug ring murder out in Port Townsend, Washington.

Hightower nodded. "I'll get her in. But remember, you've got Violet Wei, too. She's already been working on this from a secure laptop at home. And today she finally came into the office."

Claire nodded. "And you're sure she's good?"

"Define *good*." Hightower smiled.

Fitz said, "If I may, sir and madam, she was expelled from MIT at the age of eighteen, when she was a junior. They let her in when she was sixteen."

"What did she get expelled for?" Claire asked.

Fitz shrugged. "Couldn't find that, but I'd love to ask her."

"That piece we can't talk about," Hightower said. "It's part of her deal. Claire, what's the second condition?"

She finished her cappuccino and tossed the cup in Hightower's trash can. "That I have total supervisory authority over these two." She jabbed a thumb in each direction, then walked out before getting an answer.

CHAPTER EIGHT

THE BOILER ROOM was what they called the basement conference area. It had been retrofitted for human inhabitants when the Federal Government—in their infinite wisdom—decided not to build a new FBI headquarters in Seattle. Instead, they'd gotten a miniscule budget to transform part of the basement into workspaces.

That was fine by Claire. She was comfortable here, and it was what they had.

A relic of the building's origins, the centerpiece was a massive steel table that had seen years of use. Five worn leather chairs surrounded it. No windows broke up the pale concrete walls, giving the room a basement feel despite its high-tech functions. A large display screen took up one wall, its glow bouncing off the exposed pipes and brick. The scent of old paper mixed with fresh coffee, dust, and worn leather spoke to the room's history and present uses.

When Claire arrived, Fitz was sitting with his feet up on the conference table, head in a book, sipping nervously from a giant can of some energy drink that looked like it was made for young spring breakers, not aging Englishmen.

In one corner, a modern desk stood out with its two blinking computer screens, constantly refreshing with new information. Sitting at the desk and looking like she might be sucked into one of the screens was a tiny woman with straight black hair.

"Are you Violet?" Claire called.

No response.

"Violet Wei?"

Still no response.

Fitz nodded in the affirmative at Claire, then clapped his hands once loudly, trying to get Violet's attention.

Nothing.

Claire walked across the room and looked over her shoulders. She was running different programs, one on each of the two monitors, switching back and forth between them at lightning speed. The desk was covered with snack wrappers and empty cans, causing Claire to wonder how she'd managed to make such a mess in so little time.

She touched her shoulder and Violet recoiled. "Just a sec."

Claire waited.

More clicking.

She waited.

"Okay, done." Violet turned to face her. "You're Agent Anderson?" Her words were short and clipped, as though damn near every syllable was an inconvenience.

Claire nodded. "What were you working on?"

Violet scrunched up her nose. "Many things, most of which you'd find insanely boring." She hit *Enter* on one of the keyboards on her desk. Something dinged and, on the far wall of the conference room, a huge screen lit up. "That's our virtual whiteboard," Violet said, pointing back without turning. "I can feed any and all info from the case into it and organize it any one of a hundred ways. Both older records and newer stuff."

"That's great."

Violet shrugged. "I've been told I'm always the brightest, just not always the brightest ray of sunshine."

"Noted." Claire had still not seen Violet's face. It was like speaking to a Cousin Itt with jet-black hair.

"Here's the deal," Violet said, still facing her computers, "let me do my computery thing and I'll make your job easier. I'll make many of your problems disappear. I'll anticipate a hundred others and quash them before they happen." She paused, thinking. "Couple nights ago I had a random date with a guy on that dating app, *Dreamboat*. He was bragging about speaking five languages. I told him I speak dozens. English, Chinese, and about twenty different coding languages. He said those didn't count, but the world is run on code and—"

"*Melanie?*" It was Jack's voice.

Claire saw Violet's face for the first time as she turned to look in his direction. Behind her thick glasses, Claire thought she read surprise in her eyes.

"Oh, so you're *that* Jack." Violet returned to her screens. "My real name's Violet, by the way."

Jack stood in the doorway, a confused look passing over his face briefly. "Alright. Violet. Got it." He found a seat at the communal desk.

Claire put the awkward moment together in her mind. Although there was no absolute rule about not dating a colleague, Claire had never seen it end well. She added it to her mental to-do list to check in with Jack or Violet—if she ever saw her face again—next time they were alone.

Claire took her seat at the head of the table just as Kiko arrived. She wore a bright outfit—a yellow suit accented with pink and orange—the only one of them not wearing black, white, or gray.

Kiko stopped in the doorway, surveyed the room, then ran up and hugged Claire, not giving her time to stand up. "Hey, fairy godmother," Kiko said. "Thanks for getting me out of the evidence room." She laughed loudly. "Why anyone thought I'd be good at that is beyond me."

Then, straightening her suit, she introduced herself to Jack, Fitz, and Violet, then took a seat. One thing Claire admired about Kiko was her ability to switch personas seamlessly. She'd studied to be an actor, so it made sense, but Claire thought it was also a natural ability.

"Okay," Claire said, standing. "Now that everyone knows everyone, let's get into it." She nodded toward Violet. "Do you have the—" She hadn't finished the sentence when the first case summary popped up on the giant virtual whiteboard. She didn't know if Violet was good at her job, but at least she was fast. "Thank you."

∼

It took an hour to go over the details of the three cases and to get everyone on the same page. When they'd finished, Claire paced back and forth in front of her chair. "I want to hear from everyone, but first, did anyone notice that the murders were all five days apart?"

"Could be coincidence," Jack said.

"No," Violet said, "it couldn't."

Fitz turned. "I hate to agree with Captain America here, but sure it could. Three murders total, each one five days apart. If there were five or ten, maybe, but—"

"Time of death," Violet said, her words clipped and impatient. She turned to face the room and spoke from memory. "Isaac Orion, 11PM. Time of death, Sal Cardinelli, whose body was discovered later so they can't be sure, estimated to be between 10 PM and midnight. Time of death, Marybeth Peters, between 10:30 PM and 11:30 PM."

Claire said. "Good work, Violet. The killer was aiming for 11-ish."

"But," Fitz countered, "people are creatures of habit, and if the killer is following a five-day cycle, it might be because that's what fits their regular schedule or routine, not necessarily because they're choosing that interval with any specific intent."

Violet wasn't done. She spoke staring into thin air as though it were a computer screen. "In a five-day span, or 120 hours, the probability of a murder at any given hour, presuming randomness, is 1 in 120, or 0.83%. To know the likelihood of two murders occurring almost exactly 120 hours apart we multiply the 0.83% chance by itself, landing at approximately 0.0069%. Next, to find the probability of a third murder happening 120 hours after the second, we multiply the prior probability, 0.0069%, by 0.83%, reaching a final probability of roughly 0.000057%. Assuming random murder times, the chance of three murders occurring exactly five days apart independently is 0.000057%. That's the same as the chance of finding a four-leaf clover, being dealt a royal flush in a game of poker, and having a meteorite land in your backyard while you're hosting a barbecue, all in the same day. It's a level of improbability that makes winning the lottery feel like a certainty. If we think it's a coincidence, I'm buying a scratcher."

"Bloody hell." Fitz slowly swiveled his chair towards Claire, and shot her a look of marvel. "Now I *really* need to know why this one got kicked out of MIT."

Claire was determined not to let Fitz throw them off the relevant aspects of the investigation. "Assuming the killer is aiming for *exactly* five days apart," she said, "and taking into consideration the victims, the symbols on the wall, what might it mean? The five thing."

Violet threw a picture of the symbols up on the screen just as the word came out of Claire's mouth.

Fitz chugged the rest of his energy drink and tossed the can toward the recycling bin, missing badly. "From religion: Five pillars of Islam, five Holy Wounds of Christ on the cross, five precepts in Buddhism, five books of the Torah, and from psychology we've got the five stages of grief. Even Maslow's hierarchy of needs is usually depicted as a five-tiered pyramid, with basic needs at the bottom and self-actualization at the top."

"The five senses," Violet added. "The five elements."

"The high five," Jack said, stone faced.

Kiko laughed. "And the five-dollar footlong at Subway."

"They don't have those anymore," Jack said. "Inflation."

"Laugh all you want," Fitz said. "But our killer has something to say. It may be ridiculous to *us*, but I promise it is important to them. I promise it will turn out to have a level of meaning in their life that we don't yet understand."

"And if the killer isn't done," Violet added, "we have until 11 PM tonight to stop the next murder."

Violet's words hung heavy in the room. Claire felt their weight land on her shoulders. "Fitz," she said. "I want you to get started on a real profile. Make it as long and detailed as you want. If you feel the need to include detailed analysis of Jung and Freud, fine, just make sure there's a two-page summary for those of us without two PhDs."

"Three," Fitz corrected.

"I thought you got kicked out of everywhere," Jack said.

"Nope, only Oxford and Cambridge. Your American universities will accept any run of the mill British genius."

That got a loud laugh out of Kiko, but Claire had moved on. Turning to Jack, she said, "You and I are going to Port Angeles."

Jack stood. "Already made some calls. Abbot originally told police he saw nothing suspicious. When I pressed him, he admitted that there was someone around over the last month who, while not suspicious, wasn't part of the monastery's normal routine. I told him we'd be out there later this morning."

"Great work," Claire said, "I don't suppose you have an in on a chopper?"

"No, but my BuCar is gassed and ready to go. If we leave now we can catch the 10:10 ferry."

"Excellent. Given that the murder at the monastery is the most recent and that things run on a strict routine there, memories will be fresh and it won't be difficult for the community to identify things—or people—outside the norm. Our efforts in this direction look most likely to yield a witness."

"No witnesses yet," Violet said. "At least not according to what we currently have on file. Not in any of the three murders."

"I know," Claire said. "Let's hope we can shake down some memories and come up with one."

Claire turned to Kiko, who, at twenty-three, was the youngest in the room and looked a little uncomfortable. "You're coming as well."

Kiko jumped up and reached for her coat. "Road trip!"

"And I will be staying with the computers?" Violet asked, her tone hopeful.

Claire nodded. "In case we need any information from the files."

"Anything else?" Violet asked.

"Be our information filter," Claire said. "This thing hasn't hit the news as a serial killer case yet, but it might. And there is already a lot of online nonsense about the individual murders, especially Orion's. There is endless speculation out there, and of course almost all of it is wrong. But keep an eye out. If a tenth of one percent of all the BS online can give us something to go on, I want you to find it and give it to us. Comb the internet, social media, whatever. Maybe something pops. Also, try to hunt down any other records you can find. Surveillance footage, cellphone records, anything the locals might have missed. And, speaking of locals—Seattle PD, Coos Bay, Port Angeles—get in touch with them and tell them who's in charge now."

"On it," Violet confirmed.

"Okay then." Claire made brief eye contact with each of the four members of her motley crew. "Let's jet."

CHAPTER NINE

"SO," Jack said, taking the turn out of the parking garage like he was auditioning for an F1 race, "how long you been with us probie?"

Claire knew the question was directed at Kiko, who was in the back of the SUV, but she didn't respond.

"Probationary agent," Claire said, turning her head slightly. "Russo wants to know how long you've been one."

"I don't respond to nicknames," Kiko said.

"This is her fourth month," Claire offered.

Jack sped down a steep hill, swerved around a delivery truck, and took the turn onto the waterfront road that led to the ferry. "Isn't *Kiko* a nickname?"

"He's got you there, *Vivian*," Claire said.

"I definitely don't answer to *that* name. Only my mother called me Vivian."

"Vivian, from the Latin word *vivus*, meaning full of life," Jack said. "It's nice. It suits you."

"Everyone has called me Kiko for years. It's my name now. Short for Kikuno, my middle name."

"I know," Jack said. "I looked you up. Vivian Kikuno

Greene. Age 23, graduate of University of Washington. Made me wonder how many theater majors end up in the FBI. Mother passed away when you were sixteen, at which point you spent two years in the foster system. Father wasn't in the picture from what I could tell. Must have left a big hole in your identity."

"Man," Claire said, "there's not a subtle bone in your body, is there, Jack?" Claire looked back at Kiko, who was staring blankly out the window.

"Sorry," Jack said. "I've been told I can be overly direct."

"No offense taken," Kiko said.

As Jack coasted through the loading dock and eased onto the ferry, Claire studied Kiko in the rearview mirror. Of course, Claire already knew all about her background, but she also knew Kiko wouldn't appreciate the intrusion.

Jack was directed to follow a line of cars to the left-most side of the ferry's lower level. He parked and shut off the engine. "What I don't know is, what's your background?"

"You mean like racial background?" Kiko fired from the back seat. "Why does that matter?"

Jack cracked the window, allowing some of the cool, salty air to fill the car. "Doesn't matter in the least in terms of how I treat you personally. Matters because our lives depend on knowing each other. Back in special ops, the people beside me weren't just my team, they were my lifeline. Knowing who's got your back, understanding their strengths, their fears, it's not for fun, it's what keeps you from getting killed."

Kiko chuckled and Jack turned to face her, staring her down. "I'm serious. I've walked through hell and back with my brothers and sisters, and I'd do it again without hesitation because I trust them with my life as they trust me with theirs. My dad was an Italian immigrant, my mom was a member of the Nez Perce tribe in rural Idaho. I relied on every sort of person you can imagine to stay alive overseas. I need you to know who I am, where I come from, what I've been through. We need to forge an unbreakable bond. In this line of work, we're not just colleagues; we're a band of warriors, and we stand or fall together."

Jack's eyes were locked on Kiko's and the staring match that followed was long enough to make Claire uncomfortable. It wasn't that she disagreed with the sentiment, but the intensity with which Jack had launched his monologue had been striking.

After what felt like a minute but was probably only five or ten seconds, Kiko smiled slightly. "I need some air."

She got out of the car and leaned on the ferry's metal railing, staring out at the choppy water. Claire and Jack followed her out. They were on the bottom level, but the view was still beautiful as they watched Seattle recede behind them.

"I'll go first," Jack said. "Grew up on a cattle ranch in rural Idaho. Grangeville. Like I said, mom's Nez Perce, dad was a rancher. They split when I was little so I was back and forth between the Rez and the ranch. Snagged an ROTC scholarship. Post-graduation, I dove into military intelligence, picked up Arabic and Russian. Covert ops became my world; black bag jobs, surveillance, asset recruitment. You name it, I did it. Can't spill much about those days, though. Six years in, and I found myself back home, but civilian life felt like wearing someone else's shoes. That's when the FBI came calling."

"How'd your dad end up on a ranch in Idaho?" Claire asked. "Not a lot of Italians out there."

Jack chuckled. "I was the only kid in school whose name ended in a vowel. A summer exchange program in high school brought him to Idaho and he fell in love with the wide-open spaces and the ranching life. He came back after college, worked his way from a ranch hand to owning his own place."

Claire leaned on the hood of the SUV. "So since you're keen on swapping life narratives, what's the background on you and Violet Wei?"

"Boom!" Kiko said, her voice triumphant. "I knew you two had a look."

"I'm not one to get into people's personal lives," Claire said. "But if it affects the office—"

"It doesn't," Jack said flatly, shaking his head.

"C'mon," Kiko said. "Claire doesn't miss much. Spill the beans, Russo."

Jack adjusted the collar on his crisp white button-down, appearing slightly uncomfortable for the first time. "We met on the *Dreamboat* app. Week ago."

Claire frowned. "Did you know she was—"

"FBI? No way! You think I would have dated her if I had? I didn't even know her real name, apparently."

"You know you can't—" Claire began.

"Don't waste your breath." Jack shook his head. "She broke it off, right then and there from her computer, during the meeting. 'We are no longer dating,' was her word-for-word text."

There was a long silence, then Jack said, "Hard pivot back to you, Kiko."

Kiko laughed. "Like Claire said, I don't like to talk much about my past. It wasn't a lot of fun to be me back then. Plus, you already looked me up. But to answer your question from earlier. Mom was half Black and half Japanese. My paternal granddad was a Jew from Brooklyn—that's where the 'Greene' comes from. My dad's mom was Samoan." She smiled. "When I was in theater, I was the all-purpose actor. When they needed a Black character, that was me. When they needed an Asian character, me. I even played Yente in *Fiddler on the Roof*. First Yente with dreadlocks, I think, and—if I do say so myself—I nailed it."

"She did," Claire agreed. "I saw it. Her Yente could outmatch the *Dreamboat* app any day."

"I get that." Kiko's eyes sparkled. "That's funny."

"Enlighten me," Jack said, totally lost.

"Yente was the O.G. matchmaker," Kiko said. She hunched her upper back and shifted her facial expression, making herself look a few decades older. Then she spoke with the distinct inflection of an older woman with a Yiddish-speaking background. "*Even the worst husband is better than no husband. True? Of course, true.*"

"Woah," Jack said. "When did we pick up this old lady?" He turned to Claire. "What about you?"

"I assume you already looked me up, too."

"Sure did. Small town overachiever. Separated from your husband. Three children. Norwegian background."

Claire stared at Jack.

"What?" he asked, the cocky look on his face disappearing for half a second.

Claire folded her arms. "I'm just trying to decide how much of a problem you're going to be. Fitz is already one know-it-all too many."

Jack smirked. "And when you put that level of pure arrogance in this package?" He stepped back as though inviting them to take in his muscular frame.

"Oh, *puh-leeze!*" Kiko said.

Claire laughed. "Swedish," she corrected. "On both sides. My father used to say he was more fair than pickled herring."

∼

The world outside transitioned from the bustling bumper-to-bumper trail of cars disembarking the ferry to the stark gray and green expanse of the Olympic Peninsula. It was late morning and the sun was behind a thin layer of clouds, casting a soft, diffused light over the evergreen landscape. The road ahead was a ribbon of wet asphalt, its surroundings of scattered homes and businesses blanketed by a thin layer of frost.

Crossing the Hood Canal Bridge, Claire had the sensation

of leaving the world behind. Seagulls soared and dived, catching the wind as it moved up off the bridge, then hovering in stillness as though captured on a postcard against the wide-open, panoramic views. When she was young, she spent many summer weekends fishing and camping in this area, and winter weekends exploring Hurricane Ridge with her family.

When the car hit the Jefferson county side of the water she set her memories aside. She'd need a sharp and focused mind to help catch this killer.

∽

The smell of cows struck Claire the moment she opened the car door. Glancing to her right, she saw a large fenced-in area where a couple dozen of them were milling about, some chewing on grass and some standing wide-eyed and occasionally twitching their tails. Up a slight slope, a beautiful stone monastery overlooked the cow pasture and the three barns that dotted the landscape within the fencing.

"We make both milk and cheese here," a voice said from behind her. "Grass fed."

Claire turned to see a man standing a few yards up the slope. He wore the traditional robe of the monastery, a deep brown to reflect humility and earthiness. She approached and, thanks to the cultural sensitivity training she'd had over the years, she stifled a handshake reflex, recalling that monks don't shake hands. Instead, she offered a brief smile and quick nod of her head. "Special Agent Claire Anderson."

"Hello, and welcome. I'm Brother Michael."

He looked to be a few years older than Claire, likely early fifties, but he carried the subtle signs of age gracefully, with crow's feet etching the corners of his kind, blue eyes, and strands of silver threading through his otherwise brown, cropped hair. His frame was lean yet sturdy, suggesting a life of physical labor intertwined with spiritual discipline.

Jack and Kiko appeared beside her. "These are Agents Jack Russo and Vivian Greene."

"Where's the Abbot?" Jack asked.

Claire shot him a look.

"What he means to say," Kiko said, "is we're very sorry for the loss of Sister Peters."

"And eager to get to the bottom of her death," Claire added.

"Abbot Rasmussen is ready to see you," Brother Michael said.

"Forgot my notebook," Kiko said, turning to jog back to the car.

"On the phone," Jack said, "the Abbot mentioned that someone had been around. Someone who—"

Brother Michael held up a palm serenely, but close enough to Jack's face to silence him. "Allow me to stop you there. Abbot Rasmussen can fill you in and—"

"*Ackkkk*! Help!"

Claire turned toward Kiko's scream to find the young agent slowly backing away from the SUV and from the largest bull Claire had ever seen.

The giant animal had sauntered into the parking lot, its curiosity presumably piqued by the guests. It stood between the shiny SUV and Kiko and was staring her down like she owed it money. The bull flared its nostrils, sucking air with quick gasps as it moved its head from side to side. With a forceful exhale, snot dripped down in thick, tenacious threads. Slowly weaving closer, it continued drawing breath with fits and starts, sniffing her.

"Uh, Jack?" Kiko called, her voice wavering.

"Oh no, Ferdinand is loose again," Brother Michael said. "I'll—"

"Don't worry, Kiko," Jack called out, walking purposefully toward her. "Just stop moving."

Kiko froze and, when he reached her, Jack stepped in front, positioning himself between Kiko and the bull, producing a handkerchief with a flourish. "Grew up around these guys," he explained, gently waving the cloth to redirect the bull's attention. "Back away slowly, toward Agent Anderson."

Kiko eased back until she was next to Claire, then grabbed her forearm. Her hand was shaking. "That thing is huge," she said.

"He weighs an actual ton," Brother Michael said. "But Ferdinand's really not dangerous."

Jack gently waved the handkerchief as he sidestepped away from the SUV and toward the fenced-in pasture.

Claire couldn't help but smile. The animal, seemingly captivated by Jack's impromptu bullfighting routine, stared for ten or twenty long seconds, then lumbered away, its interest waning.

When the bull was twenty yards away, Jack returned, casting a sardonic smile at Kiko. "So, are you enjoying your first visit to a ranch?"

CHAPTER TEN

ABBOT RASMUSSEN'S office was nicer than Claire had expected.

As Brother Michael led them in, she noticed the walls first, adorned with a tasteful blend of religious iconography and a few personal mementos, contrasting with the simple, unadorned floor of polished wood that creaked softly underfoot. It had a large window facing northeast, offering a nice view of the water from its perch on the second floor.

Abbot Rasmussen stood behind a large antique desk in the center of the room, a sour look across his face. "Welcome, although I'm sorry to be greeting you under these circumstances."

A faint scent of incense lingered in the air, mingling with the mustiness of old books that filled a tall, carved wooden bookcase against one wall, creating an ambiance that was both scholarly and spiritual.

Claire stepped into the center of the large room as Brother Michael excused himself. Jack stayed half a pace behind. Beside him, Kiko stood, arms at her sides, following Claire's direction to let them do the talking for now.

"Welcome, Agent Russo," the Abbot said. "We spoke briefly on the phone, did we not?"

Jack stepped forward and shook his hand. "We did. And I've read the files about Sister Peters' daily routine and habits, but I wonder, were there any recent disputes between her and other members of the monastery or locals, or—"

"There certainly were *not*," Abbot Rasmussen interrupted, "She was a beloved member of the community, both ours and the one that extends beyond our walls."

In his early sixties, Abbot Rasmussen presented a contrast to the simplicity of Brother Michael. His robes, a richer, deeper hue than those of his brethren, hinted at a penchant for subtle extravagance, adorned with discreet but elegant embroidery. His balding head, ringed with wisps of gray hair, and his slightly stooped posture spoke of years spent within the monastery's walls, yet there lingered an air of worldly savvy about him.

"We understand," Claire said. "We'll want to look at her quarters."

"Fine, fine," Abbot Rasmussen said, walking around the desk.

"Before we do," Claire continued, "Agent Russo mentioned the monastery does not have security cameras. Is that correct?"

"Here within these walls, we place our trust in a higher power," Abbot Rasmussen said. "We know that God is our security, watching over us with a vigilance no earthly device can match."

His demeanor was cordial, but somehow guarded, his eyes darting away mid-sentence, as if preoccupied by burdens unknown.

Claire folded her arms, not defiantly, just waiting. Sometimes she found that saying nothing was the best way to get someone talking. She wanted to see if he would recognize the irony in what he'd just said.

Jack was not so patient. "Was God also head of security for Sister Peters?"

Claire shot him a look, but he didn't seem to pick up on it.

Before the Abbot could reply, Jack said something that surprised her even more. "Is that a *Jaeger LeCoultre?*"

The Abbot looked surprised for half a second, then spoke quickly and, unless Claire was misreading him, a little defensively. "A gift." He cleared his throat. "It was a gift."

"What are we talking about?" Claire asked, confused.

"Nothing," Jack said. "I'm a watch guy is all. That's a nice one."

Claire glanced at the Abbot's wrist, but he'd pulled it back into his sleeve.

Noticing Claire's questioning stare, he held up his hand, allowing the sleeve to fall back, revealing a watch with a thin brown strap and a simple, stainless steel and white face. It looked like a decent watch, but not especially fancy.

Abbot Rasmussen cleared his throat again and moved toward the door. "I'll take you to her quarters."

They walked in silence to the stairwell, but when the Abbot began leading them up to the third floor, Jack paused. "Agent Anderson, you'll want to ask about the person who was around over the last month, but I'll have to catch up with you later." He held up his phone as though that might be explanation enough. Then, responding to Claire's quizzical look, he added, "Quick call. It's nothing."

Claire suspected Jack was lying, and the fact that he pulled Kiko down the stairs with him was proof. Still, as she made her way into Sister Peters' small quarters with the Abbot, she didn't mind. One of the reasons Claire was in her role was that she was good at letting people do their jobs. And, for now, she trusted Jack.

Sister Peters' room was a modest, sparsely furnished cell, embodying the essence of monastic simplicity.

"How long did she live in this room?" she asked.

"Twenty-two years."

"I was her student before then."

"At the University of Washington?" he asked.

Claire nodded, taking small steps around the room. She inspected the narrow bed and plain woolen blanket, then the small, wooden desk that held only a notebook and a well-worn Bible. The air carried the faint scent of beeswax candles and lavender, a testament to her devotion and the herbal remedies she often created. There was also a faint, sterile odor of forensic chemicals that contrasted sharply with the room's natural, earthy undertones.

She'd avoided looking at it up to that point, but she allowed her eyes to rise to take in the strange glyphs painted in white on the gray wall.

Claire knew next to nothing about languages, but even more than when she'd seen photographs of them, the symbols carried an ancient, otherworldly feel to them. For a moment her head grew light and she wavered, leaning against the wall.

"Are you alright?" the Abbot asked.

Gathering herself, Claire said, "Fine, fine. So nothing changed in her behavior?" She was eager to change the subject. "Agent Russo mentioned someone new had been around."

"Alexander Angelica. Magazine reporter doing a piece on monasteries." As he spoke, he stepped back into the hallway to give Claire more room. Standing in the doorway, he continued. "He was interested in the histories and spiritual practices of Western monasteries. California, Oregon, Washington. His focus was on capturing the details of monastic life in the modern age, how these ancient traditions have adapted and thrived amidst contemporary society. He spent a few days here, speaking to many of us, asking about our daily routines, our work with the community, and our philosophies. Sister Peters, because of her successful life before she joined us here, was of special interest."

Alarm bells ringing in her head, Claire scribbled a few notes in the small notebook she kept in her pocket. "And the name of the magazine?"

"*Contemporary Spirituality Digest*, I believe."

"And where is this reporter now?"

The Abbot shook his head. "He had finished his visit about a week before the occurrence. I believe he was headed out to Oregon to continue his reporting at the Willamette Valley Hermitage."

"Has her family been out to visit?"

"We *were* her family," the Abbot said.

Claire raised an eyebrow.

"No. She lost contact with them long ago. A source of great pain to her, which she was asking for God's help with."

Claire finished her inspection of the room and stepped out into the quiet hallway. "What was she like? Really like? What did she care about?"

Abbot Rasmussen offered a sad smile. "Sister Peters and I held different views on many things. But we always were able to converse with respect. That was one of her gifts. She truly respected all people." He led her down the hall and into the stairwell, and continued as he slowly descended. "I still remember our late night conversations about environmental stewardship and its place in religious life. Sister Peters believed in a more active role for the church in environmental advocacy, often challenging traditional views with her perspectives on conservation. Her commitment to this and other causes was both admirable and, at times, a point of gentle contention between us."

"*Gentle* contention?" Claire asked, purposefully trying to ruffle his feathers.

Abbot Rasmussen paused at the bottom of the stairs. "Gentle. *Always* gentle."

CHAPTER ELEVEN

THE SUN HAD BROKEN through the cloud cover and the courtyard of the monastery was bright as Jack led Kiko back toward the car.

"What the hell are we doing?" Kiko asked.

"Did you see that $12,000 watch?"

Kiko shrugged. "It didn't look like much to me."

"It's an understated design," Jack said, "but what is an Abbot doing with a watch like that?"

Kiko stopped and took Jack by the forearm. "You still didn't answer my question. What are we doing?"

She was on the tall side, but still he had about four inches on her. Her eyes were fiery and somehow accusatory, but not in a way that bothered him. It was as though she had aggression built into her look, and he had to admit that he liked it. "His window was cracked," Jack said. "The Abbot's."

He shook his arm free and walked around the side of the monastery. Stopping, he glanced up at the second-floor window. As before, it was cracked a few inches.

"You're not serious," Kiko said.

"You ever read *All the President's Men*?"

"Saw the movie, and I know where you're going with this. 'Follow the money,' right? But he could have gotten that watch from—"

Jack shushed her as he saw Brother Michael and another man carrying buckets toward a small barn down the slope toward the road. Brother Michael waved at them and took a few steps in their direction.

"I hear you are a great performer," Jack said. "Can you cause a bit of a distraction?"

Kiko offered up an odd look. He wasn't sure if it was a frown or a wry smile. Perhaps it was both at the same time. But without another word, she began walking briskly toward Brother Michael and the others.

"Settle a debate between me and my colleague," she called to Brother Michael.

Jack hurried to catch up with her and they stopped under the barn's old roof, which hung a few feet past a big arched entrance. Brother Michael set down his bucket. Two others, both dressed in the same plain brown robes that Brother Michael wore, put their hands on their hips and listened.

"Now," Kiko continued, "my buddy here believes that monasteries can't really exist in the modern world the way they did, say, in the 13th and 14th centuries. Obviously that is true on the one hand, as you have technologies that were not available then. But I would argue that, fundamentally, your lives are not too dissimilar."

She waved a hand at the barn then out at the fields, and Jack noticed her eyes momentarily widen at seeing the bull, despite the fact that he was now behind a fence.

"In fact," she continued, "I'd argue that fundamentally your lives are very similar. Cheese making, farming, late nights with books and candles. What would you say?" But before they could respond, she grabbed her head and dropped to her knees with a strange, guttural scream. "Ouch," she yelled.

Brother Michael dropped to his knees as well. "What is it?" he asked.

"The sun," she said, "it gives me migraines and..." she closed her eyes hard and pressed her hands into her temples... "One of them just hit hard."

"What can we do to help?" Brother Michael asked.

"I need to lie down immediately," Kiko said. "Can we go in the barn?"

Brother Michael touched her shoulder gently. "Certainly."

Kiko stood slowly, then wobbled and nearly collapsed into the arms of the two other men. They held her up, and Brother Michael took her by the left arm as they led her into the barn.

Heading for the corner, Kiko nearly collapsed onto a hay bail. Jack held back his laughter at the performance. It was a bit over the top, but she seemed to know her audience as the men looked genuinely concerned.

"I will go get Claire," Jack said.

Kiko called out, "Grab my sunglasses from the car. They always help with migraines."

"Will do."

But Jack wasn't going to find Claire, and he wasn't going back to the car. Walking backwards, eyes on the arched entryway to the barn, he made it to the wall underneath the Abbot's office.

The stone on the side of the monastery was irregular, jutting out at little angles that made it look like one of the climbing walls Jack tested himself on from time to time.

Scaling it proved even easier than he'd expected. The window to the Abbot's office was only about twelve feet above the ground, and Jack made it up in under thirty seconds.

Sliding his hand under the opening, he gripped the windowsill and pushed the window the rest of the way open. Then, yanking himself up, he pulled himself headfirst into the warm office and closed the window behind him.

Glancing back down, he saw Brother Michael emerging from the barn, but he didn't seem to suspect anything. He was probably rushing to get a glass of water for Kiko, or perhaps she'd sent him on some other ridiculous errand.

It didn't matter.

Alone in the room, Jack turned his attention to the stacks of papers on the large antique desk.

CHAPTER TWELVE

CLAIRE WASN'T sure what Jack and Kiko were up to, but she decided to keep Abbot Rasmussen preoccupied while she could to give them the benefit of the doubt.

Plus, she had more questions about the journalist. "If you don't mind, Abbot Rasmussen, I'd like to look something up on my phone and show you some photographs. Do you have a few more minutes?"

"Certainly," he said. "Would you like to return to my office?"

"I'd prefer to take a look at the outbuildings. Can we do that?" She nodded in the direction of a slope where small structures dotted the field.

Abbot Rasmussen stepped aside and gestured up a dirt path that led toward what looked like a miniature version of the monastery. It had similar stone and small windows and a similar roof.

"What is this structure?" she asked.

"It is my home," the Abbot said. "Would you like to take a quick tour?"

Claire nodded and they began walking.

She used her peripheral vision to keep pace with the Abbot

while looking at her phone to do a quick Google search for the magazine *Contemporary Spirituality Digest*. Her first instinct, of course, had been that it was fake. That their killer had been checking out his next victim under the pretense of being a reporter. She wasn't sure how the timelines would fit together, but it was worth looking into.

The website appeared to be legitimate, and she quickly found a photograph of the reporter in question. Alexander Angelica. He looked to be in his late twenties with dark brown hair in a bowl cut, making him look like one of The Beatles.

"Abbot Rasmussen, is this him?" she asked, holding out the phone.

The Abbot stopped and took the phone. He studied the photograph for longer than Claire believed was necessary. "That's him," he said, continuing to look at the image.

When he returned the phone, Claire followed Abbot Rasmussen up to his house. They paused out front and Claire held up a finger as if to say 'hold on one moment.' Scanning through the website of *Contemporary Spirituality Digest*, she looked for anything strange, but it all looked legitimate to her. Then again, she was no expert in digital forensics. She forwarded the link to Violet, attaching a quick note to check out the back end of the website in any way she could.

"You said the journalist left about a week before the murder," Claire noted. "Do you know if he has heard about the death of Sister Peters? It was reported in a few places."

"He *did* hear," replied Abbot Rasmussen. "In fact, we got a call maybe two days ago offering condolences and offering to take any of her quotes out of his article before publication, out of respect."

"Did he seem genuine to you?"

Abbot Rasmussen thought about this for a long time. "He did. I've spoken with thousands of people, both religious and non-religious. Men and women of all faiths and those who aren't religious at all. I'm not a big believer in psychology or therapy or any of those modern modalities. I don't believe they can touch the soul. But I do believe I have the ability to read men and women in their relationship with God. I don't believe this journalist could have had anything to do with this horrific crime."

Claire gave him a long look, studying the thin lines on his face. His manner of speech was overly practiced, but she was beginning to feel that it was just his way. "You'll pass along any contact information you have on the reporter?"

"Certainly," the Abbot said, unlocking the front door of his house and leading her in.

CHAPTER THIRTEEN

INSIDE THE ABBOT'S darkened office, Jack engaged *tactical insight* mode, scanning the papers on the desk, checking a few drawers, then finally landing on a large oak filing cabinet in the corner by the window. He immediately recognized the cabinet was full of standard bills, tax receipts, and the like.

What he was looking for was something that didn't fit in. And he found it rather quickly.

Toward the bottom was a file of a different color—dull brown—rather than the standard yellowish cream color of the rest of them. It was older, too, well worn, and that told Jack that, when the filing system had been updated at some point in the last few years judging by the crispness of the folders, this one had been left out.

Within two minutes of slipping into the Abbot's office he was cracking a file labeled: *Sister Peters' Contracts.*

The way his mind worked was all about efficiency: ask a question, find an answer, then on to the next question. Right now his mind had two interrelated questions: why was Abbot Rasmussen wearing a $12,000 watch, and did it have anything to do with Sister Peters or her murder?

Back in rural Idaho, Jack had been valedictorian of his high school, but he'd never thought of himself as smart. His classmate Vicky had been gifted in math and science and had gotten into all the top schools even though her overall GPA was lower than his. She actually cared about math—she worked equations in her free time, went to summer camp at Cal-Tech, and built robots for fun.

Jack, on the other hand, wasn't brilliant at math or science, history, or English. He had excelled at *getting good grades*, a wholly different kind of intelligence. He had a way of seeing what was important, eliminating what wasn't, and locking in on the crucial stuff. Within five minutes of receiving a syllabus on the first day of a new class, Jack had figured out what he needed to do to get an A. He was also impatient by nature, so naturally he looked for the *quickest* route to maintain his perfect GPA.

Vicky had once called him superficial, but he thought of himself as gifted with the skill of *tactical insight,* an intense focus that cuts out everything but what is needed to get a job done. And the mission of school had always seemed to him to be grades, not learning.

He took every shortcut imaginable to complete *mission straight-A student*, putting in the absolute minimum effort. He never cheated, though. Something inside him wouldn't allow it, even when presented with opportunities. But impatience, combined with the goal of being valedictorian, had created a kind of supercomputer within him. Like the Terminator, he'd lock onto a problem—get an A—and use the most efficient path to get there.

The one skill he *did* have—the one thing at which he was truly gifted—was languages. Maybe it was listening to his dad speak Italian to the horses and cows as a little boy, or his mom struggling to learn the language of her tribe.

Or perhaps it was stumbling into an early chatroom for gamers. He'd never needed much sleep—four to five hours a night. It had been enough then and still was, so when homework was done, he'd often stay up all hours playing multiplayer online games on his computer. Many of the early internet games had chat rooms full of international players in different timezones. Ironically, most of his formative interactions in Russian and Spanish were exchanges of insults related to the game *Counter-Strike*. By the time he was seventeen he could tell people to kick rocks in four languages.

So the second his feet touched down in the Abbot's office, Jack had gone into *tactical-insight* mode, eliminating all non-relevant information and honing in on what was important.

And the papers in his hands were exactly what he'd been looking for.

He'd been aware that Sister Peters was fairly well known in the nineties. The information he found in these folders informed him of something new.

She still received consistent royalties for her books and the option for her best-selling memoir had been picked up again only six months earlier. The folder contained royalty reports for each of the last sixteen years from two different publishers. And though no single payment had been more than $3,500, they totaled $60,000 over 16 years. Not bad, but not enough to kill for. And certainly no reason to stage an elaborate, color-coded murder of Sister Peters along with two others.

At the back of the file, Jack found an old contract from a film studio, optioning the rights to Sister Peters' memoir: *Echoes of Divinity*. As he rifled through the contract, which had a half-dozen addenda paper clipped to it, the story of the memoir took shape in his mind.

Just a year before Sister Peters joined the monastery, *Echoes of Divinity* hit the best-seller list and was optioned for the big screen. Year after year the option was renewed. He traced the trajectory of increasing amounts—from $15,000 to $25,000, each increment a testament to the growing but unmet interest in bringing the memoir to live action. Typical Hollywood, Jack knew. The most significant leap came when a new production company took over the rights in 2019, upping the option price to $50,000. The contract had been sent with a letter, promising big things and even suggesting that Meryl Streep was interested in playing Sister Peters in the film. But, like most Hollywood fantasies, nothing came of it.

What interested Jack most, however, was that the Abbot was the signatory on all the options after Sister Peters joined the monastery. She'd signed over the rights to her life's work for the benefit of the place and, apparently, that work had funded much of the monastery's operations. Jack wondered if it had also funded designer watches and other lavish lifestyle choices for the Abbot.

Jack's ears pricked. A sound outside the door.

In an instant he'd slipped beneath the desk, hugging his knees tight to his chest and lowering his head. His breaths were shallow and controlled as he watched the wall for a change of light or shadow.

The door swung open with a soft groan. The footsteps were heavy and the man was whistling a tune, some pop song Jack vaguely recognized. Not the Abbot, he thought.

A few seconds of footsteps, then a pair of scuffed sneakers shuffled past him. A hand moved toward him.

He held his breath.

The hand grabbed a silver trashcan next to the desk.

Jack heard the sound of papers being dumped into a trash bag.

It was a custodian.

The man set the can back down with a metallic clang.

Jack remained motionless, every muscle coiled in readiness. The cleaning guy seemed to linger by the desk, close enough for Jack to hear the rustle of his shirt.

Then footsteps again, and the man was gone, the door clicking shut behind him.

Jack sat under the desk, enjoying the silence. He missed special ops.

Working with the FBI was meaningful, but offered little opportunity for danger. Truth was, he'd spent most of his time doing paperwork.

He stood and returned the file to the cabinet, putting the story together in his mind.

Sister Peters had transferred her royalties to the monastery as part of her vows. Not having any children and taking the vows for life, it made sense. This meant her book earnings, speaking fees, and film rights had gone to the monastery for two decades.

The question remaining was whether the Abbot was siphoning off a percentage for himself.

A quick rummage through desk drawers and a stack of papers on a coffee table told Jack that the Abbot didn't store any personal files in this office. Most likely, he had those in his quarters, or perhaps he'd destroyed them altogether. It wouldn't be impossible to get his bank records, but it would take some time, and Jack wasn't a patient man.

But he was already fairly sure he'd find out that the Abbot was using her money for himself. If so, the only other question was whether that was connected to Sister Peters' death.

CHAPTER FOURTEEN

TEN MINUTES LATER, Claire returned to the car to find Jack leaning casually on the hood, looking as though he was posing for the cover of *Ruggedly Handsome* magazine.

Kiko, on the other hand, sat in the backseat, speaking to Jack through a rolled-down window.

Reading the confusion on Claire's face, Jack called to her, "Kiko is afraid the bull will return."

"No way. I'm not afraid," Kiko called through the window. "Just wisely cautious."

Claire walked around the car to the window and raised an eyebrow at Kiko. "Don't give me any BS. Where did you two go and what did you find out?"

"Between Jack and these bulls, I am the *least* likely to be giving you BS." Kiko glanced toward the field and, seeing no bulls in sight, slowly got out of the car to join Jack.

Claire folded her arms, squinting against the sun, which had grown bright despite the cold.

"The short version," Jack said, "is that Sister Peters has generated a ton of cash for this place over the last twentyish years. So far, I have no evidence that the Abbot has funneled any of that to himself, but his $12,000 watch speaks volumes. I'm sure Violet can get access to the financial records we need fairly quickly. And dollars to donuts, that's going to show that he is corrupt as hell."

"First of all," Claire said, "it's not as easy as you think to pull financial records. At this moment, I'm not going to ask exactly how you found out about Sister Peters generating money for this place, but I know it wasn't because you asked the Abbot."

"He literally scaled a wall," Kiko blurted out.

Claire frowned.

Jack opened his mouth, but Claire held up a single finger, silencing him. "I saw in your record that you have a concept of yourself as specializing in tactical something or other."

"Tactical insight," Jack said.

"Whatever," Claire responded. "As a military man, I'm sure you can understand the difference between tactics and strategy. So let's get something straight. On *this team*, strategy is my department. I have no doubt you are good at what you do, otherwise you wouldn't be here. But you have to do things within the confines of my overall plan. Got it?"

Jack held her gaze for a long time and opened his mouth as though he was going to say something, but Claire had a formidable gaze of her own. She had no interest in getting into a pissing contest with Jack on their first day. And she had no doubts about his talents, either. But she knew that if she didn't assert herself now, his capricious tendencies could become a problem.

She'd worked with a number of "freelancers," as they were sometimes called. Men—and they were almost *always* men— who liked to take matters into their own hands. They usually had good intentions, saving a life or solving a crime, but her job was not only to solve a crime, but to make sure it was prosecutable.

Otherwise, what was the point?

Jack and Kiko's little stunt could have jeopardized that. And she needed to let Jack know she was going to be calling everyone's shots, including his.

After a long moment, Jack nodded. "Got it," he said, and, to her surprise, he smiled. "I have no problem working for a woman, by the way. It has nothing to do with that, you know. I'm just like this."

"Got it," she echoed, and offered a quick smile back.

"So what did *you* find out, Claire?" Kiko asked.

The truth was, the visit to the Abbot's private quarters had yielded little. She'd been surprised by some of the high-end furnishings he had, which contrasted with the sparse decor in the rest of the monastery, but she had little doubt that he was genuinely mourning the loss of Sister Peters.

But before Claire could answer, her phone rang.

Violet.

Claire put it on speakerphone as Jack and Kiko huddled around to hear.

"I've got something," Violet said. "Something quite interesting. Claire, the magazine website you sent me was set up only four months ago, but it has over a hundred articles, some dating back to 2015."

"How is that possible?" Claire asked.

"What about—" Jack tried to answer, but Claire held up a hand to shut him up.

"The site was only registered four months ago," Violet continued, "and most of the content is high-end, AI-generated crap. They're not *real* articles. No one wrote them. Most of the photographs on the website are heavily edited stock photos that I was able to trace back to their original websites. Someone wanted to create a convincing-looking magazine, and they did a pretty decent job of it."

Claire leaned on the car and took a deep breath. Whenever

she got the first break in a case, something tingled inside her. Like the first sip of a really good wine, or the rush of endorphins in her brain brought on by the venti peppermint mocha she allowed herself a couple times every winter. It was pleasure, mingled with the sense that something was simply right with the world. She had no idea where this was going, but she knew that—for the first time—she had something rock solid.

"What about the reporter?" she asked.

"The reporter is the only real thing about this magazine," Violet said. "Not his name, of course. I mean, Alexander Angelica? Who comes up with that alias? But I ran the photo through an image search and figured out quickly that the reporter is a real person."

"Who?" Kiko asked.

"Oh, hey Kiko," Violet said. "How is Port Angeles?"

"They have animals here," Kiko said. "I'm personally not a fan of animals."

Violet laughed. "Not a fan of animals? That's not something you want to admit. That's like admitting you hate ice cream."

"*I* hate ice cream," Jack said.

Kiko scoffed. "You probably just hate carbs. And it's not like I'm *against* animals, like I'm morally opposed or something. But when a 2000 pound bull approaches you as though he wants to eat you for lunch, it's normal for a city girl like me to be a little trepidatious."

"Can we get back to it?" Claire asked.

"Sorry," Violet said. "The guy's name is Damian Henderson. About six months ago, just about every trace of him was erased from the internet. Social media accounts, an old blog, that sort of thing."

"So how did you find it?" Jack asked.

"Hold on a second," Violet said. "Fitz is buzzing at me."

Claire waved Jack and Kiko into the car and got in the front seat herself. She turned on the vehicle and the call automatically switched over to the car's audio system.

In the background, Violet told Fitz to hold on for a second, then said, "Damian Henderson. No criminal record. Long story short, this guy did everything he could to erase himself from the internet, but some stuff is archived and I found a little bit out about him. One old cell phone number, which we already tried. Disconnected. It was attached to an address in central Washington. But I already confirmed that the apartment building that was there at the time was leveled two years ago. A new one has been built up in its place, so it's unlikely he's still there. Pulled up his social security number, and there are no recent records of addresses or new phone numbers. Whatever is going on here, this guy decided to get off the grid around the same time they built this fake magazine website."

"Wait a second," Claire said, gripping her hands tight on the steering wheel. "You said *they*."

"Yeah," Violet said. "Even though this stuff was easy for me to figure out, it wouldn't have been easy for most people to figure out. And it's not easy to do. Particularly the way they erased most of his online footprints. Whoever is behind this is a tech person. A hacker of some sort. Someone who knows what they're doing."

"So that doesn't explain why you said 'they,'" Jack interjected. "Seems like this Damian guy is our killer. Why can't he be a tech person?"

Claire nodded along. It's exactly what she had been thinking.

"Well, I did find out one more thing about Damian Henderson," Violet said. "He graduated in 2015 with a 2.2 GPA from Central Washington State College. That makes him thirty or so, which matches what I found through social security. He flunked every math and science class he ever took. Barely graduated by passing some basic English and communications courses. Unless this plot goes back that far, and he had some ingenious plan to appear inept at math and computing, there's no way this guy is behind the technological side of this." She mumbled something under her breath and then said, "Fitz wants to say something."

Jack took the moment of silence as an opportunity. "Violet, what sort of financial records can you get us for the monastery without a warrant and without breaking any laws?"

"All of them," Violet said. "It's a non-profit, and their yearly tax statements are online. Accessible to anyone for free. I'll have them all when you get back. Anything in particular I should be looking for?"

Claire glanced at Jack, and she expected him to be smirking, but he wasn't. His attitude walked a fine line between confidence and arrogance, and, assuming she could channel his skills in the right direction, she was beginning to realize just how valuable an asset he would be.

"Well," Jack said, "assuming that he wouldn't put any obvious crimes into his tax records, look for any inconsistencies, any unexplained incoming or outgoing money, especially *outgoing*. Any expenses that don't seem reasonable."

"Got it," Violet said. "Here's Fitz."

Claire eased the SUV down the muddy dirt road away from the monastery and toward the water. There were two pieces of this case about which she was *not* an expert: technology and ancient lost languages. She had just gotten a hefty dose of the first and she was bracing herself internally for a deluge of the second.

"Hey Fitz," Claire said. "Let me guess, you traced that script back to before the Roman Empire, before ancient Egypt, before the Mesopotamians, to a long-lost civilization that answers every question humanity can muster?"

There was a long pause.

"No," Fitz said, obviously amused with himself. "I just wanted to let you know that I got us a dog."

"Wh... what?" Claire stammered.

"Dear God," Kiko groaned.

"Dog," Jack corrected. "I believe he said Dog."

CHAPTER FIFTEEN

Coeur d'Alene, Idaho

AS AFTERNOON TURNED TO EVENING, she stood in the corner of the small garage gym, breathing slowly, almost silently, and waiting.

Free weights and other equipment surrounded her. A small refrigerator hummed in the corner, filled no doubt with energy drinks, steroids, and other supplements. Shielding her from view was a giant heavy bag that dangled from a chain, nearly brushing the concrete floor.

Soon, the carrier of the Red would arrive.

Johnny "The Flame" Stadler was a 25-year-old MMA fighter who'd become a local legend before breaking onto the national scene in the last year. Although he'd lost his one light-heavyweight championship bout in the UFC, he was training for a rematch. He'd only lost due to catching the flu a week before the fight, and he'd still lasted all five rounds, only defeated by split decision. Now, odds were eight to one in his favor for the rematch.

While searching for the perfect fighter, the perfect embodiment of the Red, she'd landed on Stadler early. He wasn't the most famous fighter in the world—not yet anyway—but his power, strength, vitality, and energy burst from the screen more than any other athlete, any other human.

Unlike the professor, unlike the nun, this man could literally kill her within seconds. He'd broken three arms in professional fights using his favorite hold, the armbar. And that was just in the clips she could find on YouTube. He'd been trained in boxing, wrestling, and Brazilian jiu-jitsu; he'd even spent three months studying kung fu in China. He was physically dominant, and he'd been expertly trained to hurt people.

That meant she'd need to be even more careful than before.

She heard the front door slam. Stadler was right on time. One didn't reach his level of physical mastery without discipline, and she knew he'd be walking into his home gym between six and six fifteen for his second workout of the day.

From her hiding spot, she turned on his stereo and slowly raised the volume from the cell phone concealed in her pocket. Hacking into his new smart stereo system, which he'd bragged about on his Instagram feed, was the easy part.

She raised the volume again, and again. The music was death metal, layers of fast guitars and violent drums along with an angry singer shouting in German.

Stadler's table of protein powders and dry supplements was right next to the stereo, and she could hear the pill bottles bouncing on the table from the bass notes as they exploded from the speakers.

She couldn't hear his footsteps, but she knew they were coming. A moment later, the door leading from his laundry room to his garage creaked open. As she expected, he turned immediately and stood in front of the stereo, his back to her, surely wondering what had gone wrong with his new sound system that it would begin playing randomly.

Taking four slow, precise, silent steps, she approached him. Soft yellow light from an outdoor fixture streamed through the windows on the top half of the garage door, illuminating the dust particles hovering between them. As he turned down the stereo, she dropped to one knee and thrust the needle into his bulky calf muscle, exposed as usual beneath his knee-length shorts.

He spun around.

She leapt back.

His eyes grew wide, his jaw popping. He lunged for her, but she dodged and ran around to the other side of a workout bench. Grunting, he leapt forward and reached for her, but the etomidate hit his system and he collapsed before he reached her: a 200-pound muscled behemoth, brought down by a needle no bigger than a sliver of mechanical pencil lead.

∽

"What the hell?" He swatted at his leg like he was after a mosquito. "Who the hell are you?"

"I am the gatherer of light," she said, painting the red glyphs on the wall with her calligraphy brush. "And you've been resting for a few hours."

"You're a crazy bitch," he said. "Did the Vasquez camp put you up to this? Is this one of those Nancy Kerrigan and Tonya Harding things? Can't beat me in the ring so they have to take me out?"

She smiled, but said nothing.

She hadn't been able to move him much, but while he was unconscious she'd tied him with strong black cords, one leg to his bench press, the other to the doorknob. His wrists she'd bound together with layers of duct tape, then tied them to a heavy table leg supporting another workout bench.

"What are you writing?" he asked.

"A prayer," she said, admiring the glyphs. "It is a prayer."

She turned when she heard him struggling against the cords.

He was much weaker than normal, but still the workout bench rattled and shook. She worried that the doorknob would pop out of its socket.

She would have to get this done now, a couple hours early.

Moving back toward the corner where she'd left her duffle bag, she pulled out the second needle and knelt next to him. "Just know, I'm not doing this because you did anything wrong. You are one of the strongest men on Earth. You've been given gifts. Gifts I was not given and gifts I've had to work assiduously to give myself." She felt the Blue, the gifts she'd absorbed from the professor, forming her words.

The serene power and grace of the Black was present as well, like an endless dark cloud moving ever so slowly through the sky. But it was tinged with the precision, grace, and rectitude of the White, thanks to the virtue of Sister Peters.

Calmly, she injected the solution into his thigh.

Stadler's eyes went wide, his legs kicking for only a few seconds as his powerful light slowly dimmed.

Just as the Blue had, just as the Black had, just as the White had, the Red filled her now, made her stronger, more aggressive, more vital, more of everything she'd lacked all those years.

She drew in what he had been.

She became Red and she felt that strength surge through her veins.

But she was still not whole.

She had one more light left to absorb.

PART 2
THE FIFTH VICTIM

CHAPTER SIXTEEN

THE DOG in question turned out to be a shaggy Golden Retriever. As Claire led the way into the Boiler Room, she spied him eating what appeared to be a perfectly-sliced, medium-rare ribeye steak out of a to-go container marked with a gold foil sticker for *Le Pigeon*, a well-known French restaurant in Seattle.

Fitz was digging into a similar ribeye steak, although his appeared to have a red wine sauce drizzled over the top and a side of roasted potatoes and asparagus. Three or four other to-go containers sat in the center of the table.

Something in Claire wanted to be upset—perhaps it was the lack of control over her own office space—but she was starving, and the way Fitz waved at the containers like Vanna White presenting a new puzzle, she couldn't resist.

"Claire," he said, "I got a brined pork chop with mashed potatoes, a cold seafood appetizer—lobster, mussels, shrimp cocktail, all the good stuff—and a duck confit salad with pomegranate and various other things. Dig in."

"Typically," Claire said, "my teams decide on dinner plans together when we work late. Usually sandwiches."

Jack beelined for the banquet. Kiko made her way towards

the food slowly, keeping herself close to the door, one eye on the canine. She looked ready to run the moment the dog lost interest in the steak.

Fitz swallowed a bite of ribeye. "Forgive me, my queen," he said. "And, you're welcome. I took the liberty of ordering for everyone since you and Jack and Kiko were out in the field all day."

Claire grabbed the duck confit salad and took a few bites. Something in her dynamic with Fitz made her want to be more annoyed with him than she actually was. But she had to admit, the salad was delicious.

Jack and Kiko dug into their meals as well, and Violet joined them from another room, carrying an armful of bottled water. She handed one to each person, then sat in the corner at her computer station.

When she was halfway through her salad, Claire let out a sigh. "Okay, I'm ready to hear it."

Fitz stood. "My profile of our killer?"

"No," Claire said. She nodded toward the Golden Retriever. "How did we get a dog in the last eight hours? And who's going to be responsible for it?"

Fitz walked over and crouched next to the pooch, who was finishing up his steak. He was an older dog and had been eating slowly, methodically. "Meet Ranger," Fitz said, "the most interesting dog in the world. He was born in Eastern Washington and bred to be a truffle-sniffing dog. In fact, his owner was one of the most successful truffle men in America during the big boom of the early two thousands. Ranger was born in 2010 and by 2014 he was winning all the truffle hunting competitions."

"There are competitions?" Kiko asked.

Fitz nodded knowingly. "Absolutely. You see, just like in wine, Americans want to compete with the Europeans in the truffle business. Most people think truffles only come from France and

Italy, but that is no longer the case. Anyway, Ranger was one of the finest in the world. But when his owner died and his truffle business was shut down, he ended up working for the FBI because of his exemplary sense of smell. On tests, he was one of the best drug-sniffing dogs in the world, year after year. He's the one who intercepted that container with fifty kilos of cocaine at the Port of Seattle back in 2020. Made the papers and everything."

Claire was growing impatient. "How did he end up living in our office and eating what I'm sure is a forty-dollar ribeye steak?"

"It's my fault," Violet said from the corner. "I was in the break room earlier getting a coffee, then a Red Bull, then another coffee, and I overheard two agents discussing how he lost his sense of smell recently due to his age. They said he was going to be 'retired,' and we all know what that means."

"They were going to put him down?" Jack asked.

"Not exactly," Fitz said. "He'd worn out his use for them, so they were going to get rid of him. He'd failed his scent test two times in a row, and that's it. Now he's ours."

"That's not how this works," Claire said. "Temporary detachments don't have pets. That's not a thing."

"Can't we keep him?" Violet asked.

Kiko shot a desperate expression at Claire. "I'm not fond of animals."

"Dogs aren't animals," Violet said, "they're benevolent aliens sent here to bring humanity together."

"Technically," Fitz said, ignoring their back-and-forth, "He doesn't belong to *us*. I adopted him. But since I'm here all day..." He trailed off, tilting his head slightly and smiling at Claire, looking for approval.

She frowned, but gave him the nod he was looking for. "Just keep him away from Kiko."

"Then it's settled," Fitz said, clapping his hands together.

"Oh thanks, mom," Violet squealed. It was the most enthusiasm Claire ever heard from her.

Ranger glanced around the room, then flopped down heavily at Fitz's feet, clearly having learned that this was the man most likely to give him the food he desired.

Within a few seconds, he was snoring louder than any dog Claire had ever heard.

∼

Ten minutes later, they'd finished eating and cleared the table. It was already late, and she had to get home as soon as possible. "Let's wrap this up quick," she said. "Violet, did you get anything else?"

"I sure did," Violet said. "I looked at the last fifteen years of public financial disclosures from the monastery. Like we thought, there is no clear evidence of a crime or fraud. There's no line item that says 'twelve-thousand-dollar watch for the Abbot.' But there are unusually high expenses labeled 'miscellaneous' or 'general' or 'cash allowances.' Nothing that jumped off the screen, but a pattern of higher expenses than one would expect from someone who'd vowed poverty."

"Why would you have expected anything?" Claire asked. "I mean, what led you to notice that?"

"I compared the overall operating costs versus the expenses of a dozen monasteries based on number of residents and square footage and acreage. What I was looking for, what I am almost always looking for, are the aberrations. What I saw in the case of this particular monastery was a consistent amount of inexplicable expenses. It never jumped above forty or fifty thousand in any given year, and it was usually spread out fairly evenly across quarters. Of course, every monastery has miscellaneous expenses and cash disbursements and whatnot. This one just has more than others of similar size and number of inhabitants. I'm sure we can get a subpoena for the complete records, but that might take a bit."

"We don't need them," Fitz said, his voice full of impatience, "because there is no question in my mind: the Abbot had nothing to do with the murder of Sister Peters."

Jack stood quickly and shoved his hands in his pockets. "What makes you say that?" he asked. "I mean, we have evidence already that he *is* stealing money from the monastery. Money that came from Sister Peters. Is it too much to imagine that she found out about his breach of vows, and he killed her or had her killed to silence her?"

"Yes," Fitz said, reaching under the table to scratch Ranger behind his ears. "It is too much to imagine." Ranger lifted up from his position and pushed his head into Fitz's hand to encourage a more weighted head pat.

"And why is that?" Jack asked, his voice full of heat.

"Because it doesn't fit the profile," Fitz said arrogantly. "And it makes no sense. Sister Peters was the third victim. Do you really think the Abbot killed two others, then Sister Peters, all to conceal financial fraud?"

Claire had to agree. The Abbot had struck her as shady and probably a hypocrite, but no murderer. And even if he was, why go to such lengths?

Jack clicked his tongue. "Maybe it doesn't fit *your* profile."

"We're not going to solve this tonight," Claire said, "but let's hear your profile."

Fitz held Jack's glare for a moment, then put on a confident, professorial tone. "Our killer is young, not teenager young, but possibly not even in their thirties yet. I'd bet everything the person is a millennial. Someone who was raised on the technology I had to learn the hard way. Someone who is brilliant both technologically, as evidenced by what Violet turned up, but also on a number of esoteric subjects. I agree with Violet that there is no chance Damian Henderson, who received his diploma from a state college by the skin of his medulla oblongata, is our killer. An accomplice? Perhaps. Possibly even an unwitting one if he is as dumb as he appeared to be in school. Although we all know grades aren't everything, so that could possibly be explained other ways." He pulled out his bronze coin and began walking it between his knuckles. "No, our killer —and I don't have a sense whether it is a man or a woman—is brilliant, both technologically and in terms of religion and science and philosophy. This entire crime is about sending some sort of message. He or she does not want the victims to suffer. Etomidate to subdue them, then a massive overdose of opioids. This person is not sadistic in the typical sense. They're not looking to inflict harm. They may even think they are doing the victims a favor. We also know that this person will have a sense of mission fueled by some sort of zealotry. Religious, political, philosophical, I'm not sure. I've got calls out to a few of the leading experts in ancient religions, and if we can get this text translated, it will be all downhill from there. Then I'll have a complete profile."

Claire was considering this, and it all sounded reasonable enough, but Jack broke the silence. "I'm sorry," he said, "but that all sounds like BS to me. We know that the Abbot was stealing her money to buy fancy watches and whatnot. That's motive. He wanted to cover his tracks. He may have even worked with this Damian Henderson guy so he could have someone to pin it on."

"I'm not sure what to tell you," Fitz said, "the Abbot is innocent. Innocent of murder, anyway. Whatever you can say about him, he is a religious man and has devoted his life to the monastery. A crook, yes, he's probably also a crook. But there's no way he's behind this."

Claire stood. "I have to agree with Fitz on this. He's not our guy." She turned to Violet. "You and Jack put in a subpoena for the rest of the financial records and figure out where he got the money for that watch. Assuming he was siphoning money, maybe we can pressure him and find out more. But our main line of investigation still has to be this guy Damian. If he posed as a reporter at the monastery, we know for certain he's involved."

Violet nodded. "On it, boss, but—"

Her words were interrupted by the shrill ringing of a landline attached to a round speakerphone system in the center of the table. Kiko met Claire's eyes, and when Claire nodded, she hit the button to accept the call.

"Hello?" Claire said.

"This is Cathy, Gerald Hightower's assistant. He'd like to see you immediately."

"See who?" Claire asked.

"All of you." Cathy hung up without another word.

Claire knew that tone. Hightower was pissed about something.

Fitz, of course, was all jokes. "Do you think he wants to see Ranger, too?"

CHAPTER SEVENTEEN

"BAD NEWS," Hightower announced as Claire led the way into his office. He frowned at her, then scanned the other four as though surprised to see them.

Claire sat across from him. "You wanted us all here, no?"

Hightower had leveled his gaze on Fitz. Specifically, Fitz's chest. "You're covered in dog hair."

Fitz sat next to Claire and looked down at his ample belly in mock surprise. "Would you look at that? Weird!"

Hightower looked like Claire's Instapot the time she'd both overfilled it and left it on too long. She couldn't actually *see* the steam releasing from his ears, but she could imagine it pretty well.

"We'll get to the dog thing," Hightower said. "But first..." he jabbed a long finger at Jack, who stood with his arms folded behind Claire, flanked by Violet and Kiko. "Why do you do this to me?"

Claire turned to see the surprised expression on Jack's face. "Do what?"

"Turn me into a damn cliché."

"I..." The confident look had been wiped off Jack's face, replaced by genuine confusion.

Fitz chimed in. "He knows about the little office stunt at the monastery."

"He... how?" Jack asked.

"I'm sure I don't know *how*," Fitz said, "but he's talking about the well-worked trope of the investigator going rogue and the supervisor chastising him and telling him to play by the rules." Fitz scratched his chin. "If I had to guess, I'd say that somehow the Abbot found out you were in his office, and it turns out he's got some important friends. Abbot called a big donor who called Governor Ridley, I'd guess. FBI overstepping religious freedom, that kind of thing. Ridley calls Hightower and, well, here we are."

Jack folded his arms defiantly.

Hightower had nodded along as Fitz spoke, but now he looked just as pissed at Fitz as he had at Jack. Finally, Hightower ran a hand over his bald head. "You're a real arrogant bastard, Pembroke."

Fitz pulled his coin from his pocket and began rolling it along his knuckles. "Would you rather have a profiler who's humble and wrong, or arrogant and right?"

"It wasn't the governor," Hightower said. "The Abbot's brother-in-law, his sister's husband, is deputy chief of the WSP."

"WSP?" Jack asked.

"Washington State Patrol."

Jack was defiant. "And you're afraid of the deputy chief of the department of hitchhiking and speeding tickets?"

Hightower kicked his chair back and stood suddenly. "Those folks are on the same side as us and, even if they weren't, they can make our jobs a pain in the ass. You can't just break into someone's office because... wait, why *did* you break into his office anyway?"

"I'll answer that," Claire said. She hadn't said a word and could tell this thing was about to get out of control. The last thing she needed was a permanent beef between Jack and Hightower. "He went in because I told him to."

"Claire, don't." She felt Jack's hand on her shoulder, but waved him off.

"Jack noticed an expensive watch on the Abbot's wrist. Mentioned it to me. I questioned the Abbot on my own after directing Jack to see what he could find out. Maybe he took it a tiny bit too far, sure. But we are on a deadline here. We know someone else is going to be killed. And as a result of Jack's efforts we now know two things: first of all, the Abbot is corrupt. Second of all, he's probably not our guy. And while we're going after members of my team, sir..." she glanced down at Fitz, unable to believe the words she could feel forming on her tongue... "I told him to get the dog."

"Claire," Hightower said. "Don't BS me."

"Really, sir. He called me on my cell and I okayed it." She folded her arms. "But I think we ought to get back to what's important here."

Hightower sat heavily in his chair. "Fine, fine. I want to announce."

"Announce what?" Claire asked.

"We have to announce the killings to the public, say what we know."

"Absolutely not," Claire said. "It's too soon."

"If I might," Violet interjected, her voice timid and quiet. "I agree with Claire. I've been monitoring online conversations and so far there's nothing about them being connected. The first victim—Orion—there was a story about the weird blue room, but it didn't mention the glyphs on the wall. The Cardinelli murder hasn't even made the papers yet, not much local journalism out in Coos Bay right now, and police there run a tight ship. The monastery released a statement about the death of Sister Peters, but they didn't even mention that she was murdered. Somehow that hasn't broken either. As far as the world knows, these three deaths are not connected. We announce it and we're gonna need a staff of half a dozen people to field calls and emails with leads. And we all know most of them will be trash."

"Not to mention," Claire said, "it could spook the killer. We have a major lead now and—"

The phone on Hightower's desk rang and he tapped a button. "Yeah?"

"It's Cathy."

"You're on speaker," Hightower said.

"You said not to bother you unless something important came up."

"And?"

"I've got Sandra Friedman Bach on the line. Chief of Police, Coeur d'Alene, Idaho. Says they might have another victim."

"Another victim in..." Hightower's confusion turned to dejection. "Oh damn, put her through." The phone beeped and Hightower said, "Chief Bach, this is Gerald Hightower. You're on speakerphone and I'm here with Special Agent Claire Anderson and her team, they're leading the investigation into UnSub 19, who we're unofficially calling 'The Color Killer.'"

"I, oh, okay..." Chief Bach sounded surprised, but she quickly composed herself. "We have a twenty-five-year-old male, John Stadler. Murdered in his home gym in his garage. Markings or letters... well, not letters, I don't know what you call them but—"

"Glyphs," Fitz chimed in. "They are glyphs from an untranslated ancient language. We're working on them. And let me guess, they were red?"

"Yes," Chief Bach said hesitantly, "but I don't know who I'm speaking with."

"That was Fitz Pembroke," Hightower said, shooting an annoyed look in Fitz's general direction. "Our profiler."

"Well, he was right," Bach said. "Glyphs, in red, painted on the walls of his home gym. Manner of death is consistent with the professor and the others. I read the dossier that you sent out."

Despite the fact that the murders had not yet been connected publicly, they'd put out a notice to law enforcement agencies throughout the Pacific Northwest. But Claire hadn't expected another victim to turn up so quickly. It was still before 11 PM.

Hightower sighed. "So that's our fourth in this case. Suspects, witnesses, anything?"

"Not yet," Bach said, "but this is new. Body was found less than thirty minutes ago."

Hightower glanced at Claire, then nodded toward the speakerphone, eyes telling her to take over.

"Chief Bach. This is Claire Anderson, Special Agent in Charge. Can you be ready to answer your phone in ten minutes? We're gonna regroup here and I'll give you a call."

"Sure," Bach said, then ended the call without another word.

Claire looked up at Hightower, who'd already called out to his secretary. Eyes locked on Claire, Hightower spoke into the phone. "Press conference on The Color Killer. Tonight... Right... Right... Claire, and yeah, me, too. This is an all-hands on-deck kinda thing... one hour... good."

He hung up and, ignoring everyone else in the room, spoke to Claire. "You're welcome, Claire, I know how much you *looooove* going on TV."

CHAPTER EIGHTEEN

CLAIRE, in fact, hated nothing more than going on TV. She wasn't especially shy in her personal life and she was comfortable speaking with almost anyone one-on-one.

But TV was a different story.

Standing behind a podium next to Hightower, fielding questions from reporters who were mostly trying to score a cheap viral moment for their social media accounts, and all to support an effort she was opposed to, was not her idea of a good time.

Still, as she stood in front of the cluster of microphones and looked out over the small press room, she was strangely calm. She had a little more than a week left on the job and felt more distance from it than she ever had before.

Plus, Hightower was fielding most of the questions.

A young reporter in the front row spoke up. "Special Agent Anderson, if I may, the map? Are you seeing any pattern there that's not immediately clear?"

Violet had thrown together a map of the Pacific Northwest marked with the four murder locations so far, and they'd printed it at poster size and displayed it behind them on the small riser.

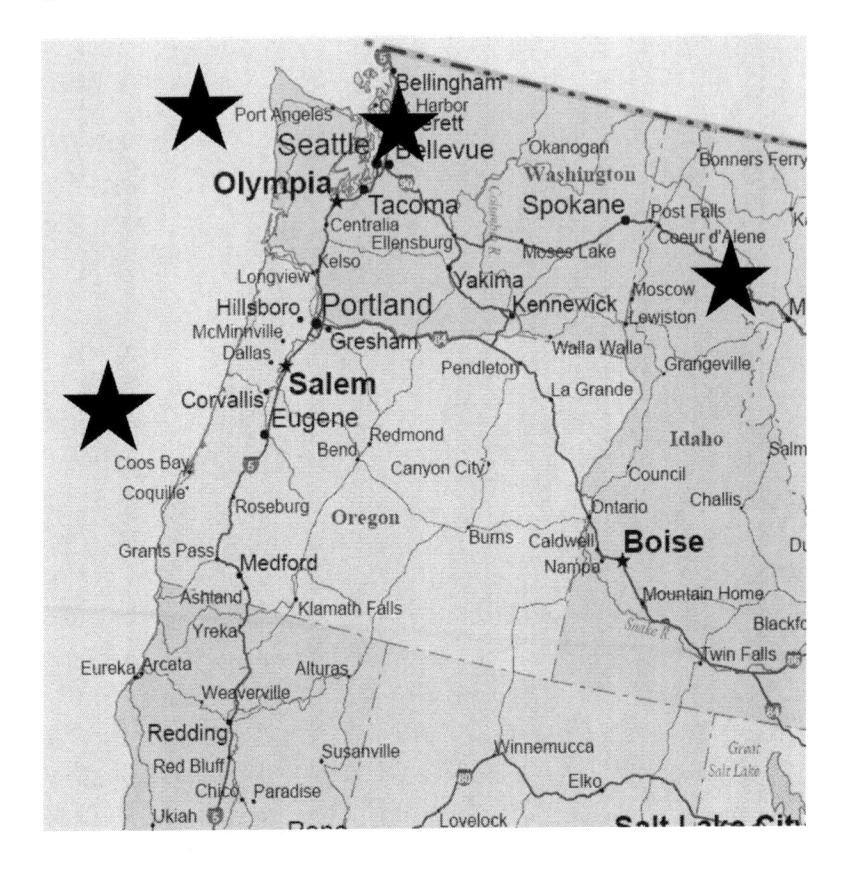

She had it memorized.
Seattle, Washington.
Coos Bay, Oregon.
Port Angeles, Washington.
Coeur d'Alene, Idaho.

"No," Claire said, "other than the obvious fact that this is a murderer who is comfortable moving around the Pacific Northwest."

"And if I might follow up," the reporter continued. "Most serial killers strike in one state, sometimes two. In a short time this killer has already committed murders in three states. So I have two related questions. First, what do you make of that?

And second—and perhaps Hightower can speak to this—how are you handling the complex jurisdictional issues?"

Claire heard herself answering as though outside her own body. "At this time, we haven't ruled anything out. Perhaps this killer likes to travel. Perhaps they have a job that takes them around the region. Like I said, we're not ruling anything in or out. We also haven't ruled out that it could be multiple killers operating in multiple locations."

It was like dry sand coming out of her mouth. Or gray paste. A few dozen words with no actual content. The point of this press conference, she knew, was to alert the public in the hope that a useful tip might come in, but not to say anything specific enough to blow their investigation. In her attempts at writing, she'd learned that detail, specificity, and clarity were crucial. In a press conference like this, mealy-mouthed vagueness ruled the day.

She nodded toward Hightower to answer his portion of the question, then thought back to her conversation with Chief Bach of the Coeur d'Alene PD, in which she'd learned that she had little of value to offer. Her officers had spoken with neighbors and friends, and no one had seen anything. Claire had sent her Fitz's preliminary profile along with photos of Damian Henderson, but she knew exactly how little good that would do.

Bach had sent over crime scene photos, which included the red glyphs she'd described on the phone. Of course, they matched the others, but were no more readable.

The only positive to come out of it was that Bach was generally cooperative. She wasn't one of those locals who got territorial. In fact, she welcomed the idea of Claire or a member of the team coming out to look into the murder.

When Claire tuned back in, Hightower was ending the conference with his usual sendoff. "We want to remind the public that this investigation is ongoing, and your assistance is crucial. If you have any information, no matter how insignificant it might seem, please contact us immediately at the number or email displayed on your screen. We urge everyone to stay vigilant and report any suspicious activity. Together, with your help, we can bring this perpetrator to justice and ensure the safety of our communities. Thank you for your cooperation and support."

∼

"Good job," Fitz said, greeting Claire in the hallway out of view of the press. "A real natural up there."

Claire wiped a line of sweat from her forehead and punched him in his arm. "Like you'd do any better."

"I'll have you know, I was head of the debate club at the Harrow School two years in a row."

She rolled her eyes and began walking down the hallway. "I gotta get home." She stopped, remembering something. "Earlier, how'd you know the glyphs would be red? Sheer genius, as usual?"

Fitz frowned. "I don't know *how* I knew. It's like I just saw it in my head."

"That's not an especially satisfying answer."

"I'm honestly worried I might be getting into UnSub 19's head a little *too* much." Fitz followed her in the direction of the elevator. "We've got Damian Henderson's picture going out to every law enforcement agency in the country, not to mention the nightly news. If he's out there, someone will have spotted him."

"Good," Claire said.

"I'm gonna take Ranger back to my place tonight."

The dog had been following Fitz and Claire looked down and smiled sadly, but said nothing. Brian had taken their family dog when he moved out and, unfortunately, that memory chose this moment to surface.

When they reached the elevator, the doors were closing and Fitz wedged his arm between them, causing a loud beep as they reopened.

"Need a lift?" Jack stood at the back of the elevator, leaning against the railing with his arms crossed.

Claire nodded. "Just heading home."

Fitz held the door to let Claire in.

"I'm gonna sleep here tonight," Jack said. "Sort through the tips as they come in. Violet, too."

Fitz spoke snidely under his breath through a fake cough. "Suck-ups."

Claire raised an eyebrow, but she was too tired to chastise Fitz or repeat her admonition about office relationships. "Good."

Jack pushed himself from the wall and stood with his finger poised over the control panel. "What floor?"

"Bottom floor parking," Claire said.

"I can push my own damn button," Fitz said defiantly.

"Why not?" Jack said, standing aside. "You push everyone else's."

"Gentlemen, please," Claire said. "You sure you want to stay the night, Jack? The tips can wait until morning."

He nodded. "I haven't settled into my apartment yet and the couch in there is more comfortable than my air mattress. I haven't committed to buying a bed yet."

"You need some rest, too, boss," Fitz said. "All joking aside. Stadler was killed roughly two hours ago. That means we have four days, five at most, before the next murder. Get your rest now because by tomorrow there will be a thousand tips and a million directions. We'll need you at your best."

Fitz patted her on the shoulder with a meaty bearpaw in the

same way she'd seen him pat Ranger. As he exited the elevator, the dog followed his every move and maintained a perfect heel.

Jack left the elevator next, leaving Claire alone for the descent.

∼

Claire walked through the underground parking garage to the sound of her own echoing footsteps, trying to remember why she let herself accept this case. It was a wonder Jack and Fitz had fit their massive egos into the elevator at the same time. Getting the two of them to work cohesively might prove more difficult than solving the case, but solving the case might depend on her being able to do so.

The pair reminded her of Sam and Sammy, two little boys she'd met during her summer working at a small daycare. They loved playing with the giant cardboard blocks together—until they didn't. Every day, without fail, tensions would rise and they'd begin fighting. Sam would become bossy and start yelling, Sammy would start stomping and throwing blocks. Eventually Claire would have to separate them and put away the blocks until after they'd eaten a snack. Just like she'd done with the little four year olds, Claire would need to figure out how to get Fitz and Jack to play together, *nicely*.

Claire's heart skipped when she perceived that someone was following her. In the same moment, the sounds in the garage changed, making her abruptly stop and turn to look behind her.

It was Jack.

She gave a sigh of relief. "Did you just run down three flights of stairs to meet me?"

He was less out of breath than she was. "I didn't need you to cover for me," he said suddenly.

She frowned, then rifled through her purse for her keys.

"With Hightower," he continued. "You said you told me to look into the Abbot. You lied to cover my ass. Why?"

Claire considered this for a moment. "You were in the army. Special ops, right?"

Jack nodded.

"You ever in command?"

"Lots of times."

Claire dropped something on the ground when she lifted out her keys and, before she could stop him, Jack bent down to pick it up.

"Anyone on one of those teams you were leading ever screw up?" she continued.

"Sure, people screwed up all the time," Jack said, inspecting the object before reaching out to hand it back to her. "Cool little lock pick set. I've never seen one like this."

"It's yours," Claire said. "I'm working this case now. But I'm about to be in a position where I'll never need to break through another door in my life."

Jack smiled and nodded a thanks, then slipped it into his back pocket.

"Anyway, as I was saying," Claire continued, "while giving your report, did you ever throw anyone under the bus?"

He opened his mouth to object to the direction of her questioning, then quietly said, "Never."

She looked him up and down. Somehow his button-up shirt was still crisp and white, even after a full day. He'd rolled up the sleeves just enough to reveal how muscular his forearms were.

Claire took out her keys. "You're obviously a good agent, Jack. But I'm running this team. And I think we understand each other."

CHAPTER NINETEEN

WHEN CLAIRE WALKED in the next morning, the team appeared as though they had been at work for hours. It was only 8 AM, and yet there were empty coffee cups strewn across the large table in the center of the Boiler Room.

Violet was at her computers in the corner, typing like a breaking news journalist on a deadline. Claire noticed that she'd added a third monitor overnight.

Jack was pacing like an expectant father about to receive twins outside the delivery room in a hospital. Fitz appeared to have just collected a food delivery because he was sliding breakfast burritos and sandwiches across the table. Ranger perked up —despite his nose blindness—as the scent of eggs, chorizo, and melted cheese wafted through the room.

The only person absent was Kiko.

Before Claire could say anything, Jack said, "We got something overnight. Well, actually, Violet got something."

Claire sat down and accepted a cappuccino from Fitz, who, thankfully, said nothing.

Violet banged her fist on the table triumphantly and spun around in her chair. Then she stood and said, "Damian Henderson. He thought he could run, and whoever is behind this thought they could hide him. No one can run, and no one can hide from me."

"Unless they are using their legs," Fitz said and, as he did, a piece of egg dropped from his mouth and bounced off his belly. Ranger deftly snapped it out of the air.

"Like you should talk, Fitz," Jack said.

"He's not wrong," Violet said. "I couldn't outrun a goldfish."

"See Jack," Fitz continued, mouth still spewing egg bits. "Violet has nothing to be ashamed of. Her mind is the fastest thing about her. It's faster than anything you've got going on—unless we consider—well, never mind. Anyway, do you think I can just turn off the profiler part of me when it comes to all of you?"

"You'd better learn to," Claire said, cutting him off before turning to Violet. "Please, start from the beginning."

Just then, Kiko walked in, waving her arms wildly and arching her back in what seemed to be some kind of dance routine. Claire didn't recognize the movements, but figured she'd learned it from TikTok or some platform capable of spreading viral content and giving it momentary relevance. Claire didn't feel old, but the more she hung around young people, the more she knew that, at best, she was out of touch with today's youth.

Claire sipped her cappuccino and watched as Kiko continued her dance across the room.

Ranger, who'd been lying next to his giant, fluffy dog bed—one Fitz had purchased with what was likely the lion's share of his first paycheck—adjusted his position having recognized the potential need to leap out of Kiko's dance path.

Arms still in midair, realizing the dance had brought her dangerously close to the dog, Kiko pivoted. The pep in her movements dulled and then stopped as she cautiously walked the last few feet to her spot at the table, looking over her shoulder to make sure Ranger was staying put. Claire buried her smile behind her coffee cup with another sip. This was the kind of thing she felt she would miss after leaving her job. The little moments of humanity that cropped up in the workplace.

Bringing her mind back to the task at hand, she asked, "What do you have, Violet?"

"Damian Henderson," Violet said. "We've got some good stuff. As easy as it is to erase social media records from the internet and hack certain databases to get rid of listings, there's a lot of stuff they couldn't get rid of. Financial transactions, government records. It was tricky because this guy changed his name a couple of years back. His real name is Damian Henderson, but now the guy goes by Kenneth Faradi. And, apparently, Alexander Angelica."

"An address?" Claire asked hopefully.

Violet shook her head. "He's either been living in hotels or renting off the grid for a while now. I did find some things through a dark web search. A couple years ago, there was a major hack of information from all sorts of random sites. Travel sites, credit card companies, and so on. Social Security numbers, emails, that kind of thing. Most of it came to nothing, but I found the name Kenneth Faradi used to book a trip to Nepal two years ago. It's a rare enough name that I'm quite sure it was him, given that he flew out of the Seattle airport. Also found two email addresses linked to that name. Jack has already put in a request to access them."

"You won't get them in time," Fitz chimed in. He swallowed what he'd been chewing and continued, speaking with a clear mouth for the first time that morning. "You just won't get them in time. We've got less than four days."

"He's not wrong," Claire agreed.

"I can hack them if you'd like," Violet said, "but that will rule out ever prosecuting the guy."

Claire shook her head. "That's a deal-breaker."

"I know. I know."

"Why would a guy like Damian Henderson travel to Nepal?" Claire asked. "Did you get anything on that?"

"She didn't," Kiko said, "but *I* did. I wasn't doing the 'Wednesday' when I came in for no reason."

"The what?" Jack asked.

Kiko leapt up and repeated her short, choreographed dance routine. "The 'Wednesday,'" she said as she wheeled her arm around, concluding the dance with a flourish. "It's trending, little bro. It's from the show *Wednesday* on Netflix, the *Addams Family* update."

"I don't own a TV," Jack said dryly.

"Wait, you what?" Kiko asked, surprised.

"How can you not own a TV?" Violet asked.

"Yeah," Kiko continued. "What do you use for staring at when you're at home?"

Fitz stifled a laugh.

Jack smirked. "I stare at books. Or sometimes just the wall." He said it with a wink in Kiko's direction, and Claire thought she saw a spark there.

Uh oh, she thought, but there was no time to unpack that now. "Kiko, what did you find about Damian, or Kenneth Faradi, or whatever his name is?"

"After Violet found the trip, I went back and looked into his college records. He took one class on Eastern religions. I got in touch with the professor of that course early this morning. A little *too* early maybe. She was annoyed at first—I think I woke her up—but she remembered him being a bit of a loner, and from what his assignments told her about him, he seemed a bit odd, too. No friends or relatives she knew of. She did have records of his assignments. They use one of those online portals where they just upload all the final papers." Out of her pocket, Kiko pulled a rolled-up stack of papers. "His five-page paper on Eastern religion and the search for meaning. Allow me to quote something..." She cleared her throat with a flourish and put on a shockingly good accent, emulating a disaffected young man in his teens. *"Eastern religions are like really really different from what we do in America. Here, everyone is always rushing and buying stuff, but in Buddhism and Taoism and all that, they just, like, live in the moment, you know? It's all about being peaceful and calm, which we totally don't do here. Americans could learn a lot from just sitting and thinking, but no one ever does that. They're too busy with their phones and their jobs that they hate. It's just so fake and empty. You can't find real happiness in a shopping mall or on some website. Real happiness is, like, in the mind, which Eastern philosophies totally get."*

She paused and looked around the room.

Claire glanced at Fitz, expecting to see an arrogant smirk across his face due to the poor grammar and shallow thoughts of young Damian Henderson, but instead he had a concerned, quizzical look, as though deep in thought.

Kiko continued reading.

"And then, there's this thing about how in Taoism, they follow the way of nature, which is so cool. Nature doesn't try to be something it's not, unlike here where everyone is trying to be something they're not, buying things they don't need with money they don't have. It's all so pointless. People here could learn from that, but they don't and never will because they're too caught up in their own world. They can't see the bigger picture, like how we're all connected and stuff. In America, it's all about me, me, me, but in Eastern thinking, it's about us, the universe, and finding your true path, which is so much deeper than any TV show or fast food chain could ever be."

Kiko set the paper on the table. "After I read the essay, I called her back and asked if she was serious. She said this actually *wasn't* the worst paper she'd received that term. I asked if she thought he would be capable of murder and she said she really didn't know, but—"

"This kid sounds like a real Holden Caulfield," Jack said.

"Huh, I guess he does stare at books," Violet said, nodding at Kiko, who looked confused by the reference.

"If I might interject," Fitz said.

"Everyone let her finish," Claire said.

"No, no, it's okay," Kiko said. "I think we are on the same wavelength here. The professor was saying that he had a major idealization of everything they studied. He wasn't just doing it to get a good grade in the class. Not that he could have."

"And that's exactly what I was going to say," Fitz said. "We could spend our time making fun of the fact that this guy can't write, but what his paper indicates to me is a hatred of American culture and a naive idealization of the ancient world and Eastern religions in general. Like Jack said with his out of character and surprisingly astute reference, he's a real Holden Caulfield. So, in theory, I'm thinking this guy could have taken the gist of someone else's doctrine and gone full Mark David Chapman on the world."

"Fitz, you realize I did *actually* graduate from high school in the United States," Jack reminded him. "It shouldn't surprise you that I've read *The Catcher in the Rye*."

"I'm sorry," Kiko said. "That was not required reading in my performing arts high school. Can somebody catch me up?"

"*The Catcher in the Rye*," Jack said. "This young whiny kid Holden complains that everyone around him is a phony the entire book."

"And Damian seems similarly disappointed and fed up with society," Fitz added. "Mark David Chapman cited *The Catcher in the Rye* as inspiration for murdering John Lennon. Poor bloke must not have finished the book. Eventually Holden regrets alienating himself, leaving room for redemption."

"Got it," Kiko said.

Claire took another sip of her coffee and stood. "Is there any way this guy learned an ancient language well enough to draw those glyphs?"

Fitz held out a bite of sausage to Ranger, who calmly took it out of his hand. "There isn't."

"Everyone around the table," Claire said, "We're going to spend five minutes eating like human beings before we get back to it."

Kiko and Jack exchanged a glance, but sat.

Fitz, who was already seated, looked down at the burrito he'd nearly finished and mumbled, "Yes, mum."

Violet's fingers danced over the keyboards before she, too, joined them.

Claire unwrapped a breakfast burrito. "The next four days are going to be intense. We were thrown together. But we're going to work together and we're going to solve this case together. Now I want to go around the room and have everyone say a couple sentences about themselves." She eyed Jack. "Someone told me yesterday that it's important to know the people you're going to battle with. I agree, and I'll start. I was born and raised in Kingston, Washington, just across the water. Basketball scholarship to UW. Married too early and had twins. Had a surprise baby later in life who's now twelve. Retiring soon to write crime novels. That's been my dream for a long time. What I love about the FBI is this. You guys. The team. What I don't like about it is, well, all the BS, the bureaucracy, and the paperwork. Kiko, you're used to being on stage. You're next."

"Well, I went over some of this in the car yesterday, but for Fitz, Violet, and Ranger, who also wasn't there, I grew up in Seattle. No dad in the picture. Mom died when I was a teenager. Drugs. Thought I would be a famous actress. That didn't work out, so here I am."

Claire nodded toward Fitz. "Your turn, Mr. Pembroke."

"Mr. Pembroke the third," Fitz corrected. He cleared his throat. "Well, where should I begin? My family's history dates back to the 1150s with the signing of the Magna Carta."

"Make it quick," Claire said.

To her surprise, Fitz grew suddenly serious. "My dad was the most respected police interrogator in England. Did special assignments for the government and the military. I was supposed to follow in his footsteps. Then gambling, alcohol, and pills. Kicked out of multiple universities, lost my share of the family fortune and ended up in America. If there was a poster child for an embarrassment to a well-clothed British family, I'd be him."

"So, we're the ones stuck with the prodigal son?" Jack asked.

Fitz smiled. "I'm never going back to England, and thank you for welcoming me with open arms, my chap. I might otherwise be pushing up daisies." He reached for a second breakfast burrito.

"Isn't that one for Violet?" Claire asked.

"I'm not eating that," Violet said. "I can't eat onions."

"Noted," Claire said.

There was a long silence in the room, then Violet said, "I've been trying to decide how many lies to bury my story in, but I won't bother. Grew up in Atlanta. Parents immigrated from China a few years before I was born. Ran a restaurant down there. I was gifted. Got into MIT. Got kicked out." She paused.

"Don't keep us on tenterhooks," Fitz said. "We *need* to know why."

"Over Christmas break one year, when most of the students and staff were gone, I networked all the school computing power toward mining Bitcoin. That was before cryptocurrencies were as popular as they are now. Managed to amass about fifty Bitcoin. Anyway, the feds gave me two options: go to prison or get four years of probation and work for them. Here I am."

"Clever," Fitz said.

"No commentary," Claire said, nodding at Jack.

"Well, everyone knows a little about my background, so I'll tell you a little bit about me personally. I like neatness, cleanliness. Showing up five minutes early means you're ten minutes late in my book. I don't think I'm a very good friend. And I know I'm not much of a boyfriend. I don't think I'll ever have kids. But every single person in this room, I would jump in front of a bullet for, because that's what you do when you're on a team."

"Wait," Kiko said. "Going back to Violet. What happened to the bitcoin? That's like three million bucks at today's prices."

"Everybody quiet," Fitz said suddenly. "I have something." He stood, reading from his phone. "My friend at Oxford got back to me. The glyphs are not translatable, but he narrowed it down. He says... wait, I'll read from his email. He says, 'Ancient script, between 1000 and 600 BC, Nepal or Pakistan, quite probably associated with one of a few lost religions. My guess, you're looking for a Luminist."

CHAPTER TWENTY

"WHAT THE HELL IS A LUMINIST?" Claire asked.

"A practitioner of Luminism," Fitz said.

She folded her arms. "That doesn't help."

"It's a religion," Fitz explained.

"That doesn't help either," Claire said.

"Violet," Fitz called across the room. "Pull up the thing we were working on earlier."

Violet tapped some keys and the screen on the wall lit up. It showed zoomed-in images of some of the glyphs from the crime scenes. Next to them were images of other ancient languages labeled Avestan, Classical Newari, and Sanskrit.

"This is what I spent much of last night working on," Fitz said. "Once I narrowed it down, I contacted my friend at Oxford. I knew the language in question had some similarities to already discovered languages." Fitz was tapping away at his phone as he spoke. Then his eyes fixed. "Bloody hell," he mumbled to himself.

"What?" Claire asked.

"Oh, bloody hell," he repeated. Ranger stood and leaned

against Fitz's leg like a service animal alerting someone who might be about to have a seizure.

"What?" Claire shouted.

Fitz opened his mouth to speak, but the intercom interrupted him. "We have something." It was the voice of Cathy, Gerald Hightower's assistant. "I've been filtering tips all morning and I think we have something. Location tip on Damian Henderson. Three different people said they saw someone who matched his description at the floating houses on Lake Washington."

Claire leapt up.

Jack was already at the door.

"Violet," Claire called over her shoulder, "you stay here with Fitz. Kiko, come with us."

～

Jack hit the gas as he turned out of the underground parking lot, his face focused and determined. Claire had taken shotgun and Kiko was in the back, bracing herself against the swift turns. The engine roared, a low growl that matched the urgency coursing through Claire's veins.

She called Hightower and Cathy connected her immediately. "Did you hear?"

"I heard. Already called the locals to tell them to stay out of the way. They've got two cars nearby and they're gonna post out at the parking lot, just in case they see him leaving."

"Good."

"Claire, be careful."

"Thanks, Hightower."

She hung up as Jack weaved the SUV through the congested streets of downtown Seattle with a precision that felt almost predatory. He danced across lanes with a navigator's grace, slipping through gaps in traffic that seemed synchronized to open just for them.

Claire called Fitz. "Finish what you were saying. I want to know what kind of lunatic we're about to collar." She plugged her phone into the charger. "You're on speaker now. Luminism. Go."

"Obscure," Fitz said, "doesn't even begin to describe this religion. You know how I like to pretend I know everything? Even *I've* never heard of it. I'm reading a Wikipedia entry."

"Give it to us," Claire said.

As Fitz read, buildings blurred into streaks of color as they shot onto the I-5 ramp. Jack's hands were steady on the wheel, movements fluid like water—every twist, every turn, every lane change executed with finesse.

"Luminism was founded around 800 BCE by a wandering sage named Bhaskar in the ancient kingdom of Gandhara, located in what is now eastern Pakistan. Bhaskar spent many years meditating in caves in the Himalayas and came to realize that the human soul was made up of five fundamental energetic elements, each corresponding to a specific color. Those colors, according to Luminism, correspond to the five-fold nature of the one true God."

As the Seattle skyline receded in the rearview mirror, giving way to the expansive blue-gray of Lake Washington, Claire swallowed a lump in her throat. Rarely did so much about a case come together so quickly.

Fitz continued reading. *"Bhaskar named these elements: Amrita (white, purity, innocence), Ananda (black, power, calm), Upeksha (yellow, bliss, joy), Tejas (red, strength, violence), and Bodhi (blue, awareness, knowledge). According to Luminist teachings written down in the ancient Sarvaprakash texts, the five elements can become imbalanced by negative traits and desires. However, through rigorous meditation, acts of service, chanting mantras, and living an ethical life, one can purify and transform the elements.*

"*Upon death, if all five elements are perfectly balanced, a practitioner can achieve Sarvaprakasha, a state of total luminous enlightenment in which the soul dissolves into eternal radiance. This ends the cycle of reincarnation and allows one to escape the suffering of contained existence.*"

Claire played the phrase over in her mind. *Escape the suffering of contained existence.*

Jack peeled off at the exit, hit the shoulder like it was the German autobahn, then cut across two lanes of traffic.

Fitz continued reading.

"*There is evidence that Siddhartha Gautama—the founder of Buddhism—came into contact with Luminist teachings, integrating some of its concepts into his formulation of Buddhism in the 5th century BCE. As Buddhism rose in prominence, Luminism gradually declined and most of its texts were lost or destroyed.*

"*However, a few esoteric Tibetan and Nepalese schools still claim to practice Luminist meditation techniques and rituals passed down through an unbroken lineage of teachers. Some scholars believe Luminism may have influenced the rainbow body concept in Vajrayana Buddhism centuries later. Though largely forgotten now, Luminism was an important precursor philosophy that shaped religious thought in ancient Asia.*"

"Fitz," Claire said, "what about translating the text so we can figure out what this maniac is trying to communicate to us?"

"Apparently there are only two living scholars of the language. One is in hospice care in Nepal. The other, in Pakistan, lives without a phone on a mountain. Violet is trying some things using AI, but she says our computers aren't fast enough."

Claire was confused, but then again there were a lot of things about Violet's job that she didn't understand. "How can artificial intelligence help translate an ancient language?"

"It can't," Fitz said. "I'd wager my family's country manor in the Cotswolds against someone cracking this language using AI. And I told Violet the same."

Jack turned into the parking lot, nodding at the two uniformed officers who leaned on the hood of a black and white.

"We're here," Claire said. She jumped out of the car. "Kiko. Address?"

"Four twenty one," Kiko said. "End of the dock."

"I'll take lead," Jack said.

"*I'll* take lead," Claire corrected.

CHAPTER TWENTY-ONE

REACHING the edge of the parking lot, Claire glanced back to confirm that Jack and Kiko were behind her. "Jack, stay at my four, Kiko, my eight."

If she was the twelve on a clock, that's what she wanted. Her right hand man and her left hand woman.

She stepped onto the long wooden dock, struck suddenly by the smell of fish. On either side of her, colorful houseboats sat in the still water of Lake Washington. They were small and simple, but she knew that even a one-bedroom live-aboard often went for well over a million dollars these days. And if the little they knew about their suspect was accurate, she didn't see how he could afford one.

A door banged closed to their right and Claire pivoted. A young couple stepped onto the dock, the man carrying a baby in some sort of chest wrap and the woman speaking loudly into a cell phone.

Claire mouthed "FBI" and waved them down the dock toward the parking lot. They hurried away.

"There," Jack said. "The red one."

Claire read the number on the side: *421*.

It stood out from the others both because it was at the end of the dock and also because it looked a little less like a boat than most of the others. In fact, it looked almost like a floating shed. But a high-end, customized shed. Roughly fifteen by twelve, it had wide French doors on both sides, a new-looking pitched metal roof, and strings of lights outlining cute windows.

Claire had made a fast calculation and decided that approaching the house immediately was their best course of action. Although they had to assume the suspect was armed and dangerous, Claire's instinct said he was neither.

"Kiko," Claire said, "watch those French doors. Jack, make sure he doesn't jump into the water off the back of this thing. I'm gonna knock."

She positioned herself in front of the door and listened carefully. She heard the gentle creaking of the dock and a faraway cry of delight from an unseen child. The house itself was still and silent.

Tap tap tap. She rapped on the single pane of glass on the top half of the door.

She heard nothing.

"Boss," Jack said.

Claire turned.

Jack was pointing up toward the roof at the back of the house. "It's got a little balcony thing off the back. Might have heard something up there and—"

Clang clang clang.

It sounded like a heavy, dull bell above them, but Claire realized right away what it was. She stepped back and saw a man bounding across the roof. Up one side of the pitch and down the other. Leaping, he landed about ten feet down the dock in the direction they'd just come from. He rolled, then sprang up.

"FBI, stop!" Claire yelled, reaching for her gun.

She took off after him, deciding not to draw. She could still hear the sounds of children playing in the park, and in this densely populated area, she'd only shoot if necessary. He was headed back in the direction of the parking lot, where the uniformed officers waited.

The man tossed something to his left into the water. His cellphone, Claire thought.

Next he turned right, cutting between two yellow houseboats and sprinting down the dock.

Claire kept pace with him, Jack and Kiko behind her.

When he reached a dead end, he leapt onto the deck of a purple houseboat, which was only a few feet from a covered area full of fishing boats. He turned his face slightly and, for the first time, she got a good look at him. His bowl haircut had grown shaggy, but it was definitely the man in the picture. Damian Henderson. Kenneth Faradi. Alexander Angelica.

"Stop!" Claire shouted. "FBI!"

Ignoring her, he leapt off the deck, barely reaching the stern of a long fishing boat that stuck out from under a tarp. He tumbled onto the boat and scrambled for the connecting walkway. Claire leapt as well, but her foot slipped and she tumbled sideways, striking her head on the boat and splashing into the water.

She lost consciousness, but only for a half second. The shock of hitting the frigid water brought her back to her senses and she quickly bobbed up, breaking the surface and gasping for air.

Head throbbing, eyes blinking away the water, she grabbed for something to hold onto.

A red life vest landed beside her. She used it to float over to the dock as Jack jumped the chasm easily and landed on the boat. Next, he deftly leapt off the boat and onto the dock.

As Claire swam over to the metal ladder, she watched as Jack caught up with Damian and tackled him from behind. Then, with a swift, fluid motion, Jack twisted the suspect's arm behind his back, using his other hand to expertly snap the cuffs in place, all while maintaining a firm grip that left no room for escape.

Kiko was right behind him, assisting Jack in leading their suspect by his elbow down the walkway toward Claire.

"You okay?" Kiko asked.

"I'm wet," Claire said. "He tossed his cellphone back there."

"I saw," Jack said. "He had no weapons on him. Nothing. Not even a wallet."

The man wasn't struggling at all and Claire gave him a hard look. "You Damian Henderson?"

He said nothing, but a slow, creepy smile spread across his face and his eyes grew wide.

He wasn't smiling at them, Claire knew. It was a smile that came from somewhere else. Somewhere she couldn't connect with, or even understand. The kind of smile she'd seen only a few times before. Once on the face of a serial killer she'd caught eight years earlier, and once on the face—which she only knew from photographs—of Thomson Flaggler, the leader of the small religious sect that had committed mass suicide when she was only a year old.

It was the smile of someone who was deeply broken.

The kind of smile that made her glad she only had a week left on this job.

CHAPTER TWENTY-TWO

"DAMIAN HENDERSON," Claire said. "Do you know why we've arrested you?"

They had gotten him back to the station and were now gathered in the little interrogation room on the second floor. Claire pressed on the bandage she'd wrapped around the right side of her head. She had a helluva lump, but no blood. And she hadn't wanted to take the time to go to the hospital while their suspect was fresh.

The young man folded his arms defiantly, but it was one of the weakest gestures of defiance Claire had ever seen. Like when Benny was six and he didn't want to take a bath, so every time she'd said it was bath time he'd folded his arms and frowned for a good ten seconds before, inevitably, heading for the tub.

Fitz stood behind her, and she could feel his eagerness to butt in. Fortunately, she'd made him promise to give her the first few minutes uninterrupted.

"We've spoken with Abbot Rasmussen. You created a fake website, a fake magazine, and spent many days there pretending to write an article. Fraud." His eyebrow flicked up slightly at this, and she continued. "You did an excellent job hiding your tracks. Looked like a real website to me. But it wasn't, was it, Alexander Angelica? Or do you prefer Kenneth Faradi?"

She waited a long time, determined to make him look up. Finally, he did. "So what?"

"You were scoping out Sister Peters' routine, and that of the other monastery residents, so you could murder her." She set a picture down before him. It showed Sister Peters' lifeless body on her bed in her little room, the white glyphs visible on the wall above the bed.

His eyes dropped. "No."

"Just like you murdered the others." She dropped a series of pictures on the desk in front of him. "Professor Isaac Orion. Sal Cardinelli. And, most recently, Johnny Stadler."

He picked up the last picture. Claire watched his eyes flick across the image, which showed the MMA fighter dead, the red glyphs on the wall behind him.

Claire noted that he hadn't even paused to look at the others.

Damian's hands trembled, the picture fluttering slightly, and he mouthed something she couldn't hear.

"What was that?" Claire asked.

"Nothing," he said.

"What did you say?" she demanded.

This time, he set the picture on the table face down and again folded his arms.

Fitz touched her shoulder and she stepped back.

Taking her by the crook of her elbow, he led her to the corner of the interview room, as far away from Damian Henderson as they could get.

Cupping his hand over his mouth, Fitz whispered, "Unless I'm wrong—which we both know I'm not—he's responding that way to the final picture because he *wasn't* there, wasn't part of that murder. Possibly didn't even know about it."

Claire knew he might be right, but something in his overconfidence made her want to disagree.

"I thought he might not be the main guy before," Fitz whispered. "Now I'm sure of it."

∼

"Damian, here's what I think happened," Fitz said. "I think you're gullible. Possibly even a moron. I don't think you can understand most of the implications of this fascinating religion." Fitz held up a printed photograph of the glyphs on the wall of the second victim. "Can you even read these?"

Damian stared blankly, but Claire noticed the smile fade slightly from his lips. After a brief chat in the hall, she'd agreed to let Fitz take the lead for a while under the assumption that Damian Henderson was an accomplice, not the killer. She'd given him twenty minutes to get something out of Damian.

"Oh *Daaa-miaaaan?*" Fitz leaned in, his voice a loud whisper. "Can you hear me? There's nothing to be ashamed about. When I was doing my A-levels I spent the better part of a year buying a young lady named Roslyn lunch every single day, only to find out she was sharing it with her boyfriend—Steve, captain of the football club—the pillock!" He sighed, as though genuinely pained by the memory. "Point is, we've all made mistakes where the heart is involved."

Claire had seen this technique many times. Sometimes accomplices were just in it for money, or because they lent some unique expertise to a plan. But, quite often, they were duped into their role because they idealized the person they were helping. If they could be made to feel like an inferior, like they'd been tricked by the real perpetrator, sometimes that was enough to get them to turn.

Claire didn't think it would work in this case. Still, she understood that Fitz had to try.

"Now," Fitz continued, "I don't know if you were sleeping with whoever is behind this, and of course, I don't want to make any assumptions about your sexual preferences, but I'm guessing you *want* to be sleeping with them. He or she is not willing to, correct? Maybe they dangled it in front of you, enticed you, made you think it might happen someday, and because you see this as a brilliant and beautiful person, that was enough to get you to do heinous things. That's how Rosalyn got my fish and chips money for three months straight." Fitz rapped his beefy index finger down heavily in front of Damian for emphasis as he spoke the last few words.

Damian looked up, his eyes wet. "But, I *didn't* do any heinous things."

"Then why did you run?" Fitz asked, his tone becoming aggressive.

Damian ran a hand through his brown hair and let out a long, thin sigh. "I was afraid," he murmured. "We don't get many visitors and I didn't know who was there. I had been sitting out on the little roof deck, taking in the sun. You know, the sun is, like, everything. We walk around all day like our little problems matter—TikTok or Facebook matter, or some crap someone said at work matters, or whether our kids do what we want matters. None of it really matters. Only the light matters." He ran a hand through his hair again. "Only the light matters."

Fitz offered a sarcastic grin. "I'm sure you're right, Damian. *Only the light matters.* I think I got the same fortune cookie as you at Panda Express last week."

Damian stood suddenly, fists clenched. Fitz didn't budge, just smiled broadly at him, daring him to take a swing.

Just as suddenly, Damian fell back into his chair.

Claire caught Fitz's attention and nodded toward the door. He followed her out into the hallway.

"We're getting nowhere," Claire said, leaning against the wall.

"We're *not* getting nowhere," Fitz said. "Every question has a purpose. He might think that only the light matters, but his *answers* are what matter to me. Don't you get it? It's not just what he says, it's *how* he says it."

"I don't think there's any chance he's going to admit to anything."

"I don't disagree with you," Fitz said, "but sometimes what they say while not admitting to anything ends up being more helpful than they can possibly imagine. Give me ten more minutes."

Without waiting for a reply, he opened the door and walked back into the room.

Claire followed reluctantly.

"This religion," Fitz said. "I've been learning everything I can about it, but I'm hoping you'll tell me more."

Damian glanced up, but didn't say anything.

"You know," Fitz said, "I studied religion. Mostly more modern ones. The history of the church in England. Luther, the Protestants. Had a little flirtation with Zen Buddhism, but, at my size, sitting still for an hour on a little cushion is, well, difficult. Plus, in the past I've preferred to get my nirvanic high from pills."

Damian cocked his head as though trying to figure out what this meant.

"Oh yeah," Fitz said, "While some try to heal their existential wounds through their belief in a particular version of God, I tried healing mine through drug addiction. Pills. Only pills. Well, booze, too. Unfortunately for me, I considered myself smarter than the pills. *Buuuut*, when you mix pills with alcohol, all sorts of stuff can go wrong. My point is, I dabbled in self medication. Now, like I said, I know a lot about religion, son, but I'd never heard of Luminism until today. It's fascinating, all of the religions and offshoots of religions that spring up and fade away. Like you said, sometimes we don't know what's really important. We've got our major religions and all sorts of little cults and side religions and whatnot. Not far from here, just across the water, a sicko tortured and killed three people at Murden Cove on Bainbridge Island. All because some young woman threw a spanner in the works of his dad's cult." He shook his head. "But there have been so many belief systems that have just—*Poof*—faded into nothing. I—"

There was a knock at the door and Violet stepped in. "Boss, can I speak with you for a sec?"

Claire nodded and stepped out into the hall as Fitz continued his monologue at Damian.

"We've got enough for a search warrant," Violet said, the moment the door closed. "I've got Damian posting about Luminism on a small, obscure message board a year ago. And, bigger than that, I've got him in Coos Bay the week before Sal Cardinelli was killed."

Claire cocked her head. "How'd you find that?"

"I've got to give Jack some of the credit on this," Violet said. "He pointed out what should have been obvious from the beginning. Whether this guy is the killer or not, we know he spent a long time scoping out the monastery. Isaac Orion would have been fairly easy to get to. Same with Johnny Stadler because he lived alone, although that would have required more physicality. But Sal Cardinelli was a cold-blooded killer. Older now, sure, but still. And he had a bodyguard. So if he spent so long scoping out Sister Peters, of course he would have spent time in Coos Bay as well. So Kiko and I began to make some calls. Turns out, our former mob boss was an amateur nature photographer. He spent a lot of time out at the Oregon Dunes National Recreation Area, which is only about twenty miles from where he lived. He loved to take pictures of it, and the park staff even knew him by name. When I sent them a picture of Damian Henderson, they recognized him as an amateur photographer as well. Which, of course, we know he wasn't. So we've got him locked in as a person of interest hanging around Coos Bay and studying the habits of our mob boss, just like he did with Sister Peters."

Claire considered this. "You and Jack get the paperwork going. We want to be able to hold this scumbag and search his houseboat."

Violet offered a single nod. "We also know he worked at a temp agency a couple years back and we're waiting on records." With that, she took off down the hall.

Back inside the interview room, Claire whispered the information about Damian being in Coos Bay to Fitz, who smiled, then began pacing, hands in his pockets, occasionally removing them to wring out his beard. "Now," he was saying. "I want to read you something. Something deeply profound. Genius level, perhaps. Will it enter into the western canon next to Homer, Dante, and Shakespeare? That's not for me to say, but I wouldn't dare to doubt it."

He cleared his throat and, making his accent a little more polished, his enunciation a little crisper, he read from the essay.

"'Eastern religions are like really really different from what we do in America. Here, everyone is always rushing and buying stuff, but in Buddhism and Taoism and all that, they just, like, live in the moment, you know?'" He paused and looked down at Damian. "Any of that sound familiar?"

The young man had no response. His eyes were locked onto the floor as though, if he stared hard enough, a trap door might open through which he could escape.

"Here's what happened," Fitz said, pulling his coin out of his pocket and passing it from hand to hand. "A while back, possibly even on the trip you took in college, you met someone. A woman, I'm guessing. She was beautiful and smarter than you, although that's not saying much. She was also charismatic, magnetic. My guess is she had a background in technology, though also a fascination with the esoteric. Ancient religions, ancient languages, particularly Luminism. You fell in love with her. She made up reasons why you couldn't be together, but you became good friends. Closer than friends. Spiritual companions, perhaps. You stayed in touch over the years. You probably had your share of little flings and whatnot, always holding out hope that someday you two might finally be together. But you have been waiting a long time. Am I getting this right?"

No answer.

"Somewhat recently," Fitz continued, "in the last year, to your surprise—as though answering your heart's deepest desires—she reached out to you. She was in the area. She had changed slightly, but that didn't matter to you. She was still the woman you loved. She asked for some help—help from *you*—and just her asking made your little heart race. You would do anything for this woman, right Damian? Head to Port Angeles and pretend to be a reporter. Scope out an old guy in Coos Bay who likes to hang at the nature preserve. It sounded like an odd plan, but I'm sure she had a breathtakingly brilliant justification for it." He stopped pacing and crouched next to Damian, so they were on the same level. "My guess is she even rented you that houseboat, always saying she'd meet you there when this was all over."

Damian kept his eyes focused on the space above and two feet past Fitz's probing stare.

"You went along because you love her. But then, after Sister Peters, after the third victim, she disappeared. You didn't know what happened. And then, when we showed you this picture of victim number four, Johnny Stadler..." He shoved the picture in front of him again. "When we showed you this picture, everything hit home. She'd ditched you. She needed you for the first three murders, but not the final two. And there *are* going to be five, aren't there?" Fitz's voice boomed as he stood up. "She doesn't need you anymore. She's left you. You're nothing. Admit it." Fitz's face was shaking with rage or, perhaps, feigned rage.

In either case his performance was imposing. "Admit it now you little bastard or the blood of the fifth victim will be on your hands!"

Claire had never seen Fitz conduct himself like this. She stepped forward and grabbed his shoulders, holding him back from attacking Damian, whom she now almost pitied.

"Lawyer," Damian said weakly. "I'm done with this. I want a lawyer."

CHAPTER TWENTY-THREE

CLAIRE NIBBLED around the edge of a chicken sandwich, catching the eye of Ranger, who'd been staring intently at it for the last five minutes. Although his yearning eyes implied he needed the sandwich more than she did, Claire suppressed the instinct to feed it to him.

She heard Fitz's loud footsteps coming down the hall and set the sandwich on the paper plate. Fitz came through the door and sat across from her, opening a plastic bottle of Coke, his second since finishing his burger and fries.

For the last twenty minutes they'd eaten dinner and talked over the case. The whole time, Kiko and Jack were sitting next to each other, eating in what Claire was beginning to think of as a silent, flirtatious magnetism. Like they just ended up near each other, whether they meant to or not. It reminded her of being in high school, when she'd angle to sit next to the boy she had a crush on in class even though she knew they wouldn't actually have a chance to talk.

She hoped she was imagining it, but she felt it. Violet hadn't turned around from her monitors.

Damian Henderson was still waiting on a public defender to arrive, but they could no longer question him.

"Assuming you're right," Claire said to Fitz, "that he's an accomplice, how does what we just heard affect your profile?"

Fitz swigged his soda and eyed Claire's chicken sandwich. "You gonna eat that?"

She frowned. "You just ate a triple bacon cheeseburger and enough fries to feed a small infantry unit."

He smiled with a fake, syrupy sweetness. "Not for me, for Ranger."

"It's got hot sauce and garlic and stuff on it. Dogs shouldn't eat the way you do, Fitz."

"I *do* plan to wipe it all off so he only gets the chicken."

Claire sighed. "Answer my question, then maybe."

Fitz took another long pull from his soda, let out a quiet belch, then stood.

"Imagine the most narcissistic person you know. Someone who is completely full of themselves, thinks the world revolves around them. Someone who fully believes they are the main character in the story of everyone's world."

Claire couldn't help herself. Scratching her chin and eyeing Fitz up and down, she said, "Hmmm, wherever would I find an example of someone like that?"

"Very funny, Claire-bear. But seriously. I'm a fairly good model. Imagine me, good at my job, smart, right? But imagine now I look like Sean Connery or Liam Neeson or—" he waved toward Jack and Kiko—"for the youngsters among us, Tom Hardy or Henry Cavill. And imagine that instead of blowing my share of my family's fortune on pills and booze, I'd invested it wisely. So you'd be looking at a gorgeous, brilliant, wealthy British aristocrat."

Claire folded her arms. "I'm having trouble imagining the 'gorgeous' part."

Fitz didn't seem to mind the banter. "Seriously, Claire. Now imagine I start a religion in which I'm the star. In which *I* am the main character."

That hung in the air for a long time, then Jack said, "But this religion is thousands of years old."

Fitz snapped his fingers. "Right. My hunch is that whoever this person is, and I believe it's a woman, was raised without religion, doesn't even think of herself as religious. Probably was an atheist and would never touch a formal religion. But the discovery of an ancient religion, something lost to everyone else... now *that's* different. That makes her special. And she *desperately* wants to be special."

"Bottom line," Claire said, taking the bun off the chicken sandwich and wiping away the cheese and sauce with a napkin, "who is this killer?"

"She's brilliant, gifted in technology like our friend over there." He nodded toward Violet in the corner. "Attractive. If not stereotypically beautiful, then charismatic. But also extremist, possibly a split personality. Possibly suffering from—and making others suffer from—a narcissistic personality disorder that includes grandiose delusions."

"Delusions about what?" Kiko asked.

"I'm gonna spend the rest of the night finding out everything I can about Luminism. But I believe our killer thinks that, when she takes out her fifth victim, she will turn into a God."

Jack stood. "Wait wait wait. That's a big leap."

Fitz waved him away like he was swatting at a fly. "You were probably too busy playing Formula 1 racer when I read the article about Luminism, so I'll give it to you again. In this religion, there are five lights, five colors relating to the five-faceted nature of God. If you perfect all of these elements, you can transcend our earthly plane. Essentially you reach nirvana, or rise to heaven, or attain some state of perfect bliss or peace. End the cycle of reincarnation. Yellow is laughter and joy. Mark my words, she will be painting the room of the next person she kills yellow."

"Fitz, what do you mean by yellow is laughter and joy?" Claire asked.

"Laughter and joy, the vibrant, outgoing, spontaneous nature of the Divine, according to Luminist beliefs. She killed Isaac Orion because he is brilliant, and she painted the room blue. She killed Sal Cardinelli because he was powerful, and she painted the room black. Sister Peters' white represented purity and innocence. And finally, the fighter Johnny Stadler embodied strength, violence, aggression, the red light of the Luminist beliefs. She believes that by killing these people, she is taking in their light and, by doing so, she will transcend the earthly plane of existence."

"Maybe," Claire said, "maybe." She didn't think Fitz was wrong. After all, his story fit with the actions of the killer and the little she'd learned about Luminist beliefs. But there was a lot more left to be learned.

And she needed to get home. She had a little internal alarm clock, and it had been going off for over an hour. Sofia sometimes stayed late when Claire was stuck at the office, but she always tried to be home to tuck Benny in at bedtime.

But there was something nagging at her. Usually, by this point in a case, she had a feel for the UnSub. Her investigation, combined with a good psychological profile and years of expertise, should have led her to an intuitive sense of the killer. Almost as though she could leave her mind and enter into theirs. But this time, despite everything, she was drawing a blank.

Even if everything Fitz said was right, she couldn't *feel* the killer as she often could.

She finished cleaning off the chicken, cut a few little bits, and held them in her hand. Ranger ran over and ate them happily. Then he sat statue-still and stared at her, waiting for more.

Claire turned back to Fitz. "I'm not quite feeling her yet. Do you know what I mean?"

Fitz finished his Coke and spun the bottle around on the table. "It's because you're too alike."

Claire felt the words like a punch to the chest. "What the hell is that supposed to mean?" she demanded.

"Our killer is not some random loser. They're successful, like you. Not only that, they're controlled. Perhaps they have a bit of a perfectionist streak. She's a bit of a Monica, as people sometimes say."

Claire stood "Wait a minute..."

But Fitz was on a roll and he barrelled right over her. "I'll see what I find tonight, but I believe this killer thinks that she is above the world, better than it somehow, and shouldn't be subject to its ridiculousness and pettiness and stupidity. She's someone who wants everything to fit together nicely, *needs* everything to fit together nicely. All the pens aligned on the desk, all the puzzle pieces fitting perfectly. Were she an FBI agent, she might retire a decade or two before her time to write novels." His voice now dripped with condescension. "Believing that she has something to say, something special, something others can't understand, she walks away from the difficult mess that is reality to create a new one in her mind. Believing she should no longer be subject to the tedious bureaucracies of the world, she quits. Sound familiar?"

Claire slapped the wall with an open palm, her frustration reaching a breaking point. Her eyes burned a hole in him. "Go to hell, Fitz." She began to move toward the door. "Kiko, Violet, and Jack, tomorrow morning, 7:00 AM. I'll see you all here."

Fitz hurried over toward the door and stopped her. "If you

want to get a feel for this person, get a feel for yourself, Claire. This is someone who could have made a massive contribution to science or technology, to anything he or she—and I still think it's a she—wanted. But instead, she quit."

Claire pushed him away, turned, and hurried out of the room.

CHAPTER TWENTY-FOUR

Kingston, Washington

"YOU SHOOT with the right trigger button, mom. The *right* trigger."

Claire fumbled awkwardly with the controller. "I... what? Where's the right trigger button?" On the screen, her character jumped backwards into a wall.

Ca-ching! Benny's computer made its familiar sound, an old-timey cash register sound that happened every time he received a micro-payment from YouTube for one of his videos.

"Moo-oom," Benny said, exasperated "you are literally the worst player in the history of video games."

Claire pressed another button, bringing up a screen called 'Inventory.' It showed a whole list of cartoonish weapons, from watermelon guns to lemon-lime grenades.

"That was the *left* trigger, mom. You shoot with your *right* trigger."

"I, umm..." Claire tried again, and this time it worked. She pressed the right trigger button on the controller and, on screen, her character, a fish wearing a bright green suit, shot a laser gun at the target, a spinning dart board that looked like a pizza, suspended in a cotton-candy sky.

She missed badly.

"Better," Benny said, laughing. "You hit the right button, at least."

His laughter was infectious, and, after the interaction with Fitz, it was exactly what she needed.

In real life she was a good shot, always testing at the top ten percent of her class. Never at the top—she'd never been at the very top in anything—but she was in the top ten percent of everything. When Brian still lived with them, he'd played video games with Benny for half an hour every night. It was their thing. Now she tried to fill that role, but aside from some Ms. Pac-Man and Donkey Kong in the arcade when she was a teenager, she knew little about gaming. Still, Benny would be a teenager soon, and that might make relating to him more difficult. She wanted to spend as much time with him as possible while he was still her little boy.

"Now," Benny continued. "See that little red circle? That's how you aim."

Claire lifted up the controller and moved her arms to the left.

Benny sighed.

"You don't *physically* move the controller, mom. See that *wire* connecting it to the box? You use the joystick."

Claire sighed and set down the controller. "It's bedtime, sweetie. We'll have to pick this up tomorrow."

Ca-ching!

"Fine," Benny said, "But I want you to practice! How can I be a famous YouTuber if I can't teach my own mom how to shoot in Fish Wars II?"

Claire chuckled. He had a point. "Just tell them I'm a poor student."

"But I want you to be good," Benny said. "Dad was better."

That hit her harder than Fitz had, but she tried not to let it show. "Dad grew up playing more video games than me. It's built into his fingers. I told you, I never had any of the Nintendos or Ataris or anything as a kid."

"Did grandma and grandpa never get you one? Because of your real mom and dad?"

Claire's chest tightened. She swallowed. "Grandma and grandpa *are* my real mom and dad. They just weren't my *biological* mom and dad. Does that make sense?"

"I know. That's what I meant, but is that why? Because of that Flaggler guy?"

"No, sweetie. We just never had the money, I guess. Plus, I wasn't that interested. I played sports instead."

He seemed content to move on and he pivoted quickly, his voice growing animated. "There's a basketball video game. *NBA 2K*. It's got all the real players and everything. We could try that." His voice was full of hope, and she could feel how much he wanted her to say yes.

"And we will. Soon I'm gonna be around a lot more, and ready to learn a new game."

Ca-ching!

~

Claire breathed in the night air and sipped her wine, a Cabernet from the Walla Walla valley. She never allowed herself more than a glass, but oh how she enjoyed that one glass.

The unseasonably warm day had settled into the low forties and she pulled up her collar against the wind. Benny had gone to bed and now, in the quiet of the night, she finally had a moment to herself.

She set her wine on the stone bench under the gazebo and grabbed her clippers from a wooden bucket. She'd come out to relax, but the roses and other bushes needed pruning before spring, and a dead offshoot on her hydrangea was bothering her as well.

As she clipped, she thought about what Benny had said. His question about her parents not wanting her to get her a video game system because of the man who'd led to the death of her biological parents. He hadn't meant to upset her. One of the things she loved most about him was that he lived his life unfiltered. And because he had such a good heart, he could get away with it. Even when he said things that might have been out of bounds in normal conversations, his intentions were always good.

She didn't know all that much about her biological parents, but she'd pulled the file on the cult leader who'd led to their deaths. He'd been an early video game developer, working for a couple of top firms in the early 1970s before, incongruously, starting a cult.

In her mind, the background of the man who led her parents to suicide meant little. Whether he'd been a dishwasher, a CEO, an airline pilot, or a video game designer before he started a twisted cult made no difference to her. But Benny had fixated on the one detail, that he'd designed video games.

She was agitated, and it wasn't only because she was thinking about her past. The argument with Fitz still lingered, and the wine was doing little to make her feel better.

She knew Fitz was right. They weren't holding the real killer. And she had little hope that Damian's conversation with his lawyer would do much to get him to cooperate.

But he wasn't right only about that. And he wasn't the first person to tell her she shouldn't leave the FBI. A couple months back, a PI named Thomas Austin had given her a plaque that read, *The World is Worth Fighting For.* It was his way of telling her to stay on the job, and she'd shoved it in a drawer.

But she'd learned early on that when she was truly bothered by something someone said, it usually meant there was at least a kernel of truth in it. Sure, Fitz could be a jerk, but the wine had mellowed her enough that she could admit to herself that that didn't mean he was wrong.

She hated the bureaucracy of the FBI, hated how little of an impact she felt she was making despite years of work and her best efforts every single day. She didn't think of herself as quitting. It was retirement, just a couple decades before it would normally come.

In her mind, she'd often gotten through the difficult times by imagining what her life could be like. Spending the mornings getting Benny off to school, her days writing and working in her garden. Being there when Benny got off the school bus. Holidays and breaks with her girls home from college. Actually being a full-time mom and still having many hours during the day to work on her passions.

It was a fantasy that was about to come true, and nothing Fitz Pembroke or Thomas Austin said was going to change that.

CHAPTER TWENTY-FIVE

FITZ WAS JUST STARTING in on his third lager by the time Kiko stopped playing coy and started flirting with Jack outright.

They had been waiting for their entrees in the all-night diner for over twenty minutes, and the drinks were going to their heads. Or maybe just to *his* head. Kiko didn't seem to drink at all, and Jack had been nursing the same Coors Light the whole time they'd been there.

Fitz had noticed a chemistry between them right away, and also something awkward between Jack and Violet. As a man with no love life of his own, trying to figure out what was going on between young people who still had a shot in life was a form of entertainment Fitz enjoyed.

Jack took a slow, cool sip of his beer. Like the hot guy in a beer commercial, he didn't drink like he was trying to get drunk. It came as no surprise to Fitz that Jack wasn't much of a drinker. He had the physique of a Greek god and his manner was tight, buttoned up. He was a man who always liked to be in control.

Which is probably why Kiko's overly flirtatious nature

appealed to him, Fitz thought. Some idioms were simply beyond reproach. Opposites attract. Always.

Freud had explained this phenomenon in terms of unresolved childhood conflicts and desires. The idea that we're unconsciously seeking to reconcile unresolved aspects of our early relationships with our parents, or trying to master past traumas through our choices in partners. Fitz's own view leaned more towards the Jungian perspective of the shadow self—we see the traits we lack or suppress in others and are drawn to them in a quest for balance, for completeness.

Jack, in his disciplined and controlled demeanor, was likely drawn to the spontaneity and openness Kiko exuded, qualities he might have repressed or never fully developed. He didn't know much about Kiko's past, but it was clear that her easygoing, over-the-top persona was a part of her personality she exaggerated out of a deep insecurity. No doubt Jack's buttoned-up look and personality—with a strong sprinkling of action hero—was like catnip to her.

Interestingly, Jack was not only Kiko's opposite, he was Violet's as well. Despite being valedictorian of his high school and speaking five languages, Jack was no genius. He was a smart enough bloke, sure, but only to a point. His pursuit of the Abbot had shown Fitz that. Violet, on the other hand, was a prodigy, and that undoubtedly appealed to Jack.

The waiter appeared and set down plates before them.

Kiko had ordered breakfast for dinner—waffles, eggs, and bacon. Jack, unsurprisingly, had ordered a chicken salad with dressing on the side and double meat—white chicken breast, no oil, no seasoning. Violet had ordered soup and pie, and Fitz, trying to decide between a healthy salad or a rare steak sandwich on garlic bread, had gone for both. He'd taken Ranger back to his apartment, fed him dinner, and left him sleeping at the foot of his futon mattress.

Violet, who hadn't spoken for some time, asked, "Are things going to be okay between you and Claire?"

Fitz smiled. "Oh, we're all sorted. She and I go back, and we have our little rows. Storms in a teacup."

Kiko grinned at him. "Was there ever anything, you know, *between* you two?"

Fitz, who had taken a long sip of his lager, fought hard to swallow. "Not on your life."

"Good," Kiko said.

"Why good?" Fitz asked, a little hurt.

"Because I'm hoping she'll end up with that Austin guy. I know he was dating some lady from the Navy or whatever but, I think she went back to the east coast."

Fitz sighed. "She told me about him, that whole thing over in Port Townsend. Not in a million years."

"Why not?" Jack asked.

Fitz rapped the table with his knuckles. "They're too similar."

Kiko laughed. "That's what she said, too. So why nothing between you and Claire, then?"

"Until recently she was married and, well, she's still married, but you know what I mean. Anyway, a rotter though I am, I respect marriage. Never would have even tried. Plus..." he leaned back and patted his belly, "...look at me. I'm not exactly much of a catch."

Kiko leaned forward. "Don't fat shame yourself. You're *distinguished* looking, a brilliant Nutty Professor type."

"I must hold my wisdom in my belly," Fitz said.

"Exactly," Kiko agreed.

Fitz smiled. A decade ago, he might have thought that Kiko was flirting with him, but he was under no such delusion now. Kiko had the kind of personality that made *everyone* think she was flirting. But Jack, with whom she was ostentatiously *not* flirting, *was* her type.

Violet, on the other hand, was quieter, always studying, watching. Like she was doing complex calculations in her head while the world buzzed on around her. And maybe she was.

"What happened with her marriage?" Jack asked.

"Not really my story to tell," Fitz said, "but it ended. Marriages end sometimes. It's just what happens. I'll tell you one thing. She is a hell of a mum. Sometimes I think if I'd had a mum more like her..." he trailed off. "Best not to go there. But no, there was never anything between us, and if you want to know about her marriage, ask her yourself. I got the sense her husband was a bit of a dumbass."

"You'd have to be to let her get away," Kiko added.

Jack finished a bite of his chicken salad, then said, "Is she always so, I don't know..."

"By the book?" Fitz asked. "Uptight?"

"I like the way she is," Violet said.

"As much as we'd like to pretend otherwise," Fitz said, "she had to be to get where she has. A woman in the FBI *still* doesn't get the same breaks as a man."

"C'mon," Jack said. "She had all the same chances I had, that these lovely ladies have." He swept a hand across the table toward Kiko and Violet.

"All I can say is this," Fitz said. "You think they would have kept her on if she'd been arrested for illegal possession of schedule two narcotics? With me they brushed it under the rug. Made me a consultant so as not to stain the shield, but I'm still working. For her, that would have been curtains."

"Plus," Violet continued. "I like rules, and order." She grew quiet, and Fitz noticed her eyeing Jack, then Kiko. "Workplaces *need* to have *rules*."

The way she said the words 'need' and 'rules' told Fitz there was a lot going on under the surface. He wouldn't have brought it up if he hadn't been two and three-quarters pints deep, but, after taking a huge bite of the steak sandwich and washing it down with the last quarter of his lager, he said, "Okay, okay, what's going on here? Let's get it out." He eyed Violet, then Kiko, then Jack.

"What?" Violet asked.

"Yeah, what?" Jack echoed.

Kiko said nothing but looked somewhere between delighted and amused.

"I'm not daft," Fitz said. "I was young once, remember?"

"When was that?" Kiko asked. "Like the 1920s or something?"

"Haha," Fitz said, "but seriously, I know I'm seeing sparks flying about."

"Can we get back to work?" Violet asked. "I got the list from the temp agency, finally. Came in as we sat down." She held up her phone. "You wanna hear where Damian worked?"

Fitz waved her away. His inebriated state made him insistent. "No more work until I know which of you is bewitched and which is doing the bewitching." The tongue tie had been a stretch and one more lager would have had him bungling it.

Violet frowned. "Fine, and I'm only going there because I know you're probably building a complete psych profile on all of us in your twisted little mind anyway, and I want to leave the absolute minimum to your imagination."

She looked at Kiko, then down at the table. "Jack and I went on two dates. A movie and dinner. *Before* I knew we'd be working together. And the minute I found out I told him we were done as long as we were on this case." She looked at him. "He failed to mention what he did for a living."

Kiko smiled broadly and punched Jack in the arm. "A movie? Dinner? Did you...."

"No," Violet said. "We did *not* hook up."

Fitz noticed a sly smile on Jack's face and a slight cock of his head. He caught Jack's eye. "What?"

"I don't kiss and tell," Jack said.

"Ohhhh," Kiko said, clearly amused. "You *kissed*. But don't worry Violet, Jack left that part out when Claire asked him about it."

Violet's cheeks flushed red. "What? Claire knows? Why tell her anything Jack? We made out for like two minutes. That's it. That's literally the entire story."

Fitz waved down the waiter and ordered another beer. That may have been the entire story *so far*, but the way her cheeks had flushed red, and the way Kiko was going over the top to appear not to care, he knew there was a lot more to the plot.

But he wasn't going to push it. "Alright, so where did Damian work?" he asked Violet.

Relieved to be changing subjects, Violet scrolled on her phone. "The temp agency he worked for did mostly low-level office stuff. He stopped working there three months ago, but his last four assignments were... okay hold on." She scrolled for a moment then read from her phone. "*Emerald City Legal Associates*. Mid-sized law firm downtown. Known for contract law, IP, boring stuff. *NeuroTech Imaging Solutions:* specializes in advanced brain scan imaging. They are known for their cutting-edge research in neuroimaging technologies and work closely with medical facilities and research institutions. *Rainier Tech Solutions*: Your basic tech startup, some app that builds apps. *Puget Sound Marketing Group:* Down on the waterfront, they're a marketing and public relations firm working mostly with corporate clients and a few athletes."

"I mean, the tech startup?" Jack said. "Could be a connection to the perp if he or she was in tech?"

"I'm gonna call around to all four tomorrow," Violet said. "Kiko, can you help with that?"

"8 AM sharp," Kiko said.

Fitz's mind was a little fuzzy, but he heard himself saying. "The brain imaging place. Pay special attention to them."

CHAPTER TWENTY-SIX

Spokane, Washington

WITH ONLY SIXTY-EIGHT hours left to go, everything was falling into place.

The top corner room of the little bed and breakfast was exactly as it had looked online. A small dresser sat beneath the lone window, which looked out onto Main Street. The bed was creaky, but she didn't mind. The old wooden floorboards and early 20th-century chandelier gave the place a charm that she would miss when she was gone.

As planned, she had cut Damian loose. He had done his job perfectly and had been everything she needed. But it was his fate to remain behind.

There was nothing she could do about that.

In fact, things had worked out better than she'd planned. She'd never intended for him to get caught, but the fact that he had been likely bought her another day or two free of scrutiny.

Not that it mattered much. She was undetectable, uncatchable. And Damian's fate had been nothing less than one more sign from the universe confirming her destiny to become what she was worthy of.

Thinking of Damian reminded her of Holden Caulfield. She'd recalled reading *The Catcher in the Rye* in high school. She'd found Holden's thinking deeply flawed. She remembered thinking she would have *never* let anyone catch her had she been in that field, even as a child.

In a way, Damian made her sick. He was like one of the children—he wanted *her* standing there to catch him. People like Damian—who trust they'll be saved—run around in the rye incapable of growth knowing they will be held and brought to safety before coming to the edge of the cliff where they would otherwise fall to their death. But she wouldn't be the one to save Damian. Standing in the way of another's fate robbed them of their chance to truly come to know themselves.

She would turn her back on the children at the edge of the field, walk a straight line through the grass, and jump off the cliff. Alone.

Gazing out the window, she took in the view of Riverfront Park. The frost of the season touched the scene, lending white highlights to the park's simple beauty. The Spokane River flowed steadily, its surface reflecting the soft light of dawn. The iconic red Radio Flyer Wagon sat quietly, a landmark resting in the calm of the morning. Barren trees lined the riverbank and, in the distance, the outline of the Post Street Bridge arched over the water. The park was serene in these early hours, with only a few early risers dotting the paths. In her youth, she'd once mocked quaint small towns like this. But she'd come to appreciate them, and part of her would miss them when she was gone.

From the armoire, she pulled out a small black duffel bag and set it on the bed. Inside were three hues of yellow paint. She hadn't been able to decide on one, but now was the time. One was a light, pale yellow, the kind that made her think of her grandmother's kitchen. The second was a dark, rich yellow that, in certain lights, had a few burnt orange hues to it. Neither felt quite right. The third?

Yes, it would be the third. She knew it the moment she looked at it.

She walked to the window, carrying a clear plastic tub, then held it up to the light.

She felt her feet on the floor, the gentle breaths in her chest.

Her entire body felt full. Blue, Black, White, and Red coursed through her veins now, giving her an almost indescribable, multi-faceted power.

There was little left to do.

She was fully prepared.

Now she would wait until the time was right.

CHAPTER TWENTY-SEVEN

CLAIRE WAS HUDDLED over a stack of files when Jack burst through the door. "Damian has agreed to talk."

Claire shot up from her seat. "Well, that's better news than we've had in awhile. What made him..."

"Apparently," Jack didn't wait for her to finish, "he met with his lawyer for a few hours last night and an hour or two this morning."

Claire eyed him skeptically. "That's it? You must have..."

Jack leaned away. "Yes, there was also the little thing about my meeting with him."

"Wait a second, what meeting?" Claire asked with a scowl. "Please don't tell me you did anything that's going to jeopardize our prosecution."

"No, no, no," Jack said. "It's not like that. You know how Fitz is brilliant and psychologically astute and all that?"

"Yeah, but hearing it from you makes me question..."

"Hey, credit where credit is due, right?" Jack continued. "Seems like Fitz had softened him up with all that stuff about being whipped."

Claire frowned. "That's not exactly what Fitz said, but okay."

"I honestly went in to threaten him a little bit," Jack continued, "but it turned out that wasn't needed. As soon as I got in the room with him, I got this deja vu type feeling. He seemed familiar. Reminded me of an old roommate. I think the kid *did* get duped. And I think he did it for love."

"So, you're saying Fitz's psychological profile on this guy is a bullseye?"

"As much as I hate to say it," Jack admitted, "yes."

"Okay then." Claire nodded, holding a straight line with her mouth to prevent a gratified smile.

"Like I was saying, my roommate was kind of like Damian so I just talked to him man to man, told him he could still turn his life around, encouraged him to give himself another shot. I don't know if that's what did it, or if his lawyer convinced him, but he's ready to talk."

Claire followed Jack down the hall, dialing Fitz from her cell phone as she walked. He hadn't yet made it into the office, giving Claire the morning to enjoy much-needed respite from him. But they'd had blow-ups before and had always made it through to the other side. And she had to admit that she wished he were here for this.

His phone went straight to voicemail and she stopped outside the door of the interview room. "Fitz, where are you? Damian is ready to talk. Get down here."

Inside the interrogation room, she found Damian looking brighter and fresher than she'd expected. His lawyer sat next to him at the end of the table, wearing a light brown suit too tight for his broad shoulders. His pinched-looking face made him look like he had just eaten something sour.

"I hear you're ready to talk," Claire said, panning her gaze from Damian to his lawyer, wondering if he would turn out to be as smarmy as he looked.

"My client has certain information that may be of interest to you," the lawyer said, standing and extending a thick, strong hand to Claire, his reach stressing the seams on his suit and making the threading briefly visible. "Malcolm C. Birdwell. pleased to meet you."

Claire shook his hand quickly, then stepped back. "Mr. Birdwell, I think you can understand that we don't have time for long negotiations. Have you spoken with McGibbons?"

Mr. Birdwell nodded. "And she has assured us that we will receive every possible consideration. My client understands that this is a time-sensitive matter and will have to proceed without drawing up a formal agreement. I've worked with McGibbons in the past, though, and I know her word is as good as gold."

Claire was relieved. Samantha McGibbons was the Assistant United States Attorney working at the US Attorney's Office for the Western District of Washington. She'd be the one responsible for prosecuting Damian Henderson and anyone else who turned out to be involved in this case. If Damian's lawyer trusted her to be lenient if he cooperated, that could go a long way.

"Then let's go," Jack said. "Let's get to it. We don't have any time to waste."

For the first time, Damian spoke. "What you said about the army, Jack... do you really think they would still take me?" His eyes were pleading as he looked up.

Jack shoved his hands in his pockets and looked down at him. "I can't say for sure, but depending on how this goes, I can put in a good word for you."

Claire knew there was no way the Army would take someone like Damian Henderson, no matter how much he cooperated. But she wasn't going to say that.

"I think you are right," Damian said. "I think I just need to learn some discipline. Sick of being dragged around by the balls by Hazel. Before her, there was Maria, and before her, there was Rebecca."

Claire's ears perked up. "Hazel? Can we begin the formal statement now?" She nodded up at a small black camera that was surveilling the room. "As you know, Mr. Birdwell, we are recording both video and audio, and you need to consent, as does your client."

Mr. Birdwell nodded, and Damian said, "Yes, that's fine."

"Tell us about Hazel," Claire said.

"And start with giving us her last name," Jack added, "and where she might be right now, buddy."

"Hazel Christopher," Damian said, his face scrunching up as he spoke. It was as though uttering the name made him disgusted with himself, but after the name hung in the air for a while, his face brightened as though he'd received a little bit of relief. "And I don't have any idea where she is. The other guy, the British guy, he was right about that. She ditched me."

Claire knew that Violet and Kiko would be watching. Chances were, within five minutes, Violet would have every possible record regarding Hazel Christopher. But Claire doubted they would find much. Damian's tracks had been well covered. She assumed Hazel would be equally effective at covering her own.

"We met about six years ago," Damian said. "It was actually at a yoga class. I was attracted to her right away. I have a thing for women who look slightly androgynous."

"Can you describe her in detail?" Jack asked.

"Yes, she's not like manly or anything. But she's lean, not especially curvy, short hair. Not like she's trying to look like a man, just not your classic blonde bombshell or anything. Main thing is, she's brilliant. She was quite advanced in yoga and I was just getting into it. We really shouldn't have been in the same class anyway. We started talking over smoothies, and I honestly couldn't tell why someone like her would be interested in someone like me."

"Did you form a relationship?" Claire asked.

"We never had sex, if that's what you're asking." Damian looked down at his hands, briefly picking at a hangnail.

"What was the nature of your relationship?" Jack asked.

"Like I told you earlier," Damian said, his voice growing dejected, "she led me around by the balls." He looked up and stared straight ahead without making eye contact. "Although I didn't know it at the time."

"Be specific," Claire demanded.

"You already know, she's into this ancient religion called Luminism, with all the colors and their meaning and everything. And I kind of am, too, I guess."

"You don't need to guess," Claire said. "We know you're into it, too."

"The religion has some interesting points," Jack said, speaking in a friendly tone.

Claire leaned back in her chair, realizing that Jack was probably right to make this interview more conversational than adversarial.

"It does," Damian agreed. "She's really right about all that Luminist stuff. I mean, I guess so anyway."

"We need to know more about your relationship with her," Claire reminded him, keeping her tone neutral.

Damian glanced over at his lawyer, who gave him a nod to continue.

"Well, we were just friends," he began. "But like on and off—we'd stay in touch online when she was traveling or when we were living in different places. We would plan to get together and I would think that things could work up to a relationship but she would just bail on me. About a year ago, she did see me in person. I was working a crummy temp job at this medical lab and was really down on myself. It was like a miracle when she showed back up and I thought, *this could be the time*. She started telling me about her plan. She calls it the Ascension. She was going to find the most advanced people in the world and merge with their light. I thought she meant like—learn from them and stuff. You got to understand, I believed damn near every word out of her mouth." He paused, shaking his head, and then looked up at Jack. "This whole thing is really really embarrassing."

"Don't worry," Jack said, "we've all been there. Well, actually, I haven't. But, I do know people who have."

Claire shot him a slightly annoyed look. "Let's get back to it," she said to Damian. "Tell me precisely what your role in the Ascension was."

"Well, you already know that I posed as a journalist to scope out the monastery. Hazel wanted me to write down the exact routines and schedules of everyone. Sister Peters most of all. I didn't know that she was going to kill her. I thought she would just 'merge with her light' in some ceremony or whatever—not to do something that would leave them dead."

Claire didn't say it out loud, but the truth was, Hazel *was* having a ceremony. She was also committing cold-blooded murder, but the glyphs, the oils, the incense, and the flowers did appear to be ceremonial. And she was fairly confident that Damian was telling the truth. "What about the others?"

"Bird watching in Coos Bay," Damian said. "Hung out at the UW gym for a bit to track that Orion guy. Then posed as a grad student for a while and went to a few of his lectures—boring as hell—but I got his schedule down, too. I even got jealous because for a minute I thought she was going to date the guy. My head was all jumbled up."

"So while you were doing all of this," Claire asked, "what exactly did you think was going to happen?"

"I thought I was going to be part of the ritual too, we were going to ascend to a higher plane of existence. We would do it together." He looked almost tearful.

From the looks of Damian, Claire thought that if Hazel appeared at this very minute, reaching out a hand for him to join her for whatever the Ascension was, he would do it. Even if it did leave somebody dead.

There was a knock at the door and Violet poked her head in, holding up a stack of papers. She waved Claire out into the hallway. "I've got something you're going to want to see."

CHAPTER TWENTY-EIGHT

VIOLET LED Claire to the Boiler Room, where the others were already gathered. Fitz was tossing pieces of popcorn into the air, smiling like a kid in front of a piece of cake each time he caught one in his mouth. And he smiled just as exuberantly when he missed one and Ranger scooped it up from the floor.

"Where were you?" Claire asked.

Fitz set down the bag of popcorn. "I felt bad about what I said last night."

"And?"

"And I drank."

Claire didn't have time for this. "Did you fall back on the pills?"

"Certainly not," Fitz said. "Never again."

"Are you sober now?"

"Sober as a priest on Christmas."

That was good enough for Claire, and her eyes landed on the large wall-mounted monitor the second she sat down.

Violet got right to it. "Damian temped at NeuroTech Imaging Solutions. They are the Pacific Northwest's leading neuroimaging technology firm. All four victims received brain scans there."

Claire's mind raced. "How did you find out?"

"Fitz's hunch," Violet said. "I called this morning and provided death certificates, which allowed them to confirm that all four were patients, though they wouldn't share anything more without a warrant."

"And if all four went there," Claire said, "then the intended fifth victim is likely a client as well."

"Exactly," Violet said. "I'm waiting on a callback from their CEO. I made it clear that we need a complete list of their clients and are not interested in waiting for a warrant."

Fitz shook his head. "It's a HIPPA violation. Even if he wanted to, he couldn't just give us all his records."

Claire felt heat rising through her chest into her face. "Let's table this for a minute. What did you find on Hazel Christopher?"

"A shocking amount," Violet said.

"Shockingly small?" Claire asked.

Violet tapped away at her keyboard. "No. I assumed we'd find almost nothing, but no. She did surprisingly little to cover her tracks."

A series of images appeared on the screen and Claire understood why Damian was mesmerized by her. She wasn't beautiful in a stereotypical sense, but she had a fascinating look.

Standing at an average height with a slender, wiry build, her hair was cut in a choppy mullet, reminding Claire of David Bowie as Ziggy Stardust, but without the glam. She wore simple black slacks, a stark white t-shirt, and no makeup. Her facial features were delicate and angular.

As Violet clicked through more photos, she summarized what she'd learned. "Hazel Christopher, age thirty-two. Grew up in the affluent Seattle suburb of Bellevue. Her parents are successful doctors, now living on Mercer Island. Hazel was gifted academically, breezing through an advanced curriculum and gaining early acceptance to the California Institute of Technology at age sixteen."

She clicked through more photos and, in each, her wardrobe was consistent: black, gray, and white. Simple, utilitarian styles like casual pants, button-down shirts, blazers, oxfords. Nothing flashy or overtly masculine or feminine. But her clothes, though simple, were high-end and pristine. She wore no jewelry beyond a single platinum band on her left ring finger. Her accessories were limited to a smart watch and rectangular framed eyeglasses.

"Cal-Tech is pretty hard to get into, right?" Jack asked.

Violet scoffed. "Nearly impossible. I got early acceptance into MIT and *I* got rejected from Cal-Tech. Anyway, during her sophomore year there, she dropped out, fell off the grid for a bit. I believe that's when she first traveled abroad. Nepal, India, and so on."

"It would seem," Fitz said, "that she had some kind of spiritual crisis. Not that uncommon among college kids. But among genius-level children who excel at math and science, well, she clearly took it to an extreme."

"I have a video," Violet said. "She was tagged on an old social media site called Bouncer."

The video showed Hazel in the background of what looked like a cocktail party. Though most of the crowd wore suits or nice dresses, Hazel wore black slacks and a white button down. She strolled from group to group casually, moving with a controlled grace that didn't expend unnecessary effort. Though she appeared engaged, she maintained an aloof, analytical demeanor, showing little emotion.

"Could she have scrubbed all this information from the web?" Claire asked.

"Absolutely," Violet said.

"Then why didn't she?" Kiko asked.

"We can get into the why later." Claire stood and walked a slow lap around the conference table. She noticed Ranger in the corner, sleeping lazily in front of a heating duct. "Now the goal is twofold. First, we need to get the list of people who received scans at that imaging center. Our fifth victim is on that list. Jack, Violet, Fitz, stay here and work on that. Second goal: find Hazel. Kiko and I will start with her parents. Mercer Island, right?"

Violet nodded. "Both doctors. Both retired."

"Kiko, do you have a suit, and can you act like a snob?"

Kiko stood, "I can act like anything you need, but why?"

"We're gonna play rich cop, bad cop."

CHAPTER TWENTY-NINE

"OH, *DAMINAAAAAN?* CAN YOU HEAR ME?" Fitz had walked three laps around Damian and his lawyer, who sat at the table in the interview room.

"I'm thinking," Damian said.

"You see," Fitz said, "you could still be charged for first degree murder. If the fifth victim is on that list and you don't share who it is when we've given you every opportunity..." He shook his head, tisking. "I'll give you a minute with your lawyer."

Fitz stepped out into the hallway and folded his arms.

"Need some help in there?" Jack asked.

Fitz glared, then shrugged.

"I thought you were an interrogation genius."

"I am, but I'm not telepathic, Jack. No one is." Fitz had spent the last ten minutes trying to convince Damian to give them the list of names of the people whose brain scans he'd furtively obtained and presented to Hazel.

Violet hurried down the hall holding a slim silver laptop. "What did he say?"

"He's having a chinwag with his lawyer," Fitz said.

The door opened and Malcolm Birdwell, Damian's attorney, poked his head out the door. "He will share the files."

Fitz made his face stay neutral, as though this is exactly what he'd expected. "Good decision. I'll join you momentarily."

Fitz waited for the door to close. "And, Bob's your uncle, I guess I am a genius," he whispered smugly, directing his comment to Jack while grabbing the laptop from Violet.

Jack threw his hands up in defeat while walking away backwards, leaving Fitz to continue the interview without him. Violet followed Fitz into the room and watched over Damian's shoulder as Fitz slid the laptop across the table in front of him.

Fitz stood back and folded his arms, allowing a slight smile to crack over his face. "You said you'd emailed the scans to yourself from a personal address while at work?"

Damian nodded and brushed his hair back from his eyes. "I set up a random Gmail account. It'll be in batches because the scans are pretty high-res."

"Drag them all onto the desktop," Violet said, "And I'll take it from there."

~

Claire pulled up to the large security gate, where a uniformed guard sat staring at his phone behind a small, glass-enclosed guardhouse.

"Can I help you?" he asked.

"Claire Anderson. FBI." She held up her ID. "They're expecting us."

"Right," the guard said. "I'll need to verify this. And your companion?"

"Vivian Greene." Claire took Kiko's ID and handed it to the guard.

Mercer Island was only about twenty minutes from their office. It was one of the richest areas in the entire country, home to both old money Seattleites and lots of new tech money, millionaires, and billionaires. During the drive from the office they'd called and found that Mr. and Mrs. Christoper were home and, thankfully, hadn't put up a fight when Claire demanded to see them at once.

"Drive on through to the second roundabout. Big stone house on the left. Tough to miss it." The guard chuckled and Claire could tell he'd made that joke a hundred times.

She was not in a joking mood. "Their daughter, Hazel," she asked. "How often does she come around?"

The guard flinched slightly. "Not often, I'm guessing. Not since I've been working here. I hear she's an odd duck. But… well, I shouldn't say more." He pressed a button to lift the gate and Claire eased up a long driveway, through one roundabout that led toward a putting green on the left and a small lake on the right. At the second roundabout, she stopped in front of one of the nicest houses she'd ever seen.

∽

"There are roughly seventeen hundred scans here," Violet said.

Fitz laced his hands behind his head and looked up at the monitor. Violet had connected it wirelessly to the silver laptop after Damian had finished adding the scans he'd stolen from the imaging center.

"I've dragged all of the individual scans into a program and, hold on…" she tapped away and Fitz saw a name appear in a search bar: Marybeth Peters. A file popped up, then an image of a scan. They were looking at Sister Peters' brain.

The image was highly detailed and vividly colored. Bright hues of red, blue, and yellow highlighted different regions, each color signifying distinct neural activities or brain structures. The intense red areas indicated regions of high metabolic activity, while the blue and green hues depicted calmer areas of lesser activity.

Fitz was no expert, but he'd taken multiple classes in neurobiology and neuropsychology and knew the basics.

The cerebral cortex was a gradient of oranges and yellows, showcasing the intricate folds and grooves of the brain's surface. Deeper structures like the amygdala and hippocampus were illuminated in purples and pinks, highlighting their roles in memory and emotional processing.

Strikingly, one area in Peters' frontal lobe exhibited an unusual pattern of heightened activity, glowing in a vibrant, almost pulsating red, which stood out against the surrounding normal activity patterns.

"There," Fitz said. "Violet. See the red area framed by those bright white lines of neural connectivity? Can you pull up Isaac Orion or one of the others?"

Violet pulled up Orion's brain scan and Fitz immediately saw the same unusual brain activity. "Now Stadler, and the mob guy."

Violet pulled up their brains scans and both had similarly intense red areas.

Jack, who'd been sitting quietly and petting Ranger, finally spoke. "What does it mean?"

"I don't know *what* it means," Fitz said. "But our fifth victim is going to have the same type of unusual brain activity."

CHAPTER THIRTY

CLAIRE HAD EXPECTED to be met by a butler or servant, or possibly an army of servants. Instead, she was met by a lawyer.

The man introduced himself as William Dimitri Butler II, and he was every bit as fancy and old money looking as his name implied.

After shaking their hands, he said, "Mr. and Mrs. Christopher are in the living room. They're happy to cooperate in any way, but I should tell you that, as their personal attorney, I am ready to step in if you cross any lines. They genuinely do not know what this is about, but it is their custom to have an attorney present at all times when discussing, well, basically anything."

Claire nodded and followed him through a long, ornate hallway.

Kiko, who had tied her dreadlocks up into an elegant bun and changed into a white skirt suit, looked like she could be working as a first year associate at the same law firm as Mr. Butler. "I understand completely," she said.

Her voice had changed slightly as well. It wasn't a phony accent, though. She just sounded twenty percent more like a highly-educated, soon-to-be-rich young professional than she normally did. Like she'd added a layer of pretentiousness and refinement to her voice that didn't come across as fake. Like she actually had it in her somewhere.

Claire was impressed.

During the car ride over, Claire explained what she'd meant by *rich cop, bad cop*. Kiko would be the more relatable one, leaving Claire to play more of a hard-ass. Since these were clearly very rich people, Claire thought it best that Kiko interact with them on that level, and given that she was somewhat close to their daughter's age, she thought it was their best bet.

Mr. and Mrs. Christopher met them in the living room. The first thing Claire noticed was a gorgeous encasement with thick glass walls holding what she thought was hundreds of thousands of dollars worth of wine. As Kiko introduced herself, Claire ignored their outstretched hands and examined the wine. She was no snob, but she loved a good Washington State Cabernet. She didn't see a single one. Every wine was either French or Italian. They didn't even have any Napa Valley Cab.

Kiko noticed as well and used it immediately in her performance. "Is that an eighty-two Mouton Rothchild?" She gestured into the wine case.

"It is," Mr. Christoper said.

Claire studied Mr. and Mrs. Christopher and could immediately see where Hazel got her likeness. Mrs. Christopher was slight and appeared anxious but was dressed in a white pantsuit not unlike the one her fellow agent was wearing. Kiko had chosen her wardrobe wisely. Mr. Christopher was barely larger than his wife, maybe five feet eight or so, and was also slightly built. He wore a classic blue suit with a brown tie and looked mildly annoyed to be alive.

"And I see a magnum of Petrus, 1961," Kiko added, as

though she was casually considering what to order off a menu at McDonald's.

She's fitting right in, Claire thought.

"Personally," Kiko continued, speaking in fluent bourgeois, "I'm in absolute heaven with a Bordeaux—the minerality, the earthiness. I haven't had the pleasure of sampling the '82 Rothchild. Perhaps you can invite me over when you open it," she added playfully. "I did, however, share the '61 Petrus with my father the last time I was in Tokyo. He's a financial analyst there. He shuttles back and forth, you know how it is. My mother is a lawyer. Stateside. You have truly exceptional taste Mr. and Mrs. Christopher."

"Thank you," Mr. Christopher said. "And it sounds like you have a very well-cultivated wine palate."

"You know, my father once said the funniest thing. My parents, they never wanted me to go into the FBI. In the throes of trying to dissuade me of doing so he said, 'With your taste in wine, Kiko, you'll never afford to live on an FBI agent's salary.' Who knows? Maybe I'll just have to go into politics."

This made Mrs. Christopher laugh. "Oh, don't do that dearie. Much too tacky."

Kiko had put the Christophers well at ease and Claire felt they would tell them anything they could about anything they knew.

"Thank you for seeing us on such short notice," Claire said, worried that her voice sounded anything but thankful. "We're going to cut right to it. When was the last time you saw your daughter, and do you know where she is now?"

Mr. and Mrs. Christopher both looked at the lawyer, who nodded slightly.

"We haven't seen her in over a year," Mr. Christopher said curtly. "And no, we do not know where she is."

Claire was no mind reader, but she had taken all the standard classes on how to tell when someone was lying. Looking up to the left, fidgeting, that sort of thing. She wasn't sure, but she got the impression he was telling the truth.

"What is this about?" Mrs. Christopher asked, her voice mousy and anxious. She reached into her pocket to retrieve a personal pocket tissue-pack and pulled out one square, holding it at the ready.

"It's very serious," Claire said. "It's—"

But Kiko interrupted, "Let's not overstate it. We don't know anything for certain, but her name came up in an important matter related to our investigation, and we're trying to find her as soon as possible."

"Don't sugarcoat it," Claire said. "Can we see her room?"

"She hasn't lived here for years," Mrs. Christopher said. She looked away and blotted the corner of her eye with the tissue.

"But I'm guessing you left her room as it was because you have so many of them," Claire said.

Mr. Christopher began walking out of the room. "Follow me upstairs."

The room matched Hazel's appearance as they'd seen it about an hour earlier on the screen. Spare, minimal, mostly black and white with a few accents of gray and blue. Even the walls were bare.

"Seems like she would have had more, I don't know, achievements or debate club trophies or things like that," Claire said.

"In our family," Mr. Christopher took his wife's hand, "excellence is expected. Beating a bunch of rotten-brained kids who eat junk food all day while watching TV in a debate or math club is not something worthy of her abilities."

"Hazel had higher ambitions," Mrs. Christopher added.

"How high?" Claire demanded.

"What she's saying," Kiko said, consolation in her voice, "is that we've learned that Hazel was certainly a high achiever. Exceptional, really. But we're concerned that she may have gotten taken in by some religious or spiritual belief systems that forced her down a dark path."

Claire watched Mrs. Christopher's eyes dance to her husband, then to her lawyer, who was standing in the doorway of Hazel's room. Kiko must have noticed this as well, because she continued, "Mrs. Christopher, I promise we're going to do everything we can to help her. But if you know something about what she's gotten into, you need to tell us, okay?"

"Hazel excelled at everything she tried," her mother said. "Obviously she wasn't athletic in a traditional way, but she earned a black belt in Kyokushin Karate, started taking college classes when she was twelve, and was always the best at everything she did."

"She's a genius," her father said matter-of-factly.

"But when she got to college... I don't know..." Mrs. Christopher's voice grew quiet. "She just started believing all sorts of the strangest things. About the world, and also about herself."

CHAPTER THIRTY-ONE

JACK STOOD AGAINST THE WALL, watching Fitz. He didn't understand how someone could have been expelled from multiple prestigious British universities, be so out of control, so sloppy, have had multiple stints with pills, be so unlikable, and still be utterly brilliant.

As Fitz leaned his hulking body over Damian, he managed to convey both gentleness and intimidation. He showed no overt aggression, but Fitz was leaning in both physically and mentally. It was almost as though, if he didn't get answers soon, his entire being would come crashing down and crush all that was Damian.

Jack was impressed, especially when Damian started spilling his guts.

"You know," he began, "it's like Hazel got this wild idea in her head. She thought that alpha wave patterns in a certain part of the brain were, like, the ultimate sign of enlightenment. Like it meant they were capable of the purest saturation of their Luminist hue. I guess she got it from twisting around something she read or something, but at the time it all seemed kinda reasonable. Cutting edge, ya know? For months,

Hazel holed up, poring over these scans, making a list of folks who've got this 'enlightened' alpha wave vibe she's so obsessed with."

Fitz had been watching Damian closely, but now shoved his hands in the pockets of his rumpled blazer and took a few lumbering steps to the other side of the table. He glanced at Jack, who wondered what the Brit was thinking. "Let me guess," Fitz said, "was it Hazel's idea for you to work at the brain imaging center?"

Jack moved his eyes from Fitz to Damian, who nodded sadly. "It was her idea," Damian admitted. "She told me her parents had cut her off financially, and we were going to save some money to travel to Tibet together."

"Right now," Fitz said, "you're guilty of aiding and abetting a serial killer in the destruction of four human lives." Fitz said this with a sigh, a sadness in his voice that surprised Jack. His usual condescending tone was gone, and it was clear he actually felt something for the victims, which Jack didn't think Fitz had been capable of.

Fitz glanced at Damian's lawyer. "Counselor, we appreciate the help, but you know how bad this can get. Despite helping us, he's looking at life in prison. I strongly urge you to wrack your client's brain for any other information."

Fitz nodded at Jack as though urging him out of the room, but Jack had one more thing to say.

"We know," Jack said, "that there is an intended fifth victim. We know it's someone who got their brain scanned." He took two steps toward Damian and put on his hardest stare. "If you know something, anything, and you don't tell us, spending the rest of your life in prison will be the best thing that happens to you in the near future."

The lawyer stood up. "Was that a threat, Agent Russo?"

Jack shoved his hands in his pockets. "Absolutely not."

He smiled at the lawyer, frowned down at Damian, and then

walked out of the room, following Fitz, who was staring at him with an icy glare.

∽

Back in the Boiler Room, Violet looked as excited as she had when explaining the entire Marvel Cinematic Universe to him on their first date. She hadn't seemed to care that he hadn't seen any of the movies, that he had no intention of watching them. She lived in a world of her own, at least as far as Jack could tell, and it's actually one of the things that had attracted him to her. She wasn't trying to impress anyone but herself.

Bounding across the room from her computer station, she said, "Damian stole 17,600 brain scans. As we already know, the first four victims were among them. I was able to run all of the scans through a program and only 230 of them had the same special brain activity that we found on the four victims."

"That *I* found on the first four victims," Fitz said.

Jack glared at him. "Is this really the time to fight for credit?" That seemed to shame him as his cheeks flushed red. "Please continue," Jack said to Violet.

"Going over the list, I eliminated some that are outside the Pacific Northwest, some others who have passed away since the scans were taken, and others who matched in the program but were false positives. That is, the area of activity in the brain scan was not as pronounced as it was in the four victims. Comparing all the brain scans, I found that those four had some of the brightest, most unusual activity in that center of the brain."

"So you've narrowed down the list to how many?" Jack asked.

Violet smiled. "We're down to 41. 41 out of 17,600. Thank you, AI."

"Send the list to Claire ASAP," Jack said. "I will text her as well to make sure she looks at it while she's in with the parents."

"I want another crack at Damian," Fitz said.

"No," Jack said. "Next, we have to get in touch with every single one of those 41 people and make sure they're safe. Call in every favor from a local cop you know, contact them in every way possible. This is about preventing more victims. Hazel Christopher is not going to choose someone at random. The next victim is on that list, and we have to stop this murder before it happens."

CHAPTER THIRTY-TWO

CLAIRE FELT her phone vibrating against her leg. Angling her body away from Kiko and Hazel's parents, she glanced down at the screen. It was a message from Jack: *Urgent. Check your email. Incoming list from Violet with 41 potential victims.*

Claire opened her email program and clicked the attachment from Violet. She immediately felt a surge of disappointment. This was phenomenal work, to be sure, but a list of 41 names and addresses wasn't the break in the case she'd been hoping for.

She knew from experience that tracking down dozens of people across multiple states was harder than it often looked on television. Holding her phone down at her side, she tuned back into Kiko and the parents. They had all moved back downstairs to the living room having found nothing to lead them in the direction of the girl that once occupied the bedroom they'd investigated.

Kiko sat, legs crossed on the sofa, leaning in toward Hazel's parents, her voice dripping with a carefully cultivated air of elitism. "Honestly, when you compare modern cinema across the globe—French, Italian, Asian—it's clear that the depth of narrative complexity and aesthetic innovation far surpasses anything produced in Hollywood these days."

How did she come up with this stuff? Claire wondered.

Swirling a glass of water as if it were a fine wine, Kiko continued, "For instance, French cinema, with its nuanced exploration of existential themes, or Italian filmmakers, who masterfully blend neorealism with poetic visuals. And let's not forget the groundbreaking storytelling techniques of Asian cinema, particularly the Japanese and Korean auteurs. It's all about the art, the unspoken words between the lines, the *mise-en-scène* that captures the essence of our existence."

Kiko was so deep into her performance, Claire wondered whether she'd forgotten why they were actually there. But the way she studied the faces of Mr. and Mrs. Christopher when she paused told Claire she hadn't yet fallen too deeply into her character. "Don't you find," she continued, her accent becoming even more pretentious, "that these films offer a more authentic reflection of the human condition, unlike the cookie-cutter narratives we're bombarded with stateside?"

"Absolutely," Hazel's mother concurred. "There's a certain *je ne sais quoi* in French cinema that American films simply cannot replicate."

"And the Italian flair for drama," the father added, "is unparalleled."

Kiko nodded, a smile playing on her lips.

Claire cleared her throat. "I hate to interrupt this riveting discussion," she said, "and Kiko, you and I are going to have a serious word about the way you tend to identify with potential suspects in a murder investigation."

Kiko stood and said haughtily, "These people did nothing wrong. They provided their daughter with absolutely every opportunity, and if in fact their daughter has even done anything, you really shouldn't put the blame on them."

Claire stifled a smile. She was so utterly convincing that it was easy to forget that they were in the middle of a murder investigation and not on a Broadway stage.

"Exactly," Hazel's mother said defensively. "I don't believe Hazel could be wrapped up in anything bad, but if she is, we had nothing to do with it."

Claire held up her phone. "I just received a list of 41 names," she said. She scanned the city field on the spreadsheet. "We have potential victims in Seattle, in Renton, in Snohomish, on Bainbridge Island, and as far east as Spokane and Coeur d'Alene, Idaho. Portland, Vancouver, Washington. Any of those cities ring any bells with you?"

When the parents said nothing, dropping their eyes to the floor, Claire walked over and crouched before them. "Look at me."

Slowly, as though both of their heads were being controlled by the same puppet master, the parents raised their eyes to Claire.

"Look in my eyes. I am not messing around," she said, glancing at her phone. "Port Ludlow. Seattle again. Dexter, Oregon. Seabeck, Washington. Do any of these locations mean anything to you? Has Hazel ever said anything about staying in any of these places, planning to visit any of these places. Or does your family have any history in any of these places?"

"No," Hazel's father said. "No, I swear it."

Claire stood and shoved her phone back in her pocket. She let out a long sigh and was about to launch into an even more threatening line of questioning when something caught her eye. In the far corner of the wine case Kiko had fixated upon when they arrived, she noticed a bottle of wine from Cascadia Cliffs Winery.

She hadn't noticed it on first glance, but now she saw that the bottle was the *only* Washington State wine in their collection. Claire had visited Cascadia Cliffs once with her husband. It had been when they were trying to reconcile, and they'd spent a weekend touring the vineyards in the Walla Walla Valley. Although they tasted some nice wines, that was the trip on which she'd decided it was definitely over.

"You have one bottle of wine from Washington State," Claire said.

"Swill," Kiko said, still in performance mode. "I wouldn't drink that with the mouth of my worst enemy. You see, just as in cinema, the French and Italians truly know how to make wine."

"We, I—" Hazel's mom stammered, and her voice had grown a little more uncertain.

Claire spun. "What?"

"Hazel gave us that bottle of wine," Mrs. Christopher confessed. "The last time she was here. She always rejected our snobbishness. Never cared about fine food or wine. We were never going to actually *drink* it. But we put it in there to remind us of her."

"And what did she say about how she got it?" Kiko asked.

Mr. Christopher's forehead creased and he closed his eyes, thinking. "Now that I think about it, she did mention something about staying out in that area. She was dating a guy, maybe. I don't know, she always played coy with that stuff. Sergei, I think was his name. But she said it wasn't serious."

Claire whipped out her phone and scanned the list again. She knew that six of the cities listed were within fifty miles of that winery. She shot a look at Kiko. "We have to get back to the office. Now."

CHAPTER THIRTY-THREE

BY THE TIME they got back to the office, Jack had already printed up detailed information on all six of the people who lived within fifty miles of the winery.

Now he stood at a cork board next to the large monitor, reading information about the six. "Byron Chang, retired physicist who worked for a chemical company in Seattle for over thirty years. Susan Baker, stay-at-home mom, age fifty-one, has seven children, the oldest of whom is thirty and the youngest of whom is nine. She posts a lot on social media about how terrible the local school board is. Christopher White, age fifty, alternate on the 1992 Olympic team in the javelin. Taught high school track and field until last year when he sort of fell off the grid. Sasha Levy, graduated high school last year and currently works at a coffee shop in Spokane. From her Instagram, it looks like she is an aspiring stand-up comedian."

Claire held up a hand. "Wait a second, why are we doing this on a cork board and not on the monitor? I want to see visuals, I want to see more information, I want to see this Instagram."

Claire glanced around the room. Fitz had his feet up on the desk, leaning back in an oversized office chair. Claire had entered in such a hurry that she had barely noticed Violet's absence. She usually sat in the corner so quietly that it was easy to forget she was there when she was.

"Violet's gone," Claire announced. "Didn't anyone notice?"

Jack shrugged. "She said she was going to the restroom."

"That was half an hour ago," Fitz said. "Now that I think about it, she's been kind of in and out today."

Kiko was sitting on the floor about a yard away from Ranger, as though trying to get comfortable with the idea that she now lived in an office with a dog. "I was in the bathroom five minutes ago," she said. "She wasn't there."

"How did we lose one of our team members?" Claire asked. The look on Jack's face told her something was up. "Jack?"

He stood. "Okay, fine. She texted me, wrote she was doing something super important and to cover for her."

"More important than this?" Claire asked.

"She assured me it was," Jack said, shrugging again.

Claire was about to explode. There couldn't possibly be anything more important than this.

Then the door swung open and Violet appeared. "Fitz, it looks like I'll be taking up residence in your family's manor in the Cotswolds, thank you very much."

"You didn't," Fitz said, bringing his feet down from the desk and nearly falling out of his chair as he hurriedly spun himself in her direction. "You couldn't have."

"Couldn't have what?" Claire asked.

"She's sorted the blasted code," Fitz said.

"Can you give it to us in *American* English, Fitz?" Jack asked.

"You really did it?" Fitz was moving across the room so fast, Claire worried he might trigger a coronary event. "You cracked the code? You deciphered the language?"

"I did," Violet said matter of factly.

CHAPTER THIRTY-FOUR

TWO MINUTES LATER, Claire stood just inside the doorway of a sixth-floor storage room she hadn't known existed.

Jack and Kiko were crammed in on her left, Fitz to her right.

Violet sat on a folding chair in front of a quietly humming device about the size of a footlocker. Violet pressed a button and a small flatscreen monitor on the wall next to the unit lit up.

"Before we go any further," Claire said, "I need to know what this thing is and where you got it."

"Through some old MIT contacts, I managed to secure one of the only Delilah prototypes. This tech is so advanced, most in the cybersecurity world don't even believe it's possible yet." Violet sounded like the recipient of a Willy Wonka golden ticket.

"Delilah?" Claire asked.

Violet nodded while running a hand over the computer. "Yes, Delilah. That's what we call her. She was developed in secret by Qubium, an Israeli tech startup out of Tel Aviv. The brains behind Qubium? They're ex-members of classified projects for the Israeli government. They've built something extraordinary—a 48-qubit processor, but it isn't just about her sheer power. It's her unique approach to error-correction, a kind of computing no one else has quite managed to figure out how to replicate."

She paused for a moment, letting the significance of her words sink in. "Delilah can shatter 2048-bit RSA encryption in just a matter of minutes. Something that's, frankly, a pipe dream for any conventional supercomputer. The secret? Its qubits remain entangled, resistant to decoherence, thanks to a proprietary method involving cryogenically frozen photonic crystals."

She leaned back, the glow of the monitor casting shadows on her face. "Delilah's got a battery backup and a rapid recool cycle. We just need to keep our usage strategic, avoid overheating, and swap out the helium-3 canisters daily. A self-contained helium-3 cryostat can maintain the stability of the 256-qubit Delilah chip for up to eight hours of EDP."

"What's EDP?" Claire asked.

"Electronic Data Processing."

Claire stared at the thing, mouth agape. The unit itself was not sleek; its crude plastic exterior betrayed none of the wonders Violet seemed to think were contained within.

Claire shifted her eyes to the small monitor when the blue glyphs from the ancient language appeared, the ones that had been written on the wall of Isaac Orion's University District Apartment. She shivered at the sight of them. She knew that languages were not intrinsically good or evil, but the sight of the jagged, aggressive lines had melded in her mind with Hazel Christopher's crimes, and the language had taken on a power inside her body. She recoiled just at the sight of it.

[glyphs]

"Essentially," Violet said, "there is no artificial intelligence powerful enough to decrypt lost languages yet. Many academics are working on it. But they're working with normal computing power. Delilah is on a different level, and it took only fifteen minutes once I got this thing working."

She tapped a button on her keyboard and the ominous glyphs transformed into English.

The Scholar Knows the Blue.

Claire swallowed hard.

Violet tapped again, and the second set of glyphs appeared, the black ones that had been written on the wall of Sal Cardinelli's home.

[glyphs]

Just as the first had, they slowly faded, replaced by the English translation.

The Ruler Embodies the Black.

Then the white glyphs that had been found on the modest stone wall of Sister Marybeth Peters' room.

The Priest is Pure as the White.

And finally, the red glyphs painted on the unfinished sheetrock of Johnny Stadler's home gym.

As the glyphs faded, Claire heard herself mouthing the words as they appeared on the screen.

The Warrior is as Strong as the Red.

The silence that followed seemed to go on forever. There was something about being the first to read an ancient language that, on its own, was breathtaking. But this was something entirely more than that.

Fitz was the first one to speak. "Bloody hell."

Jack said, "For the first time, Fitz, you and I are in total agreement. Bloody hell."

"Fitz, I'm hoping your various PhDs will tell us something," Claire said. "Assuming that we are right about the general location of the next murder, and that yellow is the final color in this system, do any of the bios Jack explained earlier connect?"

Fitz shoved his way out of the little storage room, and Claire followed him into a long nondescript hallway. The sixth floor was mostly for storage and secretarial work, all the stuff that made it possible for them to do their jobs. The hallway smelled of some kind of ammonia based chemical cleaner, and the fluorescent lights flickered above them.

Jack, Kiko, and Violet joined them in the hallway, and all eyes were on Fitz. "The Scholar, the Ruler, the Priest, the Warrior. If I try to put my mind in the ancient world, these are probably the four most important archetypal figures. And clearly, Hazel believes she has found their representations in the modern world. A brilliant professor. A powerful mob boss who ruled with an iron fist. A holy woman, not a priest exactly but someone who personifies what a good religious figure would be. And a warrior. Someone who exemplifies the targeted use of violence and aggression. She believed all of them were special because of the brain scans, then she chose well." Fitz turned suddenly. "Jack, remind me of the people you mentioned down in the Boiler Room. There was the physicist and—"

"The stay-at-home mom, the physicist, the former track athlete. I didn't get to all of them. We'd have to go back down and—"

"Who was the last one that you mentioned?" Fitz asked impatiently.

"Sasha Levy. A young woman who is an aspiring stand-up comedian."

Fitz held up a finger, silencing him. His forehead creases intensified as he fell into deep thought. He was mumbling something to himself and Claire approached trying to listen. "The Scholar. The Ruler. The Priest. The Warrior. Who would come next? The Scholar. The Ruler. The Priest. The Warrior." Suddenly, Fitz slammed an open palm against the wall. "*The Jester. The Fool.* Exemplifying the yellow, which in Luminism represents joy, exuberance, laughter. It's probably the fifth most important archetypal figure, and it matches the Yellow."

"It's Sasha Levy," Kiko said. "The stand-up comedian in Spokane."

Jack spun on his heels. "Claire, how fast can you get us a chopper?"

She was already pulling out her phone.

CHAPTER THIRTY-FIVE

"SO, what were you able to find on Sasha Levy?" Claire asked Kiko, sliding on her headset as she climbed into the helicopter.

"Hold on," Kiko said. "I've got some notes here and some stuff to pull up on my phone."

Before leaving the office, Claire had updated Hightower, provided information to law enforcement on the other side of the Cascades, and sorted out the logistics necessary for their arrival in Spokane. Kiko and Violet gathered information on Sasha Levy. Fitz took the dog out for a walk and to have himself *a think*.

Violet and Fitz had remained behind, Violet to run additional Luminist texts and images through her supercomputer, Fitz to explore and sort what the computer came up with.

Plus, Fitz hated helicopters. The poor guy did not have a body type that fit well in standard seating arrangements, let alone those inside a chopper. On the one trip they'd taken together, in addition to fidgeting constantly and jabbing an occasional elbow into Claire's side, Fitz had fiddled with his headset the entire flight. "It's making me sweat," he'd complained, taking it off and putting it back on repeatedly and causing a grating noise that rippled through the crew's headphones. Fitz had a way of leaving a lasting impression in any type of group setting.

Jack returned after helping the pilot make a final inspection before lift-off. "You two ready?" He checked that they were properly secured in their seatbelts.

Kiko flipped through her notes as the chopper rose into the air. "She's nineteen, an improv comedian who's spent her whole life in Spokane."

Claire was relieved that the headset voices came over crystal clear.

"In high school," Kiko continued, "she was pretty much the driving force behind starting an improv troupe, *The Social Whippoorwills*. They began performing at school assemblies, local gigs, and it wasn't long before they started gaining some serious traction around town. Here, I've got a video I can show you."

While Kiko pulled up the video, the helicopter reached cruising altitude.

Claire peered out the window, her gaze sweeping over the landscape. It was a bright, sunny day, and the sharp clarity of the cold air made the land below them hyper-vivid, as though it had been digitally enhanced.

Claire leaned in, staring down at Kiko's phone as she pressed play on a YouTube clip. Sasha Levy stood on a dark stage, her spotlight doing little to enhance the ambiance. It obviously wasn't a high-end production—just a small comedy club. The filming was subpar as well. But Sasha's enthusiasm and comedic chops shone through despite what the setting and video quality left to be desired. "My parents say I'm too young to be a comedian," she said, "that I should go to college..."

Claire briefly followed the words then tuned out the content, choosing to shift from the content of her jokes to focus on Sasha's face, which shone with an enthusiastic lightness that was mesmerizing. Claire didn't really know what having the "It Factor" meant, but she felt she was watching someone who had it.

Fitz strongly believed the fifth victim would be the jester or the fool. Someone who personified the qualities of the Yellow as they were believed to exist in ancient Luminist texts. And as she watched Sasha's charisma on display, she had no doubt that she was Hazel Christopher's next intended victim.

Kiko ended the video and glanced down at her notes. "Fast forward to just a year out of high school, and *The Social Whippoorwills* are an underground sensation. Their sketches, viral videos—online fandoms are eating it up. Sasha? She's at the center of it all. Her knack for diving headfirst into these wild characters, her fearless improv—she's even caught the eye of a few TV comedy scouts." Leaning back, Kiko continued, "Outside of the spotlight, she's slinging coffee part time as a barista, still hitting the stage and creating new content with her troupe. When she isn't behind the counter, she's on the stage. Her big dream? *Saturday Night Live*, maybe her own show one day. But beneath all that onstage goofiness, there's this old soul, someone who's truly herself when she's in the moment, embracing whatever creative path she's on. She has a diary-like video blog showcasing that side of her."

They hit a brief patch of turbulence, causing Kiko to pause, looking like she might be sick. When the ride smoothed out, she continued. "I've got something else. When I was gasbagging with Hazel's parents—Claire, I think this is when you were on your phone for a bit—they said something that stood out to me. I'd asked about boyfriends and they said she hadn't dated much in her life. When she was little, she had talked about being neither man nor woman, and not in the kind of gender identity way that is in the news a lot these days. It wasn't like she was born a woman and identified as a man, or vice versa. And it wasn't even like her gender was fluid. The way they described it, she did not have any gender, at least that is what she told them when she was a little kid. She told them—*bodies do not matter.*"

"What a strange notion for a child," Claire said.

"Right? Just like that—*bodies do not matter,*" Kiko repeated. "Plus, I asked Violet to run a quick search for us, and she found a Sergei in Spokane. A field hand named Sergei Kuznetsov. He files taxes, and on his W2, it says he works on a small farm. We've got an address. Another guy Hazel duped into helping her?"

Claire nodded. "Just like Damian."

~

A little over an hour later, Spokane appeared before them like a miniature model. The low winter sun cast long shadows that stretched lazily across the snow-dusted rooftops, and the Spokane River wound through the heart of downtown.

Stripped of their foliage, skeletal trees stood over the urban landscape, frost-dusted branches sparkling with reflected sunlight. The stark contrasts of the season—the deep blues of the river against the crisp whites of the snow, the jagged profile of bare branches against the steel and glass of the city's skyline—gave the scene a curious, ethereal quality.

The chopper began making its final descent over a large field just outside the downtown, the blades whipping the snow airborne into swirling eddies, momentarily obscuring the view before the aircraft settled on the ground with a gentle thud.

They hurried off the helicopter and, at the edge of the field, as the sounds of the chopper died down, a young officer greeted them and gave report. "We have two officers at Sasha Levy's apartment. No answer at the door so they got the landlord to let them in for a wellness check. No one home, no evidence of violence, forced entry, anything. Kinda messy, but they said it looked pretty much like any recent grad's first apartment."

"Thanks," Claire said. "Tell them to stay there in case she returns."

The young officer nodded, "Yes, ma'am."

"Jack," Claire continued, "you take Officer..." she pointed at the officer to her left..."I'm sorry."

"Officer Cortez," the young woman said. She was around thirty, and wore her black hair in a slicked back ponytail and, in Claire's opinion, used too much makeup for a cop.

"Apologies," Claire said, her voice hurried. "You two begin combing the downtown. Sasha Levy is supposed to perform down there at the Laugh Hut tonight." She glanced at her watch. "Within two hours, actually. So there's a decent chance she's already somewhere close, maybe having dinner or something. Check with the comedy clubs, nearby restaurants, and so on."

Jack nodded, first at Claire and then at officer Cortez, before walking in the direction of the downtown area. The other officer, a young man with pasty flesh and bright red cheeks, said, "Even in the winter, on a sunny day like this, there's a lot of people down there. Lots of foot traffic. You want me to go with them?"

"No," Claire said. "Officer... I'm sorry, what was your name again?"

"Peralta. Mike Peralta."

"Officer Peralta, if you'd take us to this address..."

Kiko handed him a slip of paper, on which she'd written the address from the W2 of the farmworker Sergei Kuznetsov.

After making brief eye contact with everyone on the team, she clapped once like a football quarterback breaking the huddle, then followed Officer Peralta to his cruiser.

CHAPTER THIRTY-SIX

THE CROWD WAS THIN, but still there were more people around than Jack expected given that it was a cold winter day. He'd never been to Spokane, but he'd heard of the famous riverfront market. He hadn't realized it would be operational in the winter.

People were dressed warmly, in thick jackets or sweaters, and most were wearing hats as well. But the sun was bright, making it a lovely day to be outside walking among the vendors. Little stalls sold locally made soaps, wine, cheese, and other arts and crafts. Glancing down at a picture of Sasha Levy he'd set as the lockscreen on his phone, he tried matching her face to those around him and came up empty repeatedly.

When he and Officer Cortez arrived at the Laugh Hut, the comedy club where Sasha was scheduled to perform in less than ninety minutes, they strolled in. Jack felt his face thawing with the warmth of the room and brought his hands to his cheeks to stop them from stinging. He looked over at Cortez, who did not seem phased in the least by the abrupt temperature fluctuation.

An older gentleman with bright twinkling eyes was setting up chairs in the small club.

"Are you the owner?" Officer Cortez asked, approaching the man briskly while Jack continued to stand in the doorway wiggling his toes to work out the tingling sensation as their feeling slowly returned. Jack could not comprehend how, in under two hours, you could fly from a temperate jungle to a frigid tundra. To him it seemed even more impossible that some humans could thrive in the latter, like Office Cortez appeared to.

"I'm the original Laugh Man of Spokane," he said. "Smith Wakefield."

Officer Cortez appeared unimpressed, "Will Sasha Levy be performing here tonight?"

"Absolutely. But, she must be very busy these days because she was scheduled to be up for a lunch set and didn't show."

"When was the last time you saw her?" Officer Cortez asked.

The man's face beamed with pride and he looked past Officer Cortez to see if Jack would be impressed. "I discovered her, you know?"

"We hear she's very talented," Jack said, stepping forward and speaking in the complimentary tone he thought the man was seeking.

"Yeah, I taught improv at the high school and she showed up when she was fourteen. *A young Jim Carrey*—I thought. I knew it right away. Impressions, physical comedy. She was a natural."

"When was—" Jack started to ask the same question that Officer Cortez had but was quickly interrupted.

"Mark my words. Yes, yes. She'll be on the big screen before you know it, too. She has gifts in comedy that I never had, that no one out of Spokane has *ever* had. That girl there is a bonafide, tried and Laugh Hut tested, solid gold, comedic prodigy."

"When was the last time you saw her?" Jack asked, his voice impatient. The man was obviously used to talking to everyone at once when he was up on stage or having no one to talk to when he was minding the Laugh Hut during off hours.

"Wait, who are you two?" he asked with a skeptical tone.

Jack stepped in front of Officer Cortez and held up his badge and FBI identification. "This is incredibly serious, sir."

"Is she okay?" The man's face dropped with worry.

"That's what we're trying to find out," Jack said.

"We just need you to tell us anything you can about when you last saw her," Officer Cortez said.

"I...I..." the man's brain was stuttering with worry. "I just saw her a few days ago. She comes in almost every night, only misses a set on occasion."

"Can you think of anywhere she would be right now, other than her house?" Jack asked.

He thought for a moment. "She stays with her boyfriend a lot. Chris Gunderson. He's a comedian, too, though not a very good one."

"Where?" Jack and Officer Cortez asked in unison.

"He lives in the old Victorian in the Browne's Addition area, that's what she told me. They've made some improvements over there. She said the place was really taking shape nicely."

"Sir, where exactly?" Officer Cortez pressed.

"Ten blocks or so west on Pacific. Big blue house that has been converted into six small apartments across from the dog park, can't miss it."

They didn't let him say another word. Officer Cortez had already sprinted out the door with Jack at her heels.

Although his body momentarily fought to move against the cold, it didn't take long for Jack to blast past her.

Three blocks from the comedy club, he hailed a cab. As he

opened the door he looked back for Officer Cortez but she was slowed at an intersection without a fast route to weave through the crowd and cars.

She waved him on.

Jack nodded back at her and got in.

CHAPTER THIRTY-SEVEN

THE SO-CALLED farm sat about ten minutes from the center of town and immediately struck Claire as too small to feed a family let alone require the employment of a field hand—the lot was an acre or two at best.

"Be alert," Claire warned Kiko as they got out of the cruiser. She pointed to the old farmhouse that sat up a gradual incline fifty feet from the parking lot. "I think there's a chance this isn't just where Sergei works. I think this might also be where Hazel has him living."

"Kind of the way she kept Damian on a chain," Kiko said. "Maybe she hired this Sergei guy or took him on as a lover and employee and used him to do the dirty work she didn't want to do."

Officer Peralta was hurrying up behind them on the gravel walkway that led from the parking lot to the dilapidated porch of the farmhouse. "Shouldn't we wait for SWAT?" he asked.

"We don't have a warrant anyway," Claire said. "We're just here to ask a few questions. Why don't you hang back?"

She turned and leveled her gaze at Peralta, who stopped in

his tracks. He looked like he was going to object, but her eyes told him there'd be trouble for him if he did.

Softening the blow, Claire said, "We need you by the radio. I don't know how cell reception is out here. We need you to be in touch with Cortez and my other agent, Russo. I need to know immediately if they find Sasha."

"Yes ma'am," Peralta nodded obediently and hurried back to the cruiser.

About ten yards from the house, Kiko stopped. "Who should I be?"

"What?" Claire was confused.

"I mean, who do you want me to pretend to be during this interview?" she asked.

Claire thought for a moment. "A badass."

"So basically, you're telling me to just be myself."

"Right."

"Got it." Kiko smiled and nodded, and they made their way up the rickety steps to the porch. Everything was quiet, save for a cold wind that blew through the old shutters and made an occasional muted whistling sound.

Claire knocked loudly and waited.

There was no answer, no movement in the house, no sound at all.

She knocked again and waited. Still nothing.

"There are no cars around," Kiko said, "and my guess is no one comes here on foot or bicycle. I don't think there's anyone home."

Claire nodded. "Let's look around."

They walked around the side of the house, and were met by a few leafless trees and dying bushes. There did appear to be plots for gardens behind the farmhouse, but they were grown over with weeds and didn't look to have been planted with any valuable crops in years. Claire was more convinced than ever that this was Hazel Christopher's hideout.

At the back of the house, there was a small staircase that dropped four steps down into what Claire assumed was a basement or cellar. At the bottom of the stairs, she rapped on the old single pane window that centered the upper half of a bifurcated door.

When there was no response, Kiko came up beside her and shone her flashlight through the window into the darkness.

What Claire saw made her breath catch in her throat.

CHAPTER THIRTY-EIGHT

"STOP MOVING THE LIGHT." Claire took the flashlight from Kiko in a hurry and scanned it back into the darkness.

There, on the far wall, above an old workbench, was a map of the Pacific Northwest. Leaving her face as close to the glass as she could, Claire picked out five little red stars on the map. She couldn't make out any of the text, but based on the locations, she thought they were Seattle, Coos Bay, Port Angeles, Coeur d'Alene, and Spokane—the spot where they now stood.

"That map is enough," Claire said. "I'm going in."

She tried the door handle and wasn't surprised to find it locked. She cursed herself for passing along her pick set to Jack.

The door was old—decades old—and Claire studied the narrow gap between its top and bottom halves. She'd spent a few weeks one summer at a farm camp that had a similar door. There, it had been the only barrier preventing the kids from sneaking into the kitchen for late-night raids, and though she hadn't been mischievous enough to join them, she knew how they'd done it.

Claire pressed her hands against either side of the upper door, careful not to disturb the fragile glass. Using friction to grip, she pushed upward. The top half of the door raised, widening the gap between the door halves even further.

"Here," Kiko said, handing Claire a rusted trowel that had been lying on the ground. "I hope you had a tetanus shot recently."

"Just help me lift up the door when I say," Claire instructed. "And, watch through the window to make sure no one is coming."

"Got it." Kiko placed her hands on the door and waited.

Claire lowered into a squat and, running the flashlight along the gap, stopped when she saw the light reflecting on the brass bolt mechanism that held the two doors together. She wedged the trowel and pushed hard against the metal.

"Now lift," Claire instructed.

Kiko lifted and Claire moved the trowel up in unison with the door's movement. She felt the bolt shift upward, away from its housing. She pulled the trowel back slowly, hoping the bolt wouldn't immediately fall back into place. Rust was on her side; the bolt didn't budge. She placed the trowel further down the bolt and pressed in hard.

"Okay now, Kiko, slowly let the door back down."

Kiko allowed the door to slide down and they heard the bolt squeaking as the metal channel moved down over the top of it.

"Now take it up again."

Claire and Kiko moved in unison, lifting up until the bolt raised completely clear of the receiving plate connected to the door's lower half. Instinctively Kiko moved back, allowing Claire to make a deft scooping movement with the trowel, which swung the top half of the door towards them.

Claire dropped the trowel as though she'd just recognized its threat, then reached through to unlock the bottom half of the door by its inside handle.

Guns drawn, they entered.

The room was dark and smelled like a lavender bouquet that

had gone moldy, having been left too long in a vase full of water. Kiko hurried to the wall and flipped on the lights.

Claire's heart hammered against her ribs as they moved cautiously through the basement, the stagnant air clinging to her like a moist, skin-tight garment. Every shadow seemed to twitch with the possibility of danger, every corner a potential hiding place for threats unseen.

"This room is clear," Claire said, nodding toward a staircase on the other end of the room.

Kiko led the way, her steps silent against the concrete floor. Claire followed, her senses hyper-aware, parsing every creak and groan of the old structure as they made their way up the stairs to the ground floor.

The main level of the house was as barren as the basement, rooms sparsely furnished with pieces that seemed like they'd been added for their utility more than actual attempts at decor.

The living room held a single, worn sofa, its fabric faded and threadbare, and a small composite wooden coffee table that bore no marks of use. Windows, their curtains drawn back, let in a weak light that did little to dispel the gloom. As they cleared each room, Claire's tension mounted, the emptiness of the house paradoxically amplifying her sense of dread. It felt as though the very walls were watching, waiting, as if the house itself was holding its breath.

They continued, methodical and thorough, checking inside closets and behind doors, under beds in the two sparse bedrooms, anywhere a person could conceivably hide. But there was nothing. No sign of recent habitation, no personal effects that might suggest someone lived there.

The kitchen was equally barren, a few mismatched cups in a cupboard, an old kettle on the stove, but nothing in the refrigerator save for a solitary, wilting carrot and a small box of baking soda with a mouth-like perforated spout, cracked open in perpetual terror, reminding Claire of the Edvard Munch painting, *The Scream*.

It was as if the house was stuck in time, a shell waiting for lives to fill it.

After clearing the last room, Claire and Kiko stood in the dim hallway, the silence between them heavy.

The tension slowly ebbed from Claire's shoulders, a mixture of relief and frustration taking its place. "There's no one here."

"Nothing but echoes and dust," Kiko said.

Returning to the basement, Claire's focus narrowed on the map once more, confirming her initial thoughts. The five locations were marked exactly as she had suspected: Seattle, Coos Bay, Port Angeles, Coeur d'Alene, and Spokane.

"Wait," Kiko said from behind her.

Claire turned to see what Kiko had discovered—a wooden door that blended so seamlessly with the paneling that it had been invisible at first glance. Claire's heart, which had just begun to settle, began kicking against her chest again as she hurried over to the concealed door.

Kiko, with practiced caution, slowly opened it, her flashlight at the ready.

From the doorway, she methodically swept the flashlight across the small room, revealing that, while devoid of any human presence, it was far from empty. Instead, what lay before them was a trove of evidence, a mountain of documents, maps, photographs, and notes that Hazel Christopher had left behind.

"Clear," Kiko announced, her voice tense.

They'd stumbled on her lair.

There, scattered and stacked with a chaotic sense of order, were the unmistakable signs of planning. Plans that detailed routes, potential hideouts, timelines, and even notes on potential victims.

It was a window into the mind of someone who had been orchestrating horror with precision and care. Among the papers, they found references to the locations on the map, each marked with a date and observations that were eerily detailed.

Claire and Kiko exchanged a look, a silent communication. They had stumbled upon Hazel Christopher's nerve center, the place where she had planned her atrocious acts.

Claire grabbed a stack of photos of Sasha Levy and quickly found what she was looking for. "She has a boyfriend."

"Already got an address," Kiko said, holding up a notepad.

Claire pulled out her cellphone. Two bars.

She dialed Jack.

Her call went straight to voicemail.

CHAPTER THIRTY-NINE

THE COMEDIAN LAY STRAPPED to the bed.

She had not wanted to subdue the boyfriend but she had known she might have to. And she had. Now the young man lay crumpled in the corner, wrists bound with zip ties, ankles duct taped together.

The room was a perfect yellow environment. The comedian was draped in beautiful yellow sheets, the color of a pale sunrise.

It was almost time.

Sitting in a small chair next to the bed, she stared down at Sasha Levy. After receiving her brain scan from Damian, she had researched her, watching every single YouTube video that the young comedian had made available to the public. In fact, she had been chosen first before any of the others.

In Luminism, it was believed that people were born with a naturally dominant color and a naturally weakest color. Yellow was her weakest. That's why it was the most important. That's why it was last.

The Blue, the dancing brilliance that some humans are capable of, that was her strongest. In fact, she was almost the equal of Isaac Orion and others like him. And yet still she had needed to absorb his light to be sure.

The Black, that quiet power that needs not rage or strength, she knew from her childhood that she possessed a vibrant density of this color within her spirit as well. That's why Sal Cardinelli had been second.

And the White had come third. That innocence and purity. The simplicity and the dedication to that which is higher. For her, this had been a more difficult find. But Marybeth Peters had been perfect.

As a child, she was made fun of for her lack of athleticism. It wasn't only a lack of athleticism, it was a lack of coordination, a lack of connection to her own physical body. She had worked on that for years studying karate. Before absorbing the Red of Johnny Stadler, she didn't know if she would have the strength to complete her transcendence. But after absorbing the Red, she no longer needed to *believe in* her destiny, she felt herself living it through the process of her becoming.

And now she would absorb Sasha Levy's Yellow, the final of her chosen five. Sasha would give her life to allow Hazel to transcend. Once she absorbed the infectious joy, the endless laughter, the spontaneous happiness that she had never possessed as a child and was still lacking, once she absorbed that light, her cycle of rebirth would end in a few days.

She didn't know whether some of the ancient stories were true, or whether some of the early mystics had transcended as she was about to. But she knew she would be the first in a long, long time.

On the bed, Sasha Levy blinked a few times. Ignoring this, then pulling a small paintbrush from her duffel bag and dipping it in the yellow paint, she carefully wrote the final glyphs on the wall above the little nightstand.

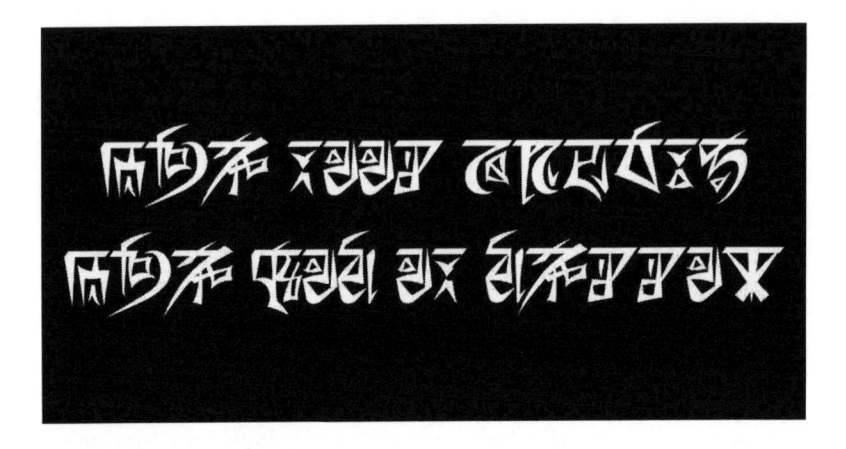

"*Abridido ala krienzo, mala en aka melieus,*" she said softly. Then she repeated the prayer in English. "The fool brings the joy of Yellow."

The yellow paint had a golden quality to it. It was the true color of joy and playfulness, but not superficiality. It wasn't ostentatious or garish; it felt rich and distinguished, almost royal. The yellow she'd chosen could not have been more perfect.

When she was finished admiring her work, she pulled out the syringe.

CHAPTER FORTY

JACK HOPPED out of the taxi and stopped. The large blue Victorian was exactly where the comedy club owner had described it.

Perched on a corner, it boasted ornate trim and a spacious wrap-around porch. In February's cold clarity, its steeply pitched roofs and ornate gables stood out against a backdrop of bare trees and a well-kept, snow-dusted lawn. The windows, framed with heavy, dark wood, reflected the bright winter sun, and smoke from the chimney hinted at the warmth within. Despite its historic stature, the house felt inviting.

Before Jack knew what was happening, his *tactical insight* mode had been initiated.

He scanned the windows of the first floor, then the second floor, then the third floor, which he guessed was an attic that had at some point in the last twenty years been turned into a small apartment when the home had been converted from a single-family to a multi-dwelling building—although its conversion was not apparent from the outside as the integrity of the building's initial design remained.

Jack had never been one of those agents who simply trusted

his gut. To him, a gut instinct could be as wrong as a faulty idea. It was just one factor he used when making a decision. But right now his gut was screaming, Sasha Levy was inside, and that he was too late.

Jogging across the street, he reached the wide staircase and bounded up two at a time. The front door was unlocked and led into what had once been a large foyer but was now a room with six little silver mailboxes in it. A small umbrella stand sat to the right and a staircase led up to the second floor. He had planned to go door to door, but a quick glance at the mailboxes told him that wouldn't be necessary. A mailbox was marked with Sasha Levy's boyfriend's name: "Gunderson, 3A."

At the second floor, he smelled bacon frying from an apartment on his right and inched through the hallway quietly. There were no stairs to bring him to a third floor but, at the end of the hall, was a door marked *3A*. He paused, pressing his ear up against it and listening. He heard nothing. A piece of him wanted to simply rip open the door or perhaps kick it in. But the disembodied voice of Claire Anderson pricked in his ear. *We need to make sure this is prosecutable.*

He knocked loudly on the door and announced himself, "Jack Russo, FBI, open up."

A long silence followed and then Jack heard a door slowly creak open behind him.

He spun around to see a young couple peering into the hall. The man was dressed in an apron and held a set of tongs. The woman was holding a baby on her hip. They looked frightened.

"Go back inside," Jack said. "FBI."

They quickly shut the door and he heard the lock click.

Turning back to the door at 3A, he tried the handle. As expected, it was locked. But it was an old door and thin. The handle seemed to be an original or possibly a replacement from early on in this mansion's history.

Jack whipped out the lockpick Claire had given to him. He

selected a slender pick and tension wrench, and inserted them into the keyhole. Methodically, he felt for the tumblers, applying gentle pressure with the wrench while nudging each pin into place. He was surprised at the quality of the feedback given that the tools were so minimal. Within moments, the satisfying click of the lock disengaging filled the silent hallway.

He turned the knob slowly and the door opened towards him, revealing a steep stairwell.

As he crept up the staircase into the attic apartment, every sense was heightened, attuned to the slightest sound or movement.

He smelled fresh paint. His pulse quickened.

Nearly at the top of the stairs, an object appeared in his peripheral vision and struck him in the temple. A cast iron pan clanged down the staircase. He staggered up the remaining stairs but, losing his balance, dropped to one knee, bringing his hand to his head and blinking away tears. He heard movement and held up his fists, but it was too late.

He felt a sharp sting in the back of his leg. Craning his neck, he saw a figure leaping away from him, saw a thick needle protruding from his calf.

He tried to yank it out, but he already felt the poison coursing through his veins. A flood of adrenaline sharpened his focus, even as the edges of his vision began to blur. As he fell from his knees flat onto his belly, what he saw seared into his consciousness with the clarity of a lightning strike. Sasha Levy was there, bound to a bed in a room that seemed too ordinary for the horror it contained.

And there, standing robotic and unyielding, with a calm that chilled his blood, was Hazel Christopher, her eyes as empty of emotion as they had been in the picture on his cell phone's home screen.

In those last seconds of consciousness, Jack's training screamed at him to act, to save Sasha, to apprehend Hazel. He told himself to reach for his gun, but he couldn't feel his hands anymore.

Instead, succumbing to the etomidate's effect, he felt himself lose the sensation of breathing.

Then everything went dark.

CHAPTER FORTY-ONE

CLAIRE KNEW something was wrong the moment they got out of the car in front of the big blue Victorian. The front door had been left wide open.

Racing up the stairs, she smelled bacon. The door to apartment 3A was open as well. Dashing up the stairs two at a time, she held her breath.

Entering the attic apartment, she shot a look right and then left. Jack lay motionless on the floor about two yards from a large bed covered in yellow sheets.

Sasha Levy lay in the bed. Barely conscious, she locked eyes with Claire as she walked in the room. In the corner, slowly coming to, was a young man who Claire assumed was Hazel's boyfriend.

Claire smelled paint and glanced up at the wall, where the familiar glyphs were written in yellow.

Kiko had come up right behind her, making a beeline to Jack's body. "Oh God, no."

"Run downstairs," Claire directed, "I don't have cell reception up here. Get someone to call an ambulance immediately."

Kiko raced from the room.

Claire knelt beside Jack. She pressed her fingers to Jack's neck, searching for his pulse. Relief washed over her as she felt the steady thump against her fingertips; he was alive. Quickly, she checked his breathing—it was shallow but present. To prevent him from potentially choking if he vomited, she carefully rolled him onto his side in the recovery position. The movement normalized his breathing and Claire left his side to check on the others.

"Claire Anderson, FBI. Are you hurt?"

Sasha shook her head no. Claire leaned over the bed to assess. The young woman's pulse was easy to feel and she was breathing normally, the effect of the poison wearing off. Sasha looked up at her with fearful eyes.

"You're going to be okay," Claire confirmed.

"Chris?" she asked weakly.

"He's okay too," Claire said.

"I'm okay." His voice was even weaker than Sasha's.

"Both of you don't worry. Ambulance is on the way."

She noticed that Jack's respirations were slowing and raced to his side. Falling on her knees hard, she shook his shoulder. "Stay with me, Jack," she demanded. She grabbed hold of his chin and shook his face then slapped his cheek. "That's it, keep breathing," she said as he took a deep breath in. Claire took in a deep breath, too, as Jack resumed a respiratory level conducive to sustaining life.

Jack was at the peak of physical health, and she knew that if anyone could survive this, he could. As long as she kept him stimulated enough to keep breathing. She noticed the small syringe protruding from his leg. Carefully, with her sleeve pulled down over her fingertips and touching as little of the surface as possible, she pulled it out of him, aware that whatever was inside had already entered his bloodstream. Jack winced slightly as she removed it. A good sign.

She heard sirens in the distance, and looked around the room.

Claire's thinking was, Hazel Christopher didn't want to kill anyone. Other than her five planned victims, she did not consider herself a killer. Quite possibly, she did not even think that she was killing those five people. She probably had created some story in which she was doing them a favor.

The sirens grew closer, and Kiko re-emerged from the stairway. "Should we try to get him downstairs?" she asked hurriedly.

"No," Claire said, "let's wait for the paramedics and a stretcher. He's alive. Isn't that right, Jack?" She shook him gently and patted him on the chest, hoping he would respond but also to keep him breathing if he couldn't.

"Everyone's alive," she said to herself. "Thank God everyone's alive."

⁓

Thirty seconds after the ambulance disappeared around the corner, Claire was back in the attic apartment. There was nothing more she could do for Jack; the medical professionals would take care of him, and his fate was out of her hands. What she *could* do was figure out what had happened, and, she hoped, find Hazel Christopher.

She'd already issued a Be-On-The-Lookout bulletin with Hazel Christopher's description and known details to all local, state, and federal law enforcement agencies in the region.

Now she updated it, highlighting that she was likely headed in a direction away from this building.

Working with the two local officers, she ordered that roadblocks and checkpoints be set up around the area for containment and capture.

After a shouting match with the local Sheriff, an intensive

manhunt was launched, leveraging all available technological surveillance, including traffic and ATM cameras.

The crime scene team was on their way, but Claire took the opportunity to look around the room. She snapped a photo of the yellow glyphs with her phone and sent it to Violet. She knew that Kiko had already filled the other team members in on what had happened. But just because they were worried about Jack, that didn't give them a reason to stop working.

Next, she looked into the open duffel bag that sat on the nightstand. Apparently, Hazel had left it while fleeing. It contained a small container of yellow paint, unopened. What surprised her, though, was something she found inside a small white box: another syringe.

Hazel had subdued Sasha and her boyfriend, whom Claire assumed she knew would both be present. And they'd found a syringe, presumably full of opioids, beside the bed.

So who was this last syringe for? Perhaps it was a precaution, a backup in case something went wrong. Or was there another Luminist color out there that Fitz hadn't learned about?

Was it for something else entirely? Or perhaps some*one* else entirely.

PART 3
LEAVING THE WORLD

CHAPTER FORTY-TWO

DAWN THE MORNING after discovering the yellow room was one of the grayest Claire had ever seen.

On the ferry ride from Kingston to Seattle, she'd forced herself to go to the top deck of the ferry and let the cold wind whip her hair across her face. Sipping her coffee in that cold wind, she'd reflected on everything she had done. She needed to understand everything she had done wrong that had landed Jack in the hospital.

Kiko had texted her multiple times late the previous night, assuring her that they'd actually done a good job. They had saved Sasha Levy and her boyfriend. Both were in the hospital in Spokane, and Jack, after being stabilized, had been flown back to Seattle, where he was now recovering only ten minutes from the FBI office.

But Kiko's texts hadn't helped.

For better or worse, she was the mother of the group—the one tasked with holding them all together and keeping them safe. And every parent knows that when your children suffer, you suffer.

She hoped Jack would be out of the hospital by the end of

the day, and that when she arrived at the office, someone would have good news to share about the location, or better yet, apprehension of Hazel Christopher.

The first thing she saw when she entered the Boiler Room, however, was not good news. On the large whiteboard on the wall she saw writing that surprised her. It was Fitz's sloppy and irregular handwriting and, at first, she was confused because she could barely read his scrawl.

When what he'd written came into view, she became livid.

Kiko: Yellow
Violet: Blue
Jack: Red
Fitz (me): Black
Claire: White

She stared at it for a long moment alone in the room. Then she turned on her heels and bounded out into the hallway.

Kiko was just returning from the restroom.

"Fitz?" Claire yelled past her into the abyss. She turned to Kiko, "Where is he?" she demanded.

"I... I don't know," Kiko stammered. "Why are you so upset?"

"Did you see what he wrote on the whiteboard?"

"I saw," Kiko said, "No big deal though, right? That's just Fitz."

Claire held up a hand, silencing her.

Just then, Ranger came loping around the corner, followed by Fitz, who had a broad smile across his face and a burrito in each hand.

"You. Get in here," Claire said, jabbing a thumb toward the open door of the Boiler Room. She didn't want to make a scene in the hall. And she knew that scenes like this were one of the reasons doors were made to close. She just hoped this door was strong enough to protect the rest of the team from the explosion she was about to let loose on Fitz.

Taking her regular seat at the large table in the center of the room, she watched as Fitz ambled in. He must have just come from the food truck that was often parked down the block because Claire recognized the logo on the breakfast burrito wrappers. Ranger, deciding that Fitz planned to stay in this room with the food, followed him in and lay by his feet staring upwards as Fitz slowly unwrapped one of the burritos before looking up at Claire.

Putting on his most polite accent, he asked, "Now, how may I help you, Claire?"

"Shut the door," she said.

"Oooh, one of *these* kinds of meetings," Fitz said.

He put down one of the burritos on the edge of the desk and made a hand gesture to Ranger, who rose dutifully and used his shoulder to push the door closed. Fitz looked up at Claire like he expected accolades.

She stared daggers at him.

"I know what you're driving at," Fitz said before taking a bite of, and then speaking the rest of his phrase through, his burrito. "It's the list of names and colors I've left written on the board."

"What is it?" Claire snapped.

Fitz swallowed and took another bite as though waiting for her to think things through.

"Isn't it obvious enough?" he finally asked.

"Explain it to me like I'm five," Claire said, her voice dripping with disdain.

Fitz slowly and methodically took three bites of his burrito, then inspected it carefully and pulled out a chunk of sausage, handing it to Ranger who took it gently then smacked a wide gaping mouth to chew. Then Fitz stood and shoved his hands in the pockets of his wrinkled slacks.

Claire could smell the stale lager on his clothes, even from ten feet away. He wasn't drunk. But the smell clung to him like he'd woken up in an alley after an all-night bender.

"Violet used her machine to translate a few texts and I read them. I was mostly right about Luminism, and about Hazel. But there was a lot—I must admit—that I had missed. If what you believe is—"

"Enough!" Claire interrupted him. "Why did you—"

"I know, I know," Fitz said, returning her interruption. "You don't have to say it. *Why did you do that, Fitz? That is not okay, Fitz. You can't psychoanalyze fellow agents, Fitz. And you certainly may not pair them with a color philosophy from an ancient religion that is currently being used by the most wanted serial killer in the United States.* Am I getting it right?"

Claire nodded.

"Now will you please let me explain?"

Claire folded her arms, begrudgingly willing to give him the benefit of the doubt, if only for the next few seconds.

"My job is to try to get inside the mind of a killer. To do that, I need to think how she thinks. Take Hazel Christopher. If you believe that people come in five archetypal qualities which reflect the fivefold nature of God, then everyone you meet will fit into one of these five boxes. She would think Kiko is spontaneous and funny and full of life, and would see her as a yellow, reflecting the joyful part of existence."

Anticipating Claire's objection, Fitz held up a hand.

"Please, please let me finish," he said. When she remained silent, he continued, "Violet is a prodigy. A genius not unlike Hazel herself. She has a mind that is once in a generation. She's blue. Jack has strength and aggression. He was an excellent athlete and still is. He's the red. And as much as I would love to say that I am a blue, I believe she would count me as a black. When you read deeply in the Luminist texts, you find out that the powerful are not always those who are actually in charge. It is more of a style of personality, of being, that makes one think one is above everyone else. If you are a wise black, you're often put in positions of power because you wield it benevolently. When it goes wrong, as it has in my case, you turn it on yourself and it leads to deeply self-destructive behavior."

He paused, waiting for her to object, but when she didn't, he continued.

"And that leads to you, Claire. You said yourself that you were inspired by Sister Marybeth Peters when you had her as a teacher. That's because, in some ways, you two are alike. Not in specific life choices, but in the way you see and approach the world. You believe that everything should be clear and clean and simple and precise and black and white. And, just as Marybeth Peters left the world to live in her little contained monastery, you are leaving the FBI to live in small town bliss. There, you're thinking you can flee to your cozy little house, and stay protected from the rest of the world. You'll hide behind the insulation of Puget Sound, naively believing you won't have to face reality ever again."

Claire stood, knocking her chair back. "Shut the hell up," she said, jabbing a finger at Fitz.

But Fitz was on a roll. "And the more I think about it, the more I think that Hazel Christopher, too, embodies the structure of the white. There is no doubt she is brilliant in certain ways, but she isn't the blue she thinks she is. Intellect is not the driving force behind her motivations. I believe she is either misreading the Luminist texts, or herself. Maybe she doesn't realize how her actions reflect her rejection of the chaos in the world. Seeking transcendence is her way of trying to control it. She's trying to place order and simplicity where it doesn't belong. Hazel is trying to reach an unobtainable nirvana through what she is calling the Ascension. Just like you hope to reach yours, Claire. Retiring to little Kingston, your Shangri La."

Claire felt her face flush.

"Can you two stop it, please?" It was Violet's voice.

Claire turned to see her and Kiko standing in the doorway. They'd cracked it without her even noticing.

They stepped into the Boiler Room and Violet continued. "You're reminding me of my parents arguing about BS in the kitchen of their restaurant while something was left on the stove to burn. Stop it! None of this is helping Jack. None of this is helping us catch Hazel Christopher."

Claire sighed deeply, her cheeks still warm.

Violet took her usual seat by her computers in the corner.

Kiko tried to break the tension. "Are you two sure you never dated?" she asked. "You argue like a couple who have hurt each other very deeply in the past and can't let it go."

Fitz let out a volcano of thunderous laughter. "I do like to say that opposites attract, but Claire and I are just too bloody opposite. We would murder each other on a first date."

"There would never be a first date," Claire said. "To date you, I'd have to fumigate you. Would you mind showering before you come to work next time?"

"With me, it's a package deal," Fitz said. "Take the genius, endure the stench. Fortunately," Fitz leaned back in his chair and placed his hands behind his head, letting out a sigh of satisfaction as he let his belly drop forward, "the juice is worth the squeeze."

"Enough of this," Claire said. "Violet, can you give us an update?"

"Absolutely. Reports have been filtering in from all around the state, and even some from the Oregon and Idaho State Patrol are in on this now as well. There have been a few calls and a few possible sightings, but so far, nothing solid on Hazel Christopher. But everyone is looking, Claire. I promise, everyone is looking."

"And Jack?" Kiko asked. "Any update?"

Violet turned slowly and gave Kiko a strange look. "He's going to be okay."

A silence hung in the room, and then Fitz cleared his throat loudly as he sat forward again. "I'm sorry," he said, "but there's only one thing left to do. Try to figure out who Hazel Christopher's next victim will be. Because I have no doubt she is going to find one soon."

CHAPTER FORTY-THREE

THE GRAY MORNING had broken into a grayer afternoon and an even grayer evening. On the ferry ride home after a long and unfruitful day, a sadness had settled throughout Claire's body, like the gray was flowing from the February sky and had saturated her entire being.

In her early thirties she had been diagnosed with a mild case of SAD, seasonal affective disorder. It was fairly common in the area. Despite its beautiful summers, the winters in the Pacific Northwest were grayer than almost anywhere in the country.

Every year, Claire told herself she would make a point of visiting Hawaii or Florida or Southern California—really anywhere she could go to get some sun on her skin in the winter. But every year, something came up: one of the kids got sick, or money was tight, or a case at work kept her in the office, or Brian, her husband, just simply didn't want to bother.

As she walked into her house, she told herself that within a week, the job would be done, and she would be able to travel in the winter whenever and wherever she wanted. She wouldn't have much money, but she could travel cheaply, perhaps stay with a friend or rent a cheap Airbnb. One way or another, this would be her last February in which she didn't take a trip.

So, why wasn't that thought making her feel any better?

The effects of the argument-turned-lecture with Fitz had lingered the rest of the day, despite the fact that they had moved on. After putting the fight behind them, they had buckled down and done everything they could to locate Hazel Christopher and figure out who the next victim might be.

The problem was, even after going through the list of patient's brain scans closely, they didn't land on anyone who was a good match for Hazel's next mark. Violet and Fitz had spent the better part of the day looking through the bios of everyone they could, and they didn't see anyone as clearly marked as yellow as Sasha Levy had been. Not to mention, they had been in touch with every single person whose brain scan information had been compromised. All were on alert, and those with the area of heightened activity were all under protection.

The more Claire thought about it, the more she believed Hazel Christopher would be forced to use something other than brain scans to choose her next victim.

Standing at the bottom of the stairwell, she heard Benny's excited voice. He was recording a video. She walked quietly to the top of the staircase and knocked on his door. He answered it with a huge grin across his face and then dove in for a hug. It was as though all the gray slowly melted away from her, like he was a ray of sunshine whose light warmed her from the inside.

"I really missed you," he said.

"Will you show me what you're working on?"

"Sure, mom," Benny said. "Pull up a chair—and *stayawhile*."

He had said it like an old-time bartender. Claire never knew where he learned to say half the things he did. Benny pressed play on his computer, and a video popped up. Immediately it was clear it was a parody of one of those infomercials that asks you to make a donation for a good cause. Benny was doing an overly-dramatic voiceover. "499 out of 500 children suffer from an incurable disease," he said on the video. "Lack of Down syndrome." Sad, somber music played over the video, which cut between a screen showing an image of the statistic, and shots of Benny playing video games or playing in the park happily. Then the voiceover continued. "As tragic as it is that so many children suffer from not having Down syndrome, there's something you can do to help. Like and share this video, and I will give 10% of all ad revenue received to one of the millions of children in America suffering from a lack of Down syndrome." The voiceover ended, and the final shot of the video was of Benny standing in front of his computer holding up a sign that read, "My parents are incredibly lucky to have me."

By the end, Claire was laughing out loud. "What the heck was that, son?" she asked.

"It's a parody, Mom."

"I got that," she said, "but I guess I really don't get it."

"That's one of the things about my channel. It isn't for every kid with Down Syndrome, and it isn't for you. It's for anyone who's into gaming and humor and wants a good laugh."

"Hey, wait. What do you mean it isn't for me?" Claire whined. "I might not be into gaming, but I *do* like humor and *do* want a good laugh."

"I know Mom," Benny feigned a reassurance even more exaggerated than his mother's feigned hurt, "the channel is for you too, don't worry."

"You really are funny, you know," Claire said.

"Do you think it's too offensive, though?" Benny asked.

"No," Claire said. "I think everyone will get that it is a joke. You're saying that you don't want to be looked on as a special case, as someone who needs help or special treatment, right?"

"That's right," Benny said. "I've seen enough sad infomercials. I'm not a victim; I'm happy the way I am."

Claire felt the tears rising to her eyes and hugged Benny

long and hard. "You are a great light on YouTube and in the world," she said, "and I love you very much."

"I guess I'd better turn myself off then," Benny booped himself on the nose with his index finger. "Don't want to waste electricity, you know?"

"Huh? Don't you dare!" Claire's smile shone through her mock admonishment. "No one better ever turn off my Bean-Bean!"

CHAPTER FORTY-FOUR

HAZEL SAT STRAIGHT BACKED, staring down at her little silver laptop. After Spokane, she had fled west. She hadn't thought she would end up needing her backup location, but she was glad she had reserved it anyway. She'd been safe here for over 48 hours and felt close to finding the next partner in her Ascension.

She didn't generally watch the news, but the situation forced her to do so. She needed to know what they knew about her. It turned out they knew a lot. And her face was all over the television, all over everything.

Online, hundreds of message boards had popped up about her. People were speculating about her motives and intentions. Her hand-painted glyphs were now being viewed in countries all around the world.

And yet here she sat, alone, eating a small salad topped with canned chickpeas, lemon juice and olive oil drizzled on in lieu of a dressing. She'd always eaten light. She had become a vegetarian over ten years ago. Food meant little to her and would, very soon, mean even less.

Those who have left the world no longer need nourishment.

Since most of the law enforcement officials in the Pacific Northwest had been told about what she'd done, she knew many would be interested in meeting her. But she was only interested in meeting the rest of one small group. It was the core team from the FBI: Violet Wei, Vivian Greene, Fitzgerald Pembroke III, and Jack Russo, the only one of them she'd seen in person.

Finally, there was Claire Anderson.

In many ways, she was the most interesting to Hazel. A small town overachiever who played basketball for the University of Washington. She appeared to be a well-balanced person, exceptional in nothing, good at everything.

Without getting to know her a little bit more, Hazel couldn't be sure of her Luminist hue. But the pictures of her online—her intense face, her sometimes pinched forehead—made Hazel think she was a fairly rudimentary white. Someone who saw things in black and white, good and evil, and wanted the edges to be clearer than they were.

She decided to look up videos to see if she could get a better sense of Claire Anderson.

Opening up a YouTube window, she watched a couple of press conferences of the FBI agent. Yes, she was definitely reflecting White. Not a good fit. Nothing ever fit as cleanly as Hazel would have liked. But she had no doubt she'd find the right person soon. She was safe here for at least another 48 hours.

She would take Yellow soon.

And then would come the final Ascension. Delayed, yes, but still her destiny was inevitable.

CHAPTER FORTY-FIVE

CLAIRE SAT ALONE in the Boiler Room. She hadn't been able to sleep and had called in Sofia early that morning to help Benny get off to school. She'd taken the early ferry and now sat alone in the office in the dark, thinking.

Despite the fact that there were no windows in the office, she knew that dawn was breaking. The first sounds of footsteps from overhead told her that the early morning staff was beginning to arrive.

It had been 72 hours since anyone had seen Hazel Christopher. After Spokane, she had vanished like smoke over a campfire.

After a flurry of activity and public interest, the world seemed to have lost its interest in Hazel Christopher, The Color Killer. Was it just her, or was the world's attention span getting shorter and shorter?

She and the team had looked into every crevice of Hazel Christopher's past. They'd interviewed her parents twice more, her high school classmates and teachers, old friends, and distant relatives. But they found nothing. No clue as to where Hazel Christopher was.

Claire could not deny that Hazel had done a phenomenal job of covering her tracks. She had cut off contact with almost everyone in her life years ago. Many people who knew her reported that they got the sense Hazel had left them behind, was leaving her old life behind having decided that she was above them, above it all.

Above everything.

She heard Kiko's voice approaching, loud and boisterous, even though it was only 6:30 in the morning. "That's a bunch of BS," she was saying.

But it wasn't an argument, at least not a sour argument. It sounded like good-natured banter. But she couldn't hear who Kiko was speaking with. A moment later, Jack appeared in the doorway with Kiko standing a little too close to him.

"Oh, hi, Claire," Kiko said. "You're here early."

Jack cleared his throat. "Good to see you, Claire."

"I heard you'd gotten released," Claire said. "Glad to see you're feeling better."

Of course, she'd known that something might be up between Jack and Kiko, but with only a few days left on the job, she couldn't bring herself to care. Soon it wouldn't be her problem anyway.

"What were you two talking about?" Claire asked.

"Religion," Kiko said.

"You know how I like to keep religion and politics out of the office," Claire said. "I respect anyone's views, but none of them will help us solve this crime."

Kiko flipped on the lights, causing Claire to blink rapidly.

Jack sat at the head of the table, and Kiko sat at the other end, as far away from him as possible, which Claire interpreted as a weak attempt to show her that there was nothing going on between them.

"Jack was saying that he is a very religious person," Kiko

said. "And I was saying that Hazel Christopher is, in her own way, a very religious person as well."

Jack's face grew serious. "And I took offense at that. I really did. What she believes and what any sane religious person believes, of any faith, have nothing to do with one another. She is twisted and sick and deranged. She's taken what Fitz assures me is a false interpretation of an ancient and benign religion and twisted it to her own ends. When I pray on Sundays, I'm seeking help from above, for me and for everyone else in the world. What she's doing has nothing to do with that."

Kiko looked like she was going to argue, but Claire could tell it was a mischievous form of argument. It was banter. It was flirting.

"And I agree." It was Fitz's voice.

Claire turned to see him standing in the doorway.

"Jack and I don't agree on much," he continued, "but on this he is quite right. I've never been much of a religious man myself, but I've known people of all faiths. Towering men and women of genius and conviction and self-sacrifice. Hazel Christopher is quite the opposite."

Fitz lumbered in and sat next to Jack, patting him on the back. "Good to see you again, Agent Russo."

Ranger, who apparently had been investigating something in the hallway, trailed in a few moments later. Claire suspected the dog might be less interested in Fitz when he didn't have some form of meat at hand.

They sat in silence, only broken by a few mumbles in salutation when Violet joined them in the room. Claire couldn't stop thinking about what Fitz insinuated the day before. He'd said that she was a lot like Hazel Christopher, and now he was speaking as though Hazel Christopher was the most selfish person he'd ever studied.

So, what did that make her?

Jack broke the silence. "Damian's lawyer finally relented.

They signed off on the plea agreement, and he says he's going to talk again. I think we should go ahead and ask him a few more questions."

"I don't think we can get anything more out of that bastard, but it's worth a shot," Fitz agreed.

"You two handle that interrogation, okay?" Claire said. "I'm going back to Hazel's parents one more time. Kiko, you come with me, okay?"

"Will do," Kiko said. Even Kiko's voice was dripping with fatigue. Her normal enthusiasm faded quickly when the thought of speaking with Hazel's parents was floated. Claire knew she would try, but they'd already tried. They had tried everything.

Claire stood. "Look, team, it may feel like I am just running out the clock here, but I promise I'm still trying. Sometimes you have to keep trying even when you know you're going to fail."

Jack stood up and shot a look at her. "Don't talk like that. We don't know we're going to fail. We might feel like we are going to fail, because we've failed a lot. But one break, one idea, one new lead is all we need. You might get it out of Hazel's parents, and we might get it out of Damian." He nodded in Violet's direction. "Or maybe one of the 100,000 tips she's getting every day will lead somewhere. Let's not give up."

In that moment, Claire felt buoyed by his enthusiasm. "You're right, Jack. Thank you for that." Then, turning to Kiko she said, "You ready?"

Kiko nodded.

"All right," Claire said. "Let's jet."

∼

They were halfway to the Mercer Island estate of Hazel's

parents when something landed in the center of Claire's chest. It was a wave of guilt like she'd never felt before.

What the hell was she doing?

She had left Benny to get ready for school with Sofia, all to pursue a case she knew was going nowhere. She had let the fact that Jack sustained an injury on her watch get the better of her, taking it personally as if her failure reflected on every moment of her life, and she had to punish herself by coming into the office early.

Damn it, Fitz! Claire felt her mind trying to squirm away from her feelings. But she had to admit that maybe she *was* more like Hazel Christopher than she would like to believe.

She had decided that Hazel's plan was to use the extra syringe they'd found in her duffle bag on herself. After taking the life of Sasha Levy and becoming the Yellow—or whatever nonsense she believed—Hazel had planned to take her own life. *The Final Ascension*, it was called in the literature Fitz had been reading. Whatever the original author of the Luminist texts had in mind when describing the path of The Final Ascension, in Hazel's interpretation it meant she would be leaving the world behind.

And Claire had to admit that's exactly what she was doing. Leaving the FBI.

But this feeling in her gut, this guilt, it came with another feeling, an intuition. If she was like Hazel Christopher, maybe Hazel Christopher was like her.

She tried to let Fitz's assessment of her sink in. Tried to think of all the times she found herself thinking things in black and white and what motivations that led her to.

Maybe she'd misinterpreted her husband's feelings when their son was diagnosed, and his questions had been less about disappointment and more about him adjusting to an unfamiliar circumstance. She'd taken his disappointment personally and treated him like a criminal repeatedly for the way she thought he felt about their son.

When bad things happened, like Jack getting shot up with poison, she blamed herself personally. And, who did she punish? The person she thought was responsible, herself. All these years she'd spent with the FBI and what was her greatest motivation for leaving? It wasn't the job, she was good at the job. And sure she had other things she wanted to do with her time, too, but she liked the work part of the job. What she was especially angry with was its bureaucratic BS. The way it would squeeze her and waste her time.

Claire landed on an epiphany about herself. Her MO was to hone in on the source of an attack, perceived or actual, then fight back personally. She'd perceived attacks from her husband, herself, the FBI—she'd find what would hurt them the most, then go in for the strike.

And when Claire put herself in Hazel's shoes, she understood. Hazel would blame Claire's team for stopping her in Spokane. And if she took it personally...

"Oh, God. Kiko," she shouted, "turn around. Drive me to the ferry right now."

"What?" Kiko asked.

"Don't ask questions," Claire said, "just drive."

Kiko swerved to the right and took the exit, driving like a woman possessed.

Claire was already on her phone, dialing Sofia. It rang and rang, but no answer.

"Oh, God," Claire said to herself. "Oh, God, no."

CHAPTER FORTY-SIX

HAZEL LIKED Claire Anderson's little study. It was neat and tidy, with everything in its place. Pens in a row, notebooks aligned with corners of the desk at ninety degree angles.

On the wall there was a small framed map of central Washington with a single pin in it marking the town of Moses Lake. Hazel didn't know what that meant, but she knew it held some special significance that Claire Anderson was focused on, and Hazel could appreciate that.

She slid open a desk drawer and shuffled through a few papers. At the bottom of the drawer she found a wooden plaque with a metal plate etched with the words, *The World is Worth Fighting For*.

Hazel contemplated the sentiment. She couldn't have disagreed with it more thoroughly. The world was a limited hellhole, a dumpster for the fallen to thrash around within.

A place to leave, not fight for.

And she believed that Claire would agree with this, which is why the plaque was hidden away at the bottom of a drawer and not displayed proudly on the wall.

She leaned back in her chair, staring at the aphorism on the framed t-shirt on the wall. *Commitment yields excellence, but only love yields transcendent performance.*

Hazel felt *this* was an intriguing sentiment.

As a teenager, she had been excellent at math and physics and had been one of the youngest people ever to be accepted to Cal-tech. She had been committed and been excellent, but she had never actually *loved* math and science.

In her junior year, when she began reading philosophy and religious texts and had her first existential and spiritual struggle, Hazel had realized that she had never *loved* anything she'd done.

To transcend the world as she was about to do, love was needed. Love of the divine, love of perfection, love of the immortal future of her spirit.

Claire Anderson's t-shirt couldn't have said it any better.

Hazel stood, walking silently across the room. At the doorway, she stepped over the body of the 20-something babysitter. Hazel had given her a double dose, and she would be down for at least half an hour before she'd need another.

Listening to the delighted squeals from upstairs, she knew she'd made the right decision. The YouTube videos of Claire had led to YouTube videos of her young son. And two minutes of one of his videos was all she'd needed to realize that he was, in fact, a perfect embodiment of the Yellow on Earth.

Benny was charismatic and funny and innocent and playful and enthusiastic. His light burst through the computer screen and told her that she had made a mistake pursuing Sasha Levy from the beginning.

A child. Only a child could truly represent the sheer delight of being alive that the ancients had written was the true nature of the Yellow.

She was so fortunate that she'd failed with Sasha Levy.

This child would be better in every way, and she couldn't wait to gather his light.

She picked up her duffel bag and silently began ascending the stairs.

CHAPTER FORTY-SEVEN

JACK STOOD with his arms folded, leaning on the wall as he watched Fitz become his father.

After learning a bit about Fitz's background, he had Googled Fitz's father and found that Fitz had actually undersold just how famous his father had been. Fitzgerald Pembroke, II had become the youngest Police Inspector in London before *Jack's* Fitz could add a roman numeral to the Pembroke name, and had risen through the ranks to become not only the most famous officer in England but a famous personality on television as well.

The more he'd read about Fitz's father, the more he understood the man before him. Overweight and poorly dressed, but brilliant. And as he hammered away at Damian, back and forth between thunderous accusations and soft, gentle whispers of understanding, he saw Damian cracking before him.

And it wasn't even that Damian was trying to conceal anything. Fitz believed that he had knowledge that was hidden even to himself, and Fitz believed he could find a way to coax it to the surface.

"So I ask you again," Fitz was saying, "other than the three you knew about, was there never any mention of any *potential* victims?"

Damian was close to tears. "I told you a hundred times, she never talked about the victims with me, other than the mob guy and the nun and the professor. After that, I have no idea."

"Did you know that she was shagging a Russian guy at a farmhouse in Spokane?"

This got Damian's attention, and he looked up, then let his head fall down, dejected. "I didn't know that, and I don't even know if you're telling me the truth."

"He *is* telling you the truth," Jack interjected.

"Fine," Damian said. He shook his head again, opened his mouth to speak, and then closed it, going silent and folding his arms.

"There's just one more question I have," Fitz said. "Did Hazel ever talk to you about what she believed was her strongest color?"

This got Damian's attention. "Blue," he said.

"And you've studied the Luminist texts some. Did you think she was correct?"

"It's not for me to say, she knew a hundred times more than me."

"Take a guess," Fitz commanded, his voice again growing loud.

"When I began learning about Luminism, I thought her dominant color might be White. I mean, I couldn't even read the texts, but the way she explained it... she sounded like a White."

"And you are correct," Fitz said. "She's delusional about herself. She doesn't know who she is. Did you ever do something to make her mad? Did anybody ever do something that made her mad?"

Damian considered this. "She had this little statue thing that seemed like it was pretty important to her. She got super mad at me and another person over it. She told me a higher up Luminist priest or something gave it to her. She said it represented the blue's moment of ascension. I guess it made her pretty mad when I said it looked like a tiny white angel. I mean, it looked like a little piece of white opalite molded into an angel to me. Anyway, when I said it, she told me to never contact her again. We made up after that, but it took awhile."

Fitz leaned into Damian's face, practically spitting his breath onto the man. "And the other person? Tell us what happened there."

"Whelp, I can't prove nothing but the thing got broken at a Luminist meeting when a lady moved her purse and knocked it off the table. It shattered when it hit the ground. The next week the lady came to the gathering crying about how every object in her home had been split in two and someone had even bashed in one of her car headlamps. I think Hazel had something to do with it. But I can't prove it. I'm sorry I can't help you more."

"Thank you, Damian." Fitz sounded sincere. "I think you've given us something to go on."

With that, Fitz left and Jack hurried out behind him.

∼

"What do we have to go on?" Jack asked.

"Who do you think she blames for stopping her from killing Sasha?" Fitz asked.

"Me?" Jack asked.

Fitz eyed him wearily. "I'm thinking it's the person who leads this team that she would blame. Claire is the one who's been on TV. The press conference."

"Okay," Jack said, his tone indicating he needed more of an explanation.

"She broke every object belonging to a woman who ruined a

figurine depicting her final ascension. What do you think she will do to a woman who ruined her *actual* final ascension? She's going to find another Yellow, one that's connected to Claire."

∽

Claire had left her car on the Kingston side of the water. Sometimes she drove it on, but sometimes when the ferry line was backed up, she parked it in a reserved spot and ran onto the ferry, catching a taxi on the other side. So when the ferry docked, she was the first off the boat, sprinting to her car a quarter mile away and then speeding through Kingston.

Her house was a midsize waterfront that she purchased with her husband over twenty years ago before the housing prices had shot up throughout the area. Only a mile from the ferry, on clear days—and when she had time—she would walk. But today she let her foot fall heavy on the accelerator, peeling along Shoalwater Place before cutting into the opposite lane to take a sharp left onto West Kingston Road.

From the ferry, she'd called Sofia five more times and emailed Benny as well. She hadn't yet let him get his own cell phone, a decision she now regretted more than anything.

Zipping in and out through traffic, swerving into the opposite lane, she used her voice commands to continue calling Sofia. She knew that the babysitter hadn't gone out of range because the call continued to ring and ring before eventually going to voicemail.

Just after the little roadside park she turned down her driveway going way too fast and scraped the bottom of her car against a rise in the concrete created by roots from a nearby cedar tree. For over a decade, her husband had said he would fix it, but he never had.

Cursing his name she slammed on the brakes and jumped out of the car, then dashed to her front door. It was unlocked, and the first thing she saw when she entered was the tangled brown hair of Sofia.

Claire gasped.

Sofia lay face down, half of her body in Claire's office and the other half protruding into the hallway.

∽

Having tried Claire's cellphone twice, Jack hurried from the interrogation room toward the Boiler Room with only one thought racing through his mind: How would Hazel find a place to stay undetected for multiple days in the immediate area? He tripped over Ranger, who'd chosen to sleep in the doorway over the bed Fitz bought, but caught himself before his face hit the floor, only lightly spraining his wrist. He stood and shaking out his wrist, he hurried across the room to Violet, whose head was dancing back and forth between her two main monitors.

"What's up?" Violet said before Jack could say anything.

"We think Hazel might be coming after us. Possibly Claire herself, possibly Kiko, if Fitz is right about her color on this Luminist theory stuff, which I still think is BS."

Violet cocked her head. "You mean you think that Hazel could come after Kiko as the final piece in her puzzle or whatever?"

"Yes."

"Kiko just called and apparently she's on her way back to the office. Claire got dropped off at the ferry."

"We need to find Hazel. Have we checked all the hotels, all the Airbnbs?"

"We've checked everything," Violet said. "No one under that name has checked in anywhere."

Jack paced, wracking his brain. He knew that Hazel wouldn't go anywhere under her real name, of course, but nothing in all their research had turned up any aliases.

Violet seemed to be reading his thoughts. "We've also sent images of her to every hotel in the Pacific Northwest, asking them to be on the lookout. We've even gotten a few dozen tips, but they've all gone nowhere. Either the person of interest had already checked out, or we sent hotel staff up, and it wasn't Hazel occupying the room after all, and a bunch of the tips were just pranks. Even though interest in this has died down a little over the last 48 hours, we're still getting tons of information. The problem is that most of it is wrong."

"My guess is that she would avoid hotels. If she had a backup plan, it would be a house she already owns or that someone she knows owns."

"We interviewed everyone she knows," Violet said, "and she didn't seem to know many people from the last few years."

"What about an Airbnb or VRBO?" Jack asked. "Those are more anonymous to check into."

"We checked all those," Violet said. "The registrations, at least. If she has an alias, we can't get far without knowing it."

"She's in one of them, I know it," Jack said. "It's just that we don't know what name she reserved it under. To what extent do you have access to the databases?"

"I have top level access to their reservation system. I can search for names only. And that alone took a lot of convincing. No way I'm getting into the personal information sections."

"And you searched both of her parents' names, and Damian's name, and Sergei's name, and everyone else associated with the case?"

"We searched everything we could think of."

She nodded and Jack shoved his hands in his pockets, walking a lap around the table. He walked another, and then another, thinking through every piece of the case he could remember. Everything Damian had said, everything Claire had said, and every report he had read.

Jack then crouched next to Ranger and scratched him

behind the ears. Ranger looked up with his big wide brown eyes. Jack had always loved dogs. Because he moved around so much, he'd never been able to care for one himself as an adult, but the fact that Fitz had brought Ranger into his life actually made him very happy. He'd always thought that dogs had an ancient wisdom, like they had been the same for thousands of years as humanity had developed and changed and fought wars and invented technologies. They were still just very special, ancient creatures.

He stood up suddenly. "Bhaskar," he said.

"What?" Violet asked, turning.

"Bhaskar is the name of the wandering sage who founded Luminism. He was said to have perfected the five-fold nature of God and ascended directly to heaven. Did you try that name?"

Violet didn't respond. She was already typing.

"By the hammer of Thor!"

"What the hell does that mean?" Jack asked.

"A person named Bhaskar reserved a small house in Poulsbo, just across the water from us, a number of times this year."

"When are the reservations for?" Jack asked.

Violet turned and looked into his eyes. "One of the reservations spans today's date. She could be there now. And that's only ten minutes from—"

"Claire's house," Jack said. "We need to be there. Now."

CHAPTER FORTY-EIGHT

EVERYTHING INSIDE CLAIRE wanted to sprint up the stairs, but she stuck to her training. She looked down at Sofia, who was slowly rolling onto her side. Claire dialed 911 on her cell and, as her eyes locked on Sofia's, she held a finger up to her lips. Sofia nodded in understanding.

Claire whispered a hurried message to the 911 operator, then placed the phone next to Sofia, who was slowly coming to.

Pulling out her firearm, Claire crept along the edge of the staircase.

She had learned from her teenagers that the staircase creaked if you used the center of the steps. Only after a couple of years in college had they admitted to sneaking out occasionally as teenagers. They told her how they'd always been able to sneak back up to their bedroom by deftly avoiding the *creakers*, as they called them, and using the edge of the staircase where their footfalls would be silent. They pointed out a few places between the stairs and their room—creakers they'd learned to avoid as well.

Claire, pausing halfway up the stairs, heard Benny's voice. She could not make out his words but she would know that tone anywhere. She knew he wasn't creating a YouTube video or gaming, he was using the wrong intonation for that. He was speaking with someone, but Claire couldn't hear who. Her pace, her pulse quickened and she continued up the stairs. Three paces from his door, she stepped on a loose floorboard, causing a creak to pierce the silence. The twins hadn't warned her of this one. She heard movement inside the room.

Bounding forward, she burst through the door, gun at the ready.

Claire turned the gun to the ground immediately. She saw her son, who was draped in a yellow silk wrap, looking up at her, his eyes filled with terror. Hazel Christopher, syringe in hand, arm around Benny's neck, was hugging him close to her.

Controlling her breathing as much as she could through the torment, Claire said, "Let him go and you can have me."

Hazel Christopher was holding the syringe only an inch or two from Benny's arm. She knew Hazel could quickly poison her son. But she didn't know whether the syringe held the sedative she used on her victims before decorating their rooms, or whether Hazel had decided to pick up the pace and give the lethal injection first.

"Slowly lower the syringe," Claire demanded. "We can talk this out."

Benny was shaking, and everything in Claire wanted to take the shot at the small portion of Hazel's head that poked out from behind Benny's. But she couldn't do that. It was far too risky.

Hazel had an odd look in her eye. "Benny was just showing me some of his videos.

He told me about how he is already making decent money monetizing them on YouTube. He really is a ray of light in the world."

"And he's going to stay that way," Claire said.

Benny's computer suddenly erupted with a loud *CA-CHING* sound.

All three of them turned their gaze to the computer for a split second.

Benny, sensing Hazel's grip loosening, swung his elbow back into her stomach, knocking her onto the bed. Claire leaped forward and grabbed Benny by the arm and yanked him out of the room and down the hall. Pushing him forward, she shoved him into the bathroom and slammed the door.

When she turned around, Hazel was sprinting down the hallway. "Freeze," she shouted, lifting her weapon, but it was too late.

Gripping the handrails tightly, Hazel vaulted down the stairs three at a time, using her hands to propel herself forward with each leap. Landing on the first floor with a thud, she raced toward the front door.

Claire took a step down the stairs to follow her, then turned back.

She decided to look after her son instead.

∼

The helicopter blades cut through the February morning with a steady, rhythmic beat, echoing across the Puget Sound. Jack watched as Seattle's skyline shrank behind them, the Space Needle, a slender spire, receding into the distance. Below, the waters of the Sound lay calm, a vast expanse of gray reflecting the overcast sky, dotted with the occasional ferry chugging its way between shores.

"Try her again," Kiko said.

"I have tried her three times," Jack said.

"She can take care of herself," Fitz said, sounding more like he was trying to reassure himself than the rest of them. "As sure as eggs are eggs, she can."

Jack shot him a look. As much as Fitz railed against Claire, Jack thought he also idealized her.

When Jack had pulled Fitz out of the interrogation, Fitz insisted on coming along. By then, Kiko had returned to the office, so all four of them hopped in the chopper.

Jack pointed at the beach. "That's the one in front of her house," he said to the pilot through his headset. "We can land there."

Fitz had refused to wear a headset for the flight and was sitting there looking very uncomfortable, plugging his ears with his fingers.

"There's nowhere to land there," the pilot said. "The closest place to land is the high school football field, which is a mile or two from her house. That will have to do."

"That will *not* do," Jack said. "You've got some rappelling equipment. I'll use that."

The pilot took his eyes off the sky for a moment to glance back at Jack.

Jack held his gaze.

The pilot got the message. There was no point in resisting.

CHAPTER FORTY-NINE

"BENNY!" Claire called, running up to him and hugging him. "I'm so sorry that happened. I'm so sorry. After this week, I'm never leaving here again. I'm never leaving this house. Never leaving you." She heard herself sobbing along with Benny. "Did she hurt you? Are you okay? Did that needle touch you at all?" Her words came out like an avalanche tumbling down a mountain. She held him back and was looking him over with her eyes and her hands to rule out even any minor injury.

Benny pulled away. "No, I'm okay. She didn't hurt me. But you might if you keep poking at me like you are." He swatted at her hands until she stopped touching him. "She said she was a friend of Sofia's at first, and then I didn't know what was happening. We talked about gaming, and then she pulled out the needle, and—" His voice cracked; he stopped talking.

She brought him in for a hug, which he allowed. She hugged him for a long time.

Then suddenly, he pulled away. "Mom, it's okay. You have to go after her."

She looked Benny in the eyes and, without another word,

took off down the hallway and bounded down the stairs. Sofia was conscious and Claire heard sirens in the distance. "Paramedics are on their way," she said, grabbing her cellphone before bolting out the front door.

Hazel hadn't left a car in her driveway, which made Claire think that she had either taken public transportation like a taxi or Uber or had walked here from the ferry. That was the most likely possibility. So Claire took off on foot toward the ferry, thinking perhaps she would get lucky. As she ran along the side of the road, she yanked her cell phone from her back pocket and dialed Jack. His phone went straight to voicemail, so she dialed Fitz.

The call picked up and she could hear bits of Fitz's voice, but Claire couldn't make out a word he was saying. She did know, from the noises in the background, he was on a helicopter. She had heard a chopper overhead while in the house with Benny but assumed it was a news helicopter or possibly a bird from the Navy.

She looked back toward her house and spotted the helicopter, which was now coming down in front of it. "I am on foot pursuing Hazel Christopher," she yelled into the receiver on the off chance he could hear her.

Continuing to run towards the ferry, Claire felt a wave of relief when she saw Hazel and confirmed she'd picked the right direction.

Ahead was a very short bridge that crossed over a tiny inlet before the road veered right along the waterfront. It ran about half a mile to the ferry. Claire spied Hazel coming to the edge of the bridge and taking that right.

Thinking quickly, Claire also veered right, heading down onto the beach. She knew that the water was shallow enough to run across here, and she had guessed right that Hazel was heading for the ferry. Or at least for downtown Kingston. It was possible she had parked a car there and walked the rest of the way to Claire's house to avoid raising the neighbors' suspicions by parking an unfamiliar car in her driveway.

Trudging along the beach, she kept an eye on Hazel, being sure to stay about a hundred yards back to not call attention to herself. Hazel ran quickly, but not gracefully, and when she reached the downtown, she took a right toward the ferry, as Claire had expected.

Shooting a look at the ferry, she saw that it was about to depart. People and cars were streaming onto it, but the line was coming to an end.

Hazel saw this as well and hurried along the walkway, reaching the boat, which didn't require a ticket when sailing away from Kingston. Claire watched her easing her way onto the boat just before the crew member raised the metal walkway that connected ship to shore. Another closed the green gate that doubled as the ferry's railing.

Hazel had been the last one to make it onto the boat, and it would soon depart.

Gathering herself, Claire increased her speed, taking off at a full sprint; some of the muscle she'd put on from her basketball years was still hard at work. But she had fallen a few hundred yards behind and had to veer up over a rocky outcropping and onto a patch of grass. She slipped on the grass, sliding in a patch of mud.

Pressing herself up, she glanced at the ferry, which had just begun to move, then sprinted up the stairs from the lawn and onto the onboarding ramp. Coming to the end of it, she pushed a young ferry worker aside and leapt onto the moving ferry, crashing into the green metal railing, then tumbling over it and onto the deck.

When she stood up, she was looking directly into the pale gray eyes of Hazel Christopher.

Claire's breath fogged in the cold air as she squared off against Hazel on the deck, water slick beneath her boots. She could feel the spray on her face, the chill biting through her jacket and the cold mud where it had soaked through her pants.

"You can ascend *with* me, Claire Anderson," Hazel offered.

"I'm not going anywhere with you."

"You should. You know you should. You hate this world as much as I do. Your husband left you because he thought your absolutely perfect yellow star of a young man—Bean-Bean, he told me you call him that—was imperfect."

Hearing the nickname she'd given her sweet boy come from the lips of this monster made Claire's heart burn.

"You're quitting the FBI because of how imperfect everything is," Hazel continued. "Come with me. Die today, and perhaps the power of my light will allow you to ascend with me."

Hazel was smaller, but Claire knew the danger of underestimating her. If Mrs. Christopher was to be believed, Hazel had a black belt in Kyokushin karate, a particularly lethal form of Japanese karate.

Without another word, Claire lunged, trying to use her size, all the weight she had—both physical and of the love for her son—aiming to overpower Hazel. But Hazel was slippery, dodging with a frustrating ease that made Claire's muscles tense with the effort to keep up.

When Hazel twisted to apply a joint lock, Claire's training kicked in, her body responding with a counter-move more out of instinct than thought.

She felt the pull, the strain against her arm, and pushed back with all her might, breaking free but feeling the sting of exertion. They traded blows, Claire's fists seeking Hazel with desperation, but each hit that landed felt like striking water, Hazel's form yielding then snapping back unaffected.

They fell apart, both panting.

Then Hazel reached into her back pocket and pulled out a syringe, the one she'd intended for Benny.

Without a thought, Claire lunged at her legs, knocking Hazel down and causing the hypodermic to go skidding across the deck.

CHAPTER FIFTY

JACK JUMPED the last few feet from the ropes and hit the beach in a tumble, deftly rolling once before springing to his feet. He turned back to assist Kiko, who had followed him down, but she already had her feet on the ground, having landed more gently than he had.

While being lowered, he'd seen Claire inexplicably running down the street, veering toward the beach, and then cutting up over an outcropping of rocks and heading toward the ferry. He didn't know what was going on.

All he knew was that he had to follow. "I'm going after Claire. You check the house."

Kiko took off toward the house as Jack sprinted along the beach toward the downtown.

He reached the city shoreline just as the ferry was slowly easing away from the dock. Shifting into overdrive, he bolted up the walkway.

He saw Claire engaged in a hand-to-hand struggle with Hazel. A chill ran down his spine recalling the image of Hazel standing over him.

The ferry was too far away for Jack to make the leap. He

thought of reaching for his gun, but the women were grappling, and there was no way he would risk discharging his weapon through their unpredictable throws.

A young ferry worker, no more than twenty-five, wearing a yellow vest and holding a walkie talkie to his mouth sat on the ground looking stunned, unable to speak.

"FBI," Jack said.

"That blonde woman just ran and jumped onto the boat. She pushed me out of the way."

"She is FBI too," Jack said. "Stop the boat immediately, get the captain to turn back." He held up a badge and gave the kid a look that said he was not messing around.

The kid stood and pressed a button on his walkie-talkie. "Captain, the FBI is here. There is a fight taking place on the boat. They want you to stop the boat and return to the Kingston dock."

On the deck of the ferry, Claire struck Hazel in the face, but the blow overextended her, and Hazel took her into a headlock. Claire stomped her heel directly on the top of Hazel's foot, and they both tumbled to the ground.

That's when Jack saw the needle.

CHAPTER FIFTY-ONE

HEART POUNDING IN HER EARS, breath ragged, Claire grappled Hazel off of her and leapt up, fighting to anticipate Hazel's next move.

A misstep sent Claire sliding, the deck betraying her with its slick treachery. She caught herself, but barely, and corrected her stance, the fear of falling—or failing—sharpening her focus.

Underneath her feet, Claire could feel the movement of the boat slowing, then reversing. She was distracted, only for a moment, but long enough for Hazel to grab the needle. When Claire looked back up, Hazel was pulling off the cap and lunging. Claire caught Hazel's wrist, stopping the needle about six inches from piercing her neck as they both fell back, crashing into the green railing, which swung open as they fell to the deck.

"Only love yields transcendent performance," Hazel said, gritting her teeth.

Claire gripped her wrist tight, pushing against the needle in Hazel's hand, still poised for injection. But she'd hit her head in the fall and her perception was becoming fuzzy.

Claire said nothing. She was using everything she had. And everything she had was waning.

She heard Jack calling out, but she couldn't make out what he was saying. Claire knew the boat was drifting back toward Jack and the dock. But, like Claire's mind and strength, Jack's voice was drifting away from her.

Piercing pain jolted her into consciousness as she felt the needle enter her neck.

The boat lurched. The movable railing that allowed passengers to board rolled open as the boat jostled into its berth. In the chaos, it had not been secured when the ferry set sail.

Then her Bean-Bean's face—smiling, a ray of light—appeared in her mind.

Only love yields transcendent performance.

Using all her core strength, she pressed herself up off the deck, throwing Hazel and rolling on top of her.

She glanced up to see Jack arguing with the ferry worker and stabbing his finger at a big red button. "Let me on!" he shouted. The button, Claire knew, controlled the heavy metal walkway that connected the entrance ramp to the deck when the ferry was parked.

Claire knew she only had five or ten seconds before the poison either incapacitated her or killed her, but at least Jack would be on board within twenty.

Rising up slightly, she gathered all her might and brought it down, striking Hazel in the face with her forearm.

Hazel spat blood at her and tried to kick her off, but Claire pressed her down by the face, rubbing her cheek into the coarse sandpaper texture of the ferry deck.

Inching sideways, Hazel brought a knee up, smashing it into Claire's rib cage. Claire howled with pain and rolled to the side, kicking her foot out just in time to knock Hazel back as the killer lunged at her.

They rolled together toward the end of the deck, Claire on

her back looking up, head dangling over the side of the boat, Hazel lying on top of her.

Claire looked up past Hazel's grimacing face at the heavy metal walkway, which was coming down at them fast. At the last possible moment, Claire used her final burst of strength to roll out from beneath her attacker.

Hazel Christopher never saw it coming.

Just as she began to push herself up, the walkway forced her head down, catching it in the space between the ramp and the edge of the boat.

Claire turned away to avoid the sight, but before losing consciousness she heard the sickening wet crack of Hazel's neck as it broke.

CHAPTER FIFTY-TWO

AS CLAIRE CAME TO, the smell of crepes, french fries, and grilled meat helped her slowly regain consciousness. She blinked three or four times before realizing she was staring at her son, Benny.

French fries, burgers, and crepes?

And Benny?

Had she died and gone to heaven?

"Bloody hell," Fitz said, "Claire, you're back!"

Fitz's voice told her she was, in fact, far from heaven.

"Oh good." Claire spoke softly, slowly turning to look over at him with a weak smile. "I thought I was in heaven."

Benny leaned in and hugged her. "Mom, you've been asleep for an hour," he said.

"58.6 minutes actually," Violet corrected.

"Oh, who cares?" Kiko said, leaning in and hugging Claire.

Claire winced from the contact. Her side ached, as did her jaw and back, and pretty much every other part of her. "Where am I?"

"The hospital in Silverdale. They said you were shot full of etomidate, just like the other victims. It's very strong, but only lasts about an hour. You should feel much better soon."

"Why do I smell delicious food?" Claire asked.

"When the ambulance took you away," Benny said, "Violet and Kiko asked me if I wanted to get some food. I couldn't decide between dinner and dessert, so they let me get both. We got burgers. *And* we got crepes."

Claire chuckled, which made her side hurt even more. "Wait," Claire said, "I told you to stay in the house."

"I did," he said, "and then Kiko came in to take care of me and Sofia. Then the ambulance came."

"Sofia? Is she okay?"

"She's in the room next door," Kiko said. "She's going to be fine. Same as you."

Benny continued. "Kiko told me that her friends were going to take care of you, and that I should come with her and she would take me to you. She wasn't like the bad lady. She told me the secret password and everything."

"You remembered that?" Claire felt her pride swell and smiled approvingly at her son.

"How could I forget *barnacle bones?*"

When he was very little, Claire had imprinted in Benny's mind that he should never trust or go with anyone he didn't know, unless they could tell him their secret password—*barnacle bones*. They'd chosen this because barnacles don't have bones and no one would ever say those two words together unless they knew their little secret. Claire had added this information to her emergency contact file with the FBI, which her teammates must have actually read.

For once, the bureaucratic system had worked to her benefit.

Claire's head was spinning, and also aching. She realized she hadn't eaten much all day, and nothing had smelled better in her life than those french fries did right now.

"Benny," she said, "will you hand me some french fries and then step out into the hall for a few minutes? Maybe you could go check on Sofia?"

Benny grabbed her a few fries and put them in her hand, but her hands were too weak to lift them to her mouth. He leaned in, gave her a little hug, and then skipped out of the room.

"Hazel?" was all Claire said as she looked up at Fitz, who glanced at Jack.

Jack cleared his throat. "The force of the descending staircase ripped her head clean off."

Claire winced. She truly hadn't wanted Hazel to die. It wasn't that she mourned her. She didn't and never would. But she had always wanted to bring her in alive so she could face her crimes in court and for the rest of her life in prison.

She knew that Jack had been pressing the button to lower the ramp, but what she didn't know was whether he realized what was going to happen. Maybe he was enacting revenge on Hazel for threatening his life, too. Maybe he took such offense to her religious convictions that he felt the world wasn't big enough for the both of them. One thing was for sure: Claire wouldn't be asking him to tally his motivations any time soon. She was glad to be alive. And whether he'd been acting within the guidelines or not, she had Jack to thank for that. However it came about, she'd been given one more day to hold Benny in her arms, and she didn't plan to take that for granted.

She looked up with concern and locked eyes with Violet. "Are there videos of it?"

Claire knew that clips of events like this were often captured by onlookers. They would be thrown up online and, when taken out of context, could be damaging for individuals as well as the department.

"I've been on my phone looking around," Violet said, shaking her head. "Nothing so far. Luckily, it was the middle of the day, so ferry traffic was light."

"I need to rest," Claire said. "Assuming I get out of here soon, we can regroup in the office tomorrow."

They all stood to leave.

"Don't expect me to get there early," Claire said, stopping them. "I'm coming in late."

"Boss, we'd be worried if you didn't," Kiko said.

"Just get some rest, Claire," Jack said. "You took some intense pounding."

Claire smiled and mouthed a thank you. "For everything," she added aloud.

Jack smiled and nodded, then followed Violet and Kiko out the door.

"And Fitz," Claire called out.

Fitz, who'd been last out of the room, poked his head back through the doorway obediently.

"Make sure Ranger is there tomorrow. I want to say goodbye to him along with the rest of you."

CHAPTER FIFTY-THREE

THE NEXT DAY, Claire shuffled out of the press room, most of her body still aching. She had done her job. She'd answered every question the journalists could throw at her, and now she was finished with her final press conference. She never wanted to talk about colors again, especially blue, black, white, red, and yellow.

Hightower and Ley greeted her in the hallway as she shut the door of the press room for the very last time.

Hightower shook her hand. "Good job," he said, "you can expect a call from Governor Ridley later today, so anticipate his commendation."

"Yes," Ley said. "Excellent work."

Before Ley could reach out for a handshake, Claire looked away shyly and held up a hand in a gesture intended to minimize the focus on her achievements. "Thank you both," she said, backing up in a way she hoped would be imperceptible.

"We're sorry to lose you," Hightower continued, ignoring her non-verbal cues. "You've given us some great work here."

She could tell that they wanted to talk further.

"Thank you," she said again, trying to sound definitive. "We'll talk later. I need to say goodbye to the team."

Claire limped down the hall and into the Boiler Room. There, Fitz, Jack, Kiko, and Violet sat gathered around the table, which now held five glasses and a bottle of champagne in the center.

"Violet," Claire said, "I hardly recognize you. I usually walk in and have to greet the back of your head."

"I thought I'd give everyone a glimpse of my resting-scowl face," she said with little inflection. "Since it's your last day and all, I didn't want my resting-smile occiput to have anyone thinking I'm glad to see you go."

"Who ever heard of a resting-smile occiput?" Kiko said, the tone of her voice sounding more dismissive than Claire thought she meant it.

"You did," Violet clapped back with equal intensity. "Right now. From me."

Claire ignored whatever was going on between them and eased into a chair, bracing her ribs from the pain as she sat, but still smiling over Violet's dry and oddly intellectual humor. "By the way, Violet, is there any chance the computer you purchased cost about five million bucks? I know the *FBI* doesn't have the budget for that."

Violet looked down at the table. "Is pleading the fifth an option for an agent? Asking for a friend."

"You used the Bitcoin you stole to buy that computer, didn't you?" Claire asked.

"Holy crap, Violet!" Kiko's voice had lost the edge Claire thought she'd detected earlier.

"Holy crap, indeed," Jack agreed.

"Bloody hell," Fitz said, "you spent five million on that thing?"

"Quantum computers ain't cheap," Violet said, her voice calm as a cucumber. "And it was never my money anyway." She shrugged. "Besides, semi-legal Israeli tech firms are easy to work with. They happily accept Bitcoin."

Claire laughed. "Look Violet, I'm not going to have my last order be to tell you to get rid of it. And nobody outside of this room knows it exists—I'm certainly not going to be talking about it with anyone on my way out the door. But if they find out about it, I don't know how you're going to convince the higher-ups to let you keep that thing, but I hope you do."

"So, you're still retiring?" Jack asked, sounding newly disappointed.

Claire nodded. "You can handle this, Jack. I'll be meeting with Hightower later, and I'll recommend you to run any crew you want. And not only that, you'll be in charge of reports for our most recent case. Consider it a lesson and a punishment."

Jack laughed. "Duly noted. Thanks for putting in a good word for me. But we are going to miss you."

"Kiko," Claire said, "you're going to do great things." She met her eyes. "Just make sure you avoid any office entanglements. Be your badass self. The FBI will take you places if you do."

She looked around the room, suddenly remembering something. "Where's Ranger?" she asked.

Fitz stood up, hands on his hips like a mother about to scold her children. "No dogs allowed. Bloody Hightower's orders. Gave Ranger the sack right there during the press conference. Said I could keep him in a kennel until the end of the day. Can you imagine? A dog that knows how to close a door sent to a kennel?"

"Maybe if you'd bought him a bed that wasn't dripping with opulence, he would have used it," Jack complained. "Then Hightower wouldn't have noticed a problem with a dog in the office, and I wouldn't be nursing this sore wrist from tripping over him."

"It's a very fine bed I got him," Fitz protested.

"Kiko, go liberate that dog." Claire gave what she thought might be her final order. "I want to see Ranger when I get back from seeing Hightower, and I don't want to see him from behind bars." She nodded at Fitz and said, "Walk me up?"

"How many floors?"

"It's twenty two stairs, Fitz. You can make it."

Fitz followed her out of the office, and they walked together to the stairwell. At the base of the stairs, she stopped him. "You were right about me. I'm too much of a perfectionist. I *was* a little bit like Hazel."

"I was wrong," Fitz said. "Probably about more things than I know. But you're nothing like Hazel, Claire. I mean, maybe you share a few commonalities, sure. But there is good, and there is evil, and I think we both know which one you are."

Claire noticed that he didn't smell like lager. "Something's different about you," she said.

Fitz shook his head. "I decided I'd take a dry spell."

She sniffed again. "Fitz, do you smell like hemp?"

He held up both hands defensively. "I took a little CBD oil to relax. Hey, it's legal here."

"Not according to the Federal Government, which includes the FBI, which signs your paychecks—for now at least."

"Anyway, I never said I was going to become a choir boy."

She sighed. "Don't let Hightower catch you smelling like that." She smiled at him. "I can't tell you how happy I am that this isn't my problem anymore."

Fitz smiled back. "You mean that *I'm* not your problem anymore."

Claire left him at the bottom of the stairs and slowly took the two flights to Hightower's office. Her boss had just finished meeting with EJ Ley, and she took the seat as Ley left the office hurriedly.

"What was that about?" Claire asked.

"We were just having a little back and forth about the future of a few FBI agents you may know. I won, and I'm pleased to share that I can offer you a permanent position as the head of a *detached* task force investigating the most heinous crimes in the Pacific Northwest. The Special-Washington-Oregon-Regional-Detachment. You'll have free reign. Less bureaucracy, less BS. It's what you always wanted, right?"

"I'm sorry you wasted your time and spent political capital," Claire said. "It's not for me."

"So you're still set on retiring?" Hightower asked. "After this huge win? You took down Hazel Christopher and, you know, our fraud division is even looking into Abbot Rasmussen out in Port Angeles. You might even bring him down in this mess."

"That's good, but yes. I'm still leaving."

"Well, we're sad to lose you. Can you give me a brief assessment of the team? Anything I should know about before you leave them with me?"

Claire nodded again. "If you want to make that task force permanent, put Jack in charge. He can handle it. He's a good leader, and he'll grow into the role as he ages. Fitz might throw a fit about Jack leading things, and Jack might lord power over Fitz, but Kiko and Violet respect them both. They will help smooth over the transition. And I probably don't need to tell you this, but never put Fitz in charge of anything."

She considered sharing what she thought she knew about the love triangle she'd seen brewing. On her first day with the team, she'd learned that Jack and Violet had gone on at least one date before this whole thing started, but now Jack and Kiko seemed to have developed a bit of a flirtation. Then there was slight tension between Kiko and Violet that Claire thought she'd noticed. But she decided to stay quiet.

"Kiko and Violet?" Hightower asked.

"They're top of the line agents. Violet is a genius and thinks outside of the box, outside of the mainframe, really. And Kiko, she will be wherever you need her, looking and sounding however you need her, always ready and willing to help get the job done. She's young and has a lot to learn, but I wouldn't be surprised if someday she's sitting where you are now."

"Good to know," Hightower said.

"Is that everything you need from me?" she asked.

"Yes, thank you," Hightower said, dismissing her from their final meeting.

Claire moved to the door.

"Wait."

A word from Hightower still had the power to stop her. "Yes?"

"Promise me one thing. You've got twenty-four more hours. Technically, tomorrow is your last day. Think about it until then?"

Claire cocked her head sideways, but said nothing.

CHAPTER FIFTY-FOUR

THE NEXT MORNING, Claire kept Benny home from school again. They spent the day cooking together, playing video games, and talking through some of what had happened.

She'd set up an appointment with a trauma therapist as well, someone with whom he could talk through the horrifying experience. But the truth was, he seemed to be doing better with it than she was. He had been inspected by the paramedics and hadn't even been bruised by the whole encounter. That was lucky. Claire hadn't been so lucky. Her ribs would be healing for weeks, and her psyche might never fully recover.

By early afternoon, Claire was sitting outside in the garden, sipping a glass of wine alone. Benny had gotten online to play with a friend. Her final divorce paperwork had arrived in the mail, but she'd left it on the kitchen counter, not wanting to enter her home office.

In fact, she'd avoided walking past it since seeing Sofia's body lying across its threshold. Thankfully, Sofia was healing as well, but the thought of nearly losing both she and Benny still ate at her.

She finished her glass of wine and stood, heading into the kitchen to prepare dinner.

Benny appeared at the sliding glass door. "What's this, mom?"

"I thought you were playing online with Sylvio."

"We got bored. What *is* this? I've never seen it before."

Claire stepped forward. "What are you holding?"

Benny ambled up to her and handed her the plaque she'd stuffed in the drawer in her office.

The world is worth fighting for.

"Oh, this. Where did you find this?" she asked.

"It was on your desk. I went in to look for you and saw it, so I picked it up. Where did you get it?"

Immediately she realized that Hazel had been in her office, looking through her stuff. That's why she'd known about the quote from the t-shirt on her wall. The thought of Hazel rummaging through her drawers chilled her. "Remember when I was away a lot a few months back? I was working on that case in Port Townsend. I was working with a man there. Detective Thomas Austin from the Kitsap Sheriff's Department. He gave it to me."

"Why?" Benny asked, his voice full of innocence.

"He was trying to convince me not to leave the FBI."

Benny sat down on the bench where Claire had been sitting, and she joined him. "Why would he want you to stay?"

"He said I was too good at this to quit. He said the world is worth fighting for, and he gave me this plaque."

Benny considered this. "Mom," he said after a long, thoughtful silence, "after this morning, I've decided that you're never going to be any good at video games."

Claire burst out laughing. They'd spent a couple hours playing Fish Wars II earlier, and she was still utterly incompetent at it. "Where did that come from?"

"All these years, I've been thinking that maybe I could teach you to be as good as me at video games, but that's never going to happen. You can't even shoot fish that aren't swimming."

She laughed despite his tone being quite serious. "You're right. I'm never going to be as good as you at video games, but I do enjoy trying to learn with you."

"I'm going to be thirteen soon," Benny said, "almost a grown-up."

"Well, I don't know about the almost a grown-up part, but you *will* be thirteen soon." "Mom, I agree with the detective."

"Why?" Claire asked.

"Are there other bad people like Hazel Christopher?"

Claire wanted to deny it, but she couldn't. She nodded slowly. "Maybe not exactly like her, but yeah, there are."

Benny reached out and took her hand. "Then the world needs you out there trying to stop them."

~

The next morning, Claire sat alone in the Boiler Room, listening to the silence.

She'd made sure to get there early to have some time alone. She'd told herself she needed to be in the room to make the decision, but the truth was she'd decided the moment Benny gave her permission.

Over the next hour, Kiko arrived, then Violet, then Jack, and finally Fitz.

And along with Fitz came Ranger. When Claire had called Hightower late the previous night, she'd had three conditions for taking on the special unit and staying on the job.

The first was that it would be permanently detached from the main hierarchy of the FBI, giving her a fair amount of freedom over which cases to take and how to manage them.

The second was that she would have ultimate say over who was and who wasn't on the task force. And the third, which was connected to the second, was that Hightower would allow Ranger to join them. He would be a permanent part of the team.

Hightower had agreed, and that had been that. She'd accepted the job.

"It's ready," Violet said.

Kiko and Violet had been working on a surprise on one of Violet's computers in the corner. Kiko said, "Claire, look up at the screen but close your eyes. You too, Fitz and Jack."

For the past two minutes, Fitz and Jack had been stuck in one of the greatest stalemates in arm-wrestling history. Although Jack was more muscular than Fitz, Fitz had about six inches of height on him and at least 100 pounds of weight. And he was using all of that weight for leverage. They had both turned beet red because neither could defeat the other.

Ranger had watched them intently for the first minute, clearly worried about Fitz, but had eventually lost interest and, for the first time ever, curled up at Claire's feet.

"Boys," Claire said. "Do as Kiko says."

After a long staredown they unclenched and slowly turned to face the monitor. Claire did so as well, closing her eyes. A long moment passed.

Then, finally, Kiko and Violet spoke at the same time. "Okay, open your eyes."

When she did, a broad smile spread across Claire's face.

On the screen was an icon of a silver FBI badge. In blocky black lettering along the bottom, Claire read the acronym: S.W.O.R.D.

It was now official. The Special-Washington-Oregon-Regional-Detachment had its own shield.

It was a permanent detachment of the FBI.

And Claire was running it.

— The End —

Thanks for reading! If you enjoyed *The Fifth Victim*, check out the next book in the FBI Task Force S.W.O.R.D. series, *We Forget Nothing*.

A NOTE FROM THE AUTHOR

Thanks for reading!

If you enjoyed this book, I encourage you to check out the whole series of FBI Task Force S.W.O.R.D. novels. Each book can be read as a standalone, although relationships and situations develop from book to book, so they will be more enjoyable if read in order.

And if you're loving S.W.O.R.D., check out my first hit series of fast-paced Pacific Northwest mysteries: the Thomas Austin Crime Thrillers.

I also have an online store, where you can buy signed paperbacks, mugs, t-shirts, and more featuring the S.W.O.R.D. team's lovable golden retriever, Ranger, as well as locations and quotations from all my books. Check that out on my website.

Every day I feel fortunate to be able to wake up and create characters and write stories. And that's all made possible by readers like you. So, again, I extend my heartfelt thanks for checking out my books, and I wish you hundreds of hours of happy reading to come.

D.D. Black

MORE D.D. BLACK NOVELS

The Thomas Austin Crime Thrillers

Book 1: *The Bones at Point No Point*
Book 2: *The Shadows of Pike Place*
Book 3: *The Fallen of Foulweather Bluff*
Book 4: *The Horror at Murden Cove*
Book 5: *The Terror in The Emerald City*
Book 6: *The Drowning at Dyes Inlet*
Book 7: *The Nightmare at Manhattan Beach*
Book 8: *The Silence at Mystery Bay*
Book 9: *The Darkness at Deception Pass*
Book 10: *The Vanishing at Opal Creek*

FBI Task Force S.W.O.R.D.

Book 1: *The Fifth Victim*
Book 2: *We Forget Nothing*
Book 3: *Widows of Medina*

Standalone Crime Novels

The Things She Stole

ABOUT D.D. BLACK

D.D. Black is the author of the Thomas Austin Crime Thrillers, the FBI Task Force S.W.O.R.D. series, and other Pacific Northwest crime novels. When he's not writing, he can be found strolling the beaches of the Pacific Northwest, cooking dinner for his wife and kids, or throwing a ball for his corgi over and over and over. Find out more at ddblackauthor.com.

- facebook.com/ddblackauthor
- instagram.com/ddblackauthor
- tiktok.com/@d.d.black
- amazon.com/D-D-Black/e/B0B6H2XTTP
- bookbub.com/profile/d-d-black

Printed in Great Britain
by Amazon